ALL OUR SECRETS

This edition published by Clan Destine Press in 2018

PO Box 121, Bittern
Victoria 3918 Australia

Copyright © Jennifer Lane

First Published by Rosa Mira Books New Zealand 2017

The right of Jennifer Lane to be identified as the author of this Work
in terms of section 96 of the NZ Copyright Act 1994 is hereby asserted.

National Library of Australia Cataloguing-In-Publication data:

Lane, Jennifer

ALL OUR SECRETS

ISBN: 978-0-6482937-9-8 (paperback)

Cover Design © Willsin Rowe
Design & Typesetting: Clan Destine Press

Clan Destine Press

www.clandestinepress.com.au

ALL OUR
SECRETS

JENNIFER LANE

CLAN
DESTINE
PRESS

For Mum

CHAPTER ONE

THE FIRST BAD THING HAPPENED BACK WHEN ELIJAH WAS FIVE. SOME people reckoned it triggered all the terrible things that happened later. But despite what they said, it wasn't Elijah's fault. He's my brother and I know everything about him, even that he was circumcised at nine months (though that's not much of a secret – the fight Mum and Dad had afterwards was loud enough for the whole of Australia to hear). I know better than anyone that he didn't mean to kill Sebastian.

It was a hot windy afternoon at the end of the Christmas holidays. Toby from next door was at our house minding the Lothums' new kitten, Sebastian, while they were at work, and Mum was supposed to be minding Toby and us. One minute Sebastian was sleeping in his shoebox bed, the next he was exploring our rug, and Elijah – oblivious to Sebastian's escape – was riding along the hall on his tricycle.

Elijah never took things slowly, and tricycle riding was no exception. He'd been born in a Coongahoola hospital record of thirteen minutes – beating Johnny Hall by two minutes – and has been in a hurry ever since. He spoke his first words ('Mama Bett' and 'God') before he was eight months old and took his first steps at tremendous speed two weeks before his first birthday. Not even skidding off our back veranda and breaking his right leg at the age of three slowed him down. I can still remember the sound of plaster scraping on floorboards as he chased me up and along the hall. It's only now that I realise he was born fast for a reason: if not for his speed, he'd never have lived to go into Year Five.

But, sadly for everyone (especially Sebastian), on this fateful afternoon Elijah's speediness worked against him.

'Here I come!' He turned his tricycle to face us. 'The fastest racing driver...'

I sat up. Toby was constructing a Lego tower, frowning in concentration.

'...in the whole wide world!' Elijah's feet were whirring on the pedals. 'Brrrrrm.'

'Slow down!' I said, uneasy about Elijah riding his trike inside. 'Smash Grandma Bett's vase, and she—'

My plea was flattened by the roar of wheels on wood.

Elijah wasn't the fastest racing car driver in the world, but he was far from slow on his little blue tricycle. I rescued as much of our Lego town as I could, sweeping my arm across the carpet as I dived off the rug and onto a beanbag. Toby grabbed Sebastian's shoebox bed and leapt into Dad's chair. That was when he realised the shoebox was empty.

Three cries sounded at once. Elijah's breathless: 'Champion of the world!', Toby's high-pitched 'Sebastian!', and the eerily baby-like scream of Sebastian himself as the wheels of Elijah's bike crushed his tiny body. It was more spine-tingling than a possum's cry, and it was the first and last sound I ever heard Sebastian make.

Then all I could hear was the dull whirr of the dusty old fan that sat on our TV.

None of us could bear to take a closer look at the corner of Grandma Bett's rug where Sebastian's black and white fur blended into the black and grey wool. His scream had been evidence enough of his fate.

'He's dead,' Toby said finally, staring at the wall. Tears slid down his cheeks, his chin quivered and his ears glowed red. This was before any of the murders. Sebastian's death was our first.

Not even three simultaneous screams had been enough to wake Mum. I found her flat on her back on top of the worn-out green bedspread, one arm flopped over the edge of the bed, an almost-empty glass bottle poking out from under the blankets. She was snoring louder than Grandma Bett snored when she had the flu, and her breath stank like one of the sprays she cleaned the bathroom with. I shook her until her red eyes blinked open and stared at me. Her hair was a tangle of knots and blue eyeliner snaked down her cheek. She didn't seem shocked when we told her what'd happened. She just mumbled something about Toby going home, and me and Elijah taking Sebastian back to the Lothums'. She wasn't even worried about how the Lothums would take the news. I wondered, for probably the millionth time, why I couldn't have a normal mum like my best friend Shelley and everyone else in the world did.

Mrs Lothum was the same age as Mum and Dad and had been made my godmother for accompanying Mum in the ambulance after she nearly gave birth to me in Woolworths. That didn't mean I liked her though. She worked at the Post Office and had a reputation for being the town's biggest gossip. She was always talking, telling me things I didn't really want to hear, and her constant questions – How's your *father?* What does your *father* make of it? Is your *father* going to be at the blah blah blah – left me feeling like a deflated balloon.

Mr Lothum was watching an old episode of *Astro Boy* on a tiny black and white TV. I didn't recognise him at first, with his bare head shining in the lamplight. I'd only ever seen him in his brown cowboy hat. He had a droopy moustache and little dents in his cheeks like cartoon cheese.

Elijah must've been nervous because after I gave him a hurry-up elbow in the ribs he spoke even faster than usual: 'I was, I was beingthefastestdriverintheworld andand Iwasgoing:brrrrrrm andhewasontherug,notinhisbedIdidn'tseehimIjustheard his – cry.'

Mrs Lothum got the message, though, because she sat down heavily on the couch and blew her nose so hard it sounded like a cow mooing. Elijah held out the shoebox that'd once been home to

9

a pair of Mr Lothum's size twelve Blundstone boots, but had since been lined with a flowery tea towel to make the kitten's bed. Inside it, wrapped in the tea towel, was the tiny squashed body of Sebastian. Mrs Lothum's arms stayed tightly crossed in front of her, so Elijah carefully placed the box down next to the *TV Guide* on the coffee table. I happened to glance over at Mr Lothum and saw tears sliding down his bumpy cheeks. Mr Lothum was crying! I didn't even know that men *could* cry.

Neither of them walked us to the door and we could still hear Mrs Lothum blowing her nose until after we'd got past the Wilsons' fence. I was so relieved to be out of their house I agreed to race Elijah home, even though we both knew he'd win.

The whole thing would've been forgotten sooner – by us, Toby, the Lothums and the rest of Coongahoola – had it not happened the same week as the screening of a horror movie at the Coongahoola Picture House. In *The Omen*, a little kid called Damien is riding his tricycle in circles around his nanny when she suddenly falls several stories to her death. Comparisons were made and even people who hadn't met Elijah started calling him Damien. People also commented on Elijah's eyes, saying that they were 'intense' or 'piercing', and, until they grew bored of it, bigger kids would tackle and hold him down, searching for the '666' birthmark under his hair.

Then there were the Baptist church people. They were always looking for something to kick up a fuss about, and that summer, apart from the screening of *The Omen*, there wasn't much.

What made things a hundred times worse was that Elijah was one of the 'River Children'. This was the name given to the group of kids born after the famous celebration of 1974 – the celebration known by those who could say the words as 'the River Picnic' (and by those who couldn't as 'that night' or 'the you know what').

The River Picnic was one of the biggest events that ever took place in Coongahoola, and even wilder than the street party the night Malcolm Fraser became Prime Minister and old Mr Buckley's Staffordshire terrier was put down. It was years before I'd hear more than snippets of what went on and I still don't know all the details. The adults spoke about it in whispers and only when they thought us kids were out of earshot. All I knew for sure, apart from the fact that Stu Bailey's wife drowned that night, in the Bagooli River, was that four times more babies than usual were born the following October and not all of them looked like their dads.

Though some kids tried to convince me otherwise, Elijah definitely belonged to our dad. He looked up at me with the same brown eyes, big and round like the eyes of the Andersons' Jersey cows. Elijah sulked with Dad's pouty lips, had a suntan even in winter and his brown hair stuck up like the Sydney Opera House no matter how many times Grandma Bett dragged a comb through it. The fact that the Muller twins, Abigail and Sammy, also shared Dad's Jersey cow eyes was something kids at school teased me about.

Anyway, some people acted like the River Children were cursed or something, and Sebastian's death didn't help. When another of the River Children, Tristan Kelly, filled his next-door neighbour's car muffler with apples, claiming 'Lucifer made me do it', Ken Knowles from the Baptist church decided to take action. He said that Elijah and Tristan's behaviour was attributable to their being River Children and he organised a meeting to decide what to do about this 'abominable' group. For all the town knew, Ken warned, all the River Children might have evil tendencies – and where would it stop? 'A kitten-killer at five – a killer of who-knows-what at ten?' he said of Elijah. But Grandma Bett helped prevent the meeting, after appealing to the parents of the River Children, who didn't want their children victimised. That Father Scott's sermon the Sunday after Sebastian's death was on the innocence of children was no coincidence, Father Scott being one of Grandma Bett's closest friends.

As it turned out, it was the River Children who had something to fear, not stupid Ken Knowles and his church. Things got scary for everyone, but the River Children copped the worst of it by far.

CHAPTER TWO

MARTHA MILLS WAS KNOWN FOR BEING TWO THINGS: COONGAHOOLA'S fattest person and Woolworths' most dedicated staff member. She had a helmet of hair that she dyed purple and, if the time it took her to eat a cream bun (fifteen seconds according to Mike from Benji's Bakery) was anything to go by, a people-sized appetite. Serving at the 10 Items or Less counter, she never let me slip past without smirking and nodding towards the Pasta, Rice and Sauce aisle, the aisle in which I was nearly born (Mum'd been buying the ingredients for spaghetti bolognaise when I decided to make my entry into the world). Purple People Eater was the kindest name I could think of for her.

'When can I start training you up, Gracie?' she'd asked once, with a wink that cut deep into her fat cheek. 'When this checkout is yours, you'll have come full circle!'

I felt hot with fury. And not just because a kid from school was standing in the queue behind me with his dad. There was no way I was going to end up like her, blathering on about the recent banana shortage or the brand of toilet paper on special. I was going to be a famous author, live somewhere far more exciting than Coongahoola, and write about things that mattered.

Whenever I saw her (and I'm not being mean, but it's very hard not to see Coongahoola's fattest person), I felt an overwhelming urge to turn and run. I didn't know why. It wasn't because she insisted that I was destined to work alongside her, as if my almost-birth during her Saturday afternoon shift meant we shared some kind of special connection. It wasn't because the folds of her enormous chin often harboured crusted icing sugar and I could never find the words to tell her. And it wasn't so I could say, 'You can't catch me!' before sprinting away at full eleven-year-old speed, although my best friend Shelley probably would've. It was just that she always gave me an uneasy feeling.

So if anyone in our town was going to stumble upon a vision of the Virgin Mary while taking their dog for a walk, it made sense that it was the Purple People Eater. Well, either her or my godmother Mrs Lothum, another person who made me feel like fleeing. But Mrs Lothum didn't have a dog. And her mind probably would've been too full of nosey thoughts for her to notice someone pale blue and holy beckoning from the sky.

Although a lot of the bad things that happened in our town can be blamed on the River Picnic, some were the result of what the Purple People Eater saw (or, 'cooked up', if you listened to Dad) near the Bagooli River. We were older then and our family had increased by a third with the arrival of the twins, Lucy and Gabriel. Or, as we called them, Lucky and Grub.

Lucy became Lucky because that was how Grub pronounced her name. It seemed fitting enough. Lucy cried so much I was convinced she was going to die, so every morning her tiny, watery eyes opened I felt she was lucky.

Gabriel was called Grub for more obvious reasons. Unlike other toddlers, he didn't move on from tasting everything he could get his little fingers on. At two, he was still supplementing his diet of Weetbix, toast, mashed vegetables and Grandma Bett's shepherd's pies with insects, dirt, leaves and whatever he could lick out from between the floorboards. By then he was so covered in grot it didn't matter what he did; he was permanently dirty.

But anyway, it was the Purple People Eater's vision that started the whole Believers thing off. I'll never forget that day. Shelley's eleventh birthday. I remember because Shelley invited me home after school for cake, and to show off the brand-new cassette player and Village People tape she'd unwrapped that morning. Shelley was a stick-thin girl like me, but unlike me she had Barbie-doll blonde hair and perfect creamy skin. (Although she complained about having freckles, you'd have to have looked through a microscope to see them.) Her parents were the normal kind you see on TV who smile, hold hands and talk to each other rather than yell, so it was more fun playing at her house than at ours. Sometimes when it was too hot to sleep I'd imagine that Shelley's parents were mine and I lived in her normal house and had everything I could possibly want, including a trampoline, like Shelley did. In my fantasy, Elijah was with me, instead of Shelley's brother Billy who was so stupid he thought that dinosaurs were still alive and roaming around Africa. Grandma Bett lived with us, too, in the Jones's two-storey brick house, because I couldn't imagine life without her. I didn't like the idea of Mum and Dad having other kids instead of us, either, so in the end I'd swap Shelley's parents for ours. Then I'd have to include the twins because no one else'd love them as much as we did, especially Grub with his Vegemite smile. In this way, my pointless fantasies would go round in circles, taking me further and further from sleep.

Shelley and I were sitting in the kitchen listening to Radio Coolio when we heard the news bulletin.

'It's the Purple People Eater!' Shelley yelled, elbowing me and turning up the radio, her sticky fingers smearing pale pink icing on the volume dial.

> '...exercising her Scottish terrier, Rusty. At approximately three thirty in the afternoon, while walking on the banks of the Bagooli River, Martha Mills alleges she saw a vision of the Virgin Mary.'

An ABBA song, the one about something being in the air that night, followed the news and Shelley and I sang along into our SodaStream bottle microphones. I forgot about the Purple People Eater until later when I was doing maths homework in my beanbag in front of the six o'clock news. It was the best thing ever, seeing Coongahoola on TV. How proud I felt, imagining kids all over Australia looking at our town: our faded Welcome to Coongahoola sign; our steelworks where my own dad worked; our deep, dark river; the gangly gum trees; the pretty banksias; the fluffy wattle trees; and our wide road, even with all the beer cans and newspapers blowing along the dusty gutters.

I wondered if Prime Minister Malcolm Fraser was watching too. Grandma Bett was watching, but she was too angry to be proud. She'd always kept a little wooden statue of the Virgin Mary on her dresser, but she'd never had any visions – and, unlike Martha Mills, she was a proper religious person. A Catholic. Her new portrait of Pope John Paul II, hanging above the lounge room table, was almost as big as the one of Jesus that smiled down at the TV. 'Utter nonsense,' she cried into the phone to Father Scott after tea. 'And of all places! The Bagooli River!'

The Bagooli River was a stretch of darkness that gleamed through the gum trees. I sometimes had nightmares that I was stranded there in the middle of the night and no matter which direction I ran couldn't find my way home. Though it was only five kilometres from the town hall, it was a place no one went to (not that the adults knew anyway). Not after the River Picnic. Not after Stu Bailey's wife drowned in it, and whatever else happened that night.

In the aftermath of the River Picnic, when Mr Kirk replaced the disgraced Mr Watson as mayor, the barbecue area next to the river had been abandoned. The kangaroos, wombats and possums returned as the trees and bushes took over again, burying the wooden picnic tables that reminded the town of that terrible night.

But the Purple People Eater's sighting changed all that. A week after she and her dog stumbled upon the Virgin Mary, the Believers invaded.

We were playing hide and go seek in the reserve when we heard the horns. Beep! Beep! Beep! Beep! Elijah and I and Elijah's best friend Michael Sanders sprinted to the top of Main Road.

'Bloody hell!' I said, catching my breath. There was a line, stretching as far as I could see, of cars, caravans and utes, all honking at the ancient Welcome to Coongahoola sign as they crawled passed it. I pressed my hands to my ears as I watched, amazed. Inside the cars were people who might as well have come from another planet. I'm sure my mouth hung open. All the women wore what looked like tea towels on their heads. I soon realised they were veils just like the Virgin Mary's. Even the kids wore them. A girl in the back of a Hillman like Grandma Bett's stared at us as her car crept by. She could've been the same age as me, but it was hard to tell with a blue veil covering half of her spotty face. She seemed to find us as fascinating as we found her, but when Elijah and Michael waved, she quickly looked away.

We watched the procession again on the news that night, all of us crowded around the new colour TV Dad'd won in a work raffle. When the TV reporter said there were more than 500 of them, Grandma Bett dropped to her knees and said ten Hail Marys.

The Believers set up camp on the bank of the Bagooli River. The gum and wattle trees were chopped down and the lantana and banksia bushes drenched in poison without a thought – said Grandma Bett – for the poor families of animals whose homes were being destroyed. All but one of the wooden picnic tables were taken apart and turned into pews. The other picnic table was spray-painted blue and used as the base for a twelve-foot high fibreglass statue of the Virgin Mary that glowed in the dark. And Mayor Kirk, who was happy to welcome newcomers to the town, showed his support for the Believers by paying for the building of a prayer room, complete with running water and toilet, beside the river.

A couple of weeks later, Coongahoola seemed like a new town. Even Woolworths looked different: the length of the queues tripled, and half the people in these queues pushed trolleys from behind long, pale blue veils. At home, Grandma Bett busied herself cleaning out every cupboard in the house, something she did when she was angry, muttering about 'the hide of the crackpots' and 'fanatics giving good honest Christianity a bad name'.

Though I never dared admit it to anyone, not even Shelley, I was excited by the Believers' arrival. Seeing women and girls walking around in ridiculous veils and long skirts made my family – Mum in Dad's old clothes, Grandma Bett in her old-fashioned dresses and me and Elijah in clothes salvaged from neighbours and bargain bins – seem almost sophisticated. And because the newcomers were considered to be 'crazy' religious people, Grandma Bett could be considered a 'normal' religious person by comparison (though I'd shared a room with her once, so I knew that she even prayed in her sleep).

The only person in Coongahoola who didn't seem to notice the invasion was Mum. It was as if she was seeing life from behind a veil of her own; she could only see what was right in front of her eyes: a 'cheating no-good husband'.

WE WERE ON THE bus home from the doctor's the day she busted Dad. I was looking out at the towering gum trees – at their silver leaves, silent and still – when I spotted our car as the bus wound around Emerson Street. Our once-white Ford station wagon was parked in front of a cream brick house. You couldn't miss it. It was older than any of us kids and had a dent in the back from where Mum backed over Dad's motorbike (a long story which Mum paid me five dollars to keep to myself). Its rusting number plate read XLB098. 'Stands for Extra Large Boy,' Dad'd once said, winking at Elijah.

'Look!' Elijah had noticed the car, too. 'What's Dad doing–' As he spoke, Elijah realised he shouldn't have. '… here?' he finished with a whisper and slowly turned around to look at Mum.

'Next stop, Andy,' Mum called out to Mr Hall, the bus driver.

'Here?' Mr Hall called back, confused. 'Sure, Nelly?'

Nelly. Mum hated being called Nelly. I think it reminded her of being called Smelly Nelly at school. She'd told me her nickname to make me feel better about Josh Napper singing 'Amazing Gracie' to me in a stupid voice during maths.

Mum nodded, though Mr Hall probably couldn't see her. Her teeth were clenched and her reddening face glistened with sweat.

My heart was hammering and my stomach felt heavy, even though Mum'd forgotten to give us lunch. I wasn't sure who I felt sorrier for – Mum or Dad. I certainly didn't feel sorry for the person whose house our car was parked in front of. The woman. I knew enough by then to know that it was a woman, and to wish that something terrible would happen to her.

The other people on the bus knew something was going on; you could tell by the way they kept sneaking glances at Mum. I hated them, the whole lot of them, for looking at Mum and at me and Elijah. For thinking things about us. Just as well Mrs Lothum wasn't on the bus – the whole world would've known by teatime.

'You two stay on and go straight home.' Mum didn't look at us as she walked up the aisle.

Elijah and I raced to the back of the bus, knelt on the sticky vinyl back seat and watched out the window as Mum stormed up the footpath towards the cream house. I wished for her sake she'd worn something nice, like the red dress Grandma Bett had helped Dad buy her for Christmas. I wanted her to look nicer than all the other mums in Coongahoola so Dad would only like her. But she was wearing Dad's grey Coongahoola Steelworks T-shirt and old baggy jeans, which hung off her as if she was a coat hanger. Although she'd attempted to comb her straw-like hair before we went out, it was still clumpy at the back.

About an hour after we'd got home, Mum came in, slammed the front door and stormed along the hallway. I was dreading the night ahead – the yelling, swearing, crying. The sound of things smashing. I wanted to go somewhere else, somewhere Mum's voice wouldn't reach, and take the other kids with me.

But there was no yelling, swearing or crying that night. Nothing got smashed. Because Dad didn't come home at all. That night, or the next. We discovered that the woman the cream house belonged to was Frannie Larson from 'Frannie's Fashion for Larger Ladies' when we heard Mum yelling about her at Mr Irwin over the back fence.

I knew Dad did some wrong things because he was always in trouble with Mum and Grandma Bett, but he sometimes gave us a dollar, which was double the amount Mum ever dug out of her purse, and he never got angry with us. I missed hearing the floorboards creaking under his boots. I wouldn't have minded listening to Mum yelling and breaking things if only I could've heard the sound of Dad's boots too.

'Maybe Mum killed him,' Elijah suggested after we hadn't seen Dad for a while. I tried to picture Dad lying squashed like poor Sebastian on a rug in Frannie Larson's house, but I couldn't. Unless she had a really big rug. But a couple of days later Elijah overheard Grandma Bett on the phone. 'Wait it out, son,' she whispered. Son! It could only be Dad. We were so relieved we painted smiling pictures of him and plastered them all over the secret room, the little room under the stairs we always escaped to when Mum and Dad were fighting. We didn't know if we'd ever see him again, but at least we knew he was alive.

CHAPTER THREE

IN THE DAYS AFTER DAD LEFT, MUM'S ANGER MELTED INTO DESPAIR, AND her howling filled every room in the house and poured out into our yard. I tried everything, but not even the little yellow flowers I picked from the Irwins' front lawn cheered her up.

Nana and Pop tried to help, too. They brought morning tea over on Mum's birthday. (It was no secret that Pop and Dad'd never got along. Pop'd been the principal of Coongahoola Central – 'Mr Butcher the Butcherer'; and Dad, one of the school's biggest trouble-makers – Robert Barrett! Mum told us that although Pop'd shaken Dad's hand on the morning of his and Mum's wedding, Pop couldn't look Dad in the eye, and let out a sob when the celebrant invited the groom to kiss the bride.) But when Pop called Dad a good-for-nothing and said Mum'd be better off raising us kids on her own, Grandma Bett said, 'I'd rather you didn't speak about my son like that,' and Nana and Pop left, taking the rest of the caramel slice with them.

Eventually Mum ran out of tears and dragged herself out of her room, but her mouth sagged and she sulked around in her dressing gown and fluffy pink bunny slippers. If not for the really bad thing that happened that Halloween, she'd probably still be slouching around today.

I was relieved that by the time the Halloween custom of trick or treating made its way from America to our town I was too old to be expected to join in. I hated the idea of performing a 'trick'. I didn't have any special talents, except maybe reading. Who'd want a ghost or zombie to sit down and read to them? That didn't stop me from wanting Elijah to go, though, because he'd promised to share his loot with me. For that reason, I'd helped him get into costume by sneaking a handful of Mum's hair gel and squishing it onto his head.

Grandma Bett didn't care that all the kids in Elijah's class were going trick or treating. She didn't care that Michael Sanders was waiting by our letterbox, looking up at our house through the two holes he'd cut into his Cowboys and Indians bed sheet. When Elijah opened the front door with his gooey hair combed flat like Damien Omen's, she pushed it closed again and led him back along the hallway.

When she saw two vampires and a fat witch running up our driveway, she quickly closed the curtains so they'd think no one was home. She was washing dishes in the kitchen when Frankenstein knocked. She sighed and answered the front door still holding a soapy baking tray.

'Trick or treat?' Frankenstein shouted, waving a half-full Woolworths bag.

'That's American nonsense,' Grandma Bett answered. 'In Coongahoola we celebrate holy occasions, thank you very much.' Then she quietly closed the door and went back to the dishes.

Of course, later she'd torment herself about this, ask God why she hadn't invited the poor dear in and given him a Johnny cake while she phoned his mother. He was on his own by that time – we later heard that he'd been with a ghost, but she'd eaten too many Chomps and thrown up all over the Valentines' agapanthus.

Frankenstein mumbled something probably not very nice about Grandma Bett, and wandered off swinging his bag of loot. I watched from the living room window, desperately hoping he wouldn't tell everyone at school what Grandma Bett'd said. He strolled up the Irwins' driveway looking less like Frankenstein and more like Nigel Holmes from Elijah's class with two toilet rolls stuck to his neck.

When I saw a photo of him on TV the next morning my arms broke out in goosebumps, then I felt so dizzy I had to lie down on the couch. I realised I was one of the last people to have seen him.

Everyone talked about Nigel after he was on TV. It was like he was everybody's best friend, even if his only real friend was Josie Armour, the ghost who ate too many Chomps. Like Josie, Nigel was one of the River Children and he dumped his school bag in the same corner of the lunchroom where all the other River Children dumped theirs, but he and Josie mostly played on their own. When Nigel hadn't come home after trick or treating, Mrs Holmes drove all the way to the end of Aimslee Crescent yelling his name out her car window. At 11 p.m. she dialed 000 and asked for Sergeant Colby. Two weeks later the sergeant, Constable Stewy and most of Coongahoola were still looking for him. Mrs Holmes and her sister sticky-taped photocopied 'Missing' posters to every telegraph pole along Main Road and thumb-tacked a whole row of them to the notice board inside Woolworths. The picture of Nigel was a school photo, possibly a year or two old because the space behind his smile where his teeth should've been was empty. His thick brown hair looked as though it'd been cut by his mum in a hurry; the left side of the fringe was longer than the right and a forgotten curl poked out from behind his left ear.

The same photo appeared on the cover of *The Coongahoola Times* where the previous ten years of Nigel's life were broken down into daily chapters. We learnt everything about him: that his favourite food was meat balls soaked in tomato sauce, that his favourite band was KISS, that he wanted to play cricket for Australia when he grew up and his hero was the bowler Dennis Lillee, that he'd had a pet kangaroo until it bit him on the knee, and that his real father was Graham Anderson's brother who'd made a trip to Coongahoola from the city especially for the River Picnic. 'The nicest kid you could meet,' his teacher Mrs Baker was quoted as saying. 'Wouldn't hurt a flea.' (Though Elijah had doubts about this last comment – he said all the boys pulled wings off cicadas, even Nigel, and if you were prepared to de-wing a harmless Black Prince, it's unlikely you'd stop at hurting a pesky flea.)

To try to forget about her final words to Nigel, Grandma Bett busied herself making sandwiches and lamingtons for the search party. To my shock, Mum helped.

'Can't get over it, Bett,' I heard her saying while she sliced a cucumber. 'Thought if there was a safe place in the world, this'd be it.'

Mum even knocked on the door of the secret room. Although we shared it with the vacuum cleaner, mop, bucket, broom, smelly rags, bottles of bleach and cans of cleaning spray, the secret room had always been our sanctuary. With the little white door closed behind us, Mum and Dad's voices sounded far away, as if all the arguing and swearing came from the Irwins' place, not ours. Sometimes we spent so much time behind the door that we carried the smells of detergent and bleach in our hair, skin and clothes. Some of the kids teased me about it at school: 'Bog girl,' hot peanut-butter-breath sang in my face, 'Gracie stinks like a bog'. It didn't bother me. Mum called Dad much worse things. And at least I smelt like a clean bog.

'Hey there,' Mum whispered, as if that's how us kids spoke in the secret room.

She crouched down and poked her head in the door. Her eyes were red and watery and she was chewing her little finger, something she did when she didn't know what to do next. 'Just wanted to tell you that we're all okay. You're safe with me and your gran so don't go worrying about it.'

'Thanks, Mum,' I whispered back. That was the first time it occurred to me that anything could happen to us – I hadn't been worried at all, just shocked and sorry for Nigel – but it was also the first time in ages Mum'd paid us any attention and I wasn't about to spoil the moment.

Mum scanned the walls behind us. I was glad we'd replaced the paintings of Dad with zombies for Halloween, though I don't think

Mum liked them because a tear ran down her cheek. I think she'd wanted to come in, but realised she wouldn't fit. I was getting too big to be in there and it'd got a lot squishier since we'd started letting Grub and Lucky in, but until I found somewhere else as peaceful, I wasn't ready to give it up.

'Who wants fish and chips then?' Mum asked, completely out of the blue. Fish and chips were usually only for birthdays or when our cousins from Sydney were visiting.

'Meeee!' Elijah, Grub and Lucky sang as they scrambled towards the door, knocking over the bucket and mop on their way. I nodded at Mum and climbed out after them.

Mum wasn't the only person who acted differently after what happened to Nigel. Everyone in Coongahoola was suddenly our friend. Parents took turns escorting us kids to and from the bus stop and made us walk along in a chain, holding hands and singing songs like 'I still call Coongahoola home' as if we were six years old. It was fun though; it felt a bit like Christmas. We couldn't walk down the street without someone asking how we were holding up. Even the Believers joined in, lifting their veils to chat to other shoppers in Woolworths. That's how Mum got talking to Bethany.

'What a sweet little boy!' Bethany said in a voice I only normally heard on TV, a loud voice with an American accent.

She was behind us in the checkout queue wearing a navy blue dress and powder-blue veil. On her face sat a pair of thick, brown glasses and below them, a smile that showed off all of her teeth. Mum looked down at Grub, chewing her handbag strap with pen ink on his face and something sticky and pink in his hair, and must've thought it was a joke. She glared at the woman then looked away.

But then Bethany put her hand under Grub's dirty chin and said, 'What lovely big eyes.' And looked over at me said, 'And this must be the beautiful big sister.'

I stared at the supermarket's dirty floor, not knowing what to say. I wasn't beautiful, far from it. I was so bony that my ribs poked out and, unlike some of the girls in my class, I didn't even have a hint of a chest. My blonde hair was frizzy and boring; Mum usually cut it level with the bottom of my neck, so it wasn't long, but it wasn't short either. Even worse, that summer it'd turned green from all the chlorine in the Coongahoola pool. My face was okay – if you squinted so you couldn't see any freckles – but you'd have to be blind to call it beautiful.

Mum nodded and mumbled a thank you. Then she noticed the spotty, bucktoothed girl, also in a powder-blue veil, attached to the woman's other hand – the girl I'd seen in the back of the Hillman the day the Believers arrived. She looked at least a year older than me and was dressed like an old lady; she wore a white, buttoned-up shirt and a long, brown skirt that swept the ground. All the Believers dressed like that and I wondered what was so wrong with their legs that they had to be covered up. The girl was looking me up and down, as if what I was wearing – my red 'Coongahoola cross-country' T-shirt and denim shorts – looked as ridiculous as her outfit. Couldn't she see that I was the normal one? I crossed my arms and scanned the aisles, pretending I was looking for someone.

'She's a dear little one,' was the best Mum could come up with. They were words Grandma Bett used when she was trying to be diplomatic, but they did the trick because the woman introduced herself as Bethany and the conversation flowed on from there.

Mum promised Bethany that until Nigel'd disappeared Coongahoola was a peaceful place to live and that the last tragedy of this scale was years ago when Stu Bailey's wife drowned. I nodded, knowing enough not to add that Stu reckoned her drowning was a gift from God.

Bethany urged Mum not to worry. 'I love this country of yours! God bless Ronald Reagan, but I wouldn't wish to be anywhere else, not even in America. God can protect you and your children. All you need to do is invite him into your home,' she said, gently patting Mum's arm.

THAT SATURDAY NIGHT MUM went out for the first time since the Andersons' wedding in the Coongahoola Town Hall six months before.

25

'Do I pass?' She spun around, her red pleated dress twirling. She even wore a ruby-red lipstick to match. Seeing Mum looking like that was a magical moment I'll never forget. Her new Olivia Newton-John record was playing, and the front door must've been open because a cool, light breeze wafted through the house. I couldn't help but stare at her, trying to preserve the image for when things turned bad. I wanted to hug her, but I couldn't because hugging was only something little kids did. Or people with normal parents, like Shelley.

Lucky and Grub can't have remembered seeing Mum dressed up before because Lucky laughed (an unusual sound that made me think of a seal), and Grub stared with his mouth open and custard dribbling down his chin.

'Ahhhh! Lovely!' Grandma Bett said. 'I knew that dress would suit you.'

'You look – nice,' I said. I was thinking 'beautiful' but was too embarrassed to say it. 'Where are you going?'

'Are you having a fling?' Elijah asked.

'Elijah! Where do you get such words? Fling!' Grandma Bett frowned.

'God no! No, I'm meeting someone – a *friend* – and a few others,' Mum said. There was a bit of lipstick on her front tooth.

'A tea towel lady?' Elijah asked.

'Surely not!' Grandma Bett cried. 'Nell?'

'Hang on to your knickers. It's just a friendly get-together. I've finally found a woman my age who isn't laughing behind my back, who I know for sure hasn't done you know what with you know who! Besides, a bit of extra protection from the bloke upstairs wouldn't hurt.'

'You are always welcome to join me at Father Scott's mass on Sundays. I thought I'd made that clear.'

'Perfectly, Bett. But it's a laugh I'm after, not hell and damnation.' Mum peered at her reflection in the oven door and fluffed up her new perm. Prettier than her hair was her smile, even with lipstick on her tooth. 'I'm off now, kids! Behave!'

We didn't need to be told. The four of us were so stunned we plonked ourselves into our beanbags and stared at the TV until Grandma Bett sent us off to bed. I didn't notice when *The Goodies* finished and *Dr Who* started; I was lost in a Mum daydream. I felt sorry for Dad. If he knew what Mum was like when she was happy he'd still be at home with us instead of stuck with Frannie in her boring house. I couldn't remember ever seeing Frannie smile.

Mum was soon attending prayer meetings twice a week. She said she could take or leave all the stuff about God, but she didn't mind the company. She said that through Bethany, or Queen Bethany as the other Believers called her (which Mum said made her laugh so much she nearly wet her pants), she was getting to know Saint Bede, their founder and leader.

'He's quite a charmer, this Saint Bede,' she said one Saturday morning as the two of us sat at the kitchen table, putting off washing up the breakfast things. 'Even if he has a beard and is bald as a bat.'

'Dad's charming. Dad's good-looking! Better than all the other blokes in this town.' I couldn't stop myself. I didn't like Mum saying that about other men, especially men with beards. Grandma Bett said that men who had beards were usually covering up bad skin.

'Yeah, that's the trouble,' Mum said, smiling. Mum being able to talk about Dad without smashing anything was one thing, smiling as she said it was another. She was wearing a new sundress, hot pink with straps that tied up at the shoulders. She'd stopped wearing lipstick because Saint Bede said make-up was a disguise that sinners hid behind, but her hair was still curly and shiny.

'So, why don't you like Dad anymore?'

'I do, Gracie, I do. It's just that we get on better when we're nowhere near each other.'

'So, you wish you didn't marry him?'

'Oh, Gracie! No, I don't wish that. But we were so young, just seventeen and still at school. We got married because – because you were coming along. We loved each other and were happy to have you, of course, but it wasn't always easy. For either of us.'

'How come?' I scraped a bit of dried Weetbix off the tablecloth with my thumbnail. I'd watched the royal wedding the year before and couldn't imagine Mum and Dad ever looking as happy as Prince Charles and Princess Diana.

'Well, your dad he was, still is, I don't know – a bit of a ladies' man, as they say. He wasn't really ready to settle down. He was just a boy really, and he'd gone off the rails after his dad died. And, well, I suppose I was just a girl.'

'Seventeen's nearly grown up,' I said. The seventeen-year-olds in the Seniors Block wore make-up and smoked cigarettes without even caring if a teacher busted them. As far as I was concerned, they were adults.

'It may seem like it to you, but what did I know about babies at that age? No offence, but having you made me realise how easy I'd had it at school. Even a double period of Modern History with Mrs Dawson was a breeze compared to the daily mission of trying to get you to close your eyes. As much of a tyrant as Mrs Dawson was, she didn't scream till her face turned purple or puke down my front.'

'Sorry.' I made a mental note to never have a baby. Not that I'd ever been tempted. I'd smelt enough of the twins' nappies to know better.

Mum didn't seem to hear me. 'I was so tired that my eyeballs ached and anything, even a TV ad for deodorant, could send me running to my bedroom, eyes streaming. After I lost the weight I'd put on while you were growing inside me, my body continued to shed fat until I felt like nothing more than a shadow.'

'Sorry!'

'Not your fault, pet. It was me. If it wasn't for your grandma, I would've taken you back to the maternity ward and begged them to take you away.'

What would've happened, I wondered, if Mum'd taken me back to the hospital? Would I have ended up with a family like Shelley's? Or with one even worse than mine?

'What about Dad? What was Dad doing?' I asked.

'Good question, Gracie!' Mum picked up a spoon and tapped it on the table. 'To start with he tried to make light of it, tried to cheer me up. But his jokes belonged in the school playground; they just made me feel more alone.' She dropped the spoon. 'After a while my crying became a sign for him to go outside and roll a cigarette. Later it was a cue to head to the pub or God only knows where.'

I wondered if God only knows where included Fat Frannie's house.

Mum stood up and started stacking the bowls and plates. 'You see, Gracie, your dad and I were doomed from the start. Every girl between fifteen and eighteen was in love with him – honestly, what chance did I ever have of keeping him to myself?'

I DIDN'T MENTION SAINT BEDE to Dad when Grandma Bett took us kids to meet him at Hartley Park. I was so looking forward to seeing Dad, I couldn't bear to think I'd make him sadder than he probably already was. I'd hardly slept at all the night before. I'd lain on top of my bedspread, thinking about Dad, imagining him arriving at the park with a smile on his face and a bag over his shoulder, telling me I'd lucked out on sitting in the Hillman's front seat because he was coming home.

Grandma Bett spread out a dusty old, green tartan blanket that used to be on our dead grandad's bed, but I couldn't sit down. My stomach tingled with butterflies and my head buzzed with all the things I wanted to say to Dad. I wanted to tell him I topped the class for my project on Aboriginal dreamtime, and that we were learning how to write essays. I wanted to say that Shelley and her brother got a new table tennis game called Pong that you played on the TV. I wanted him to know that Mum had some new clothes and she looked a bit like the Commonwealth Games swimmer, Lisa Curry. And I wanted to say that our house felt too big, too empty, without him; that things just weren't the same.

Grandma Bett poured five lemon cordials and handed out bread rolls stuffed with bananas and lemon juice. She was buttering our date scones by the time I recognised Dad's shape strolling towards us. I used to say he looked like Harrison Ford from the Indiana Jones movies but only because that's what Dad said himself. I

29

thought he was better looking than Harrison Ford, even with his two naked lady tattoos (neither of which was Mum, something I wasn't sure whether to be sad or relieved about).

'Hey, kids! Mum!' He stretched out his arms to hug us kids all at the same time, then bent down to give Grandma Bett a kiss on the cheek. He didn't look any different. His boots were shinier, maybe even new, but he looked the same.

I put my scone down on the plate next to my untouched banana roll. Dad wasn't carrying a bag on his shoulder.

'Lucky weed!' Grub said. Lucky buried her head in the blanket. She'd been so excited about seeing Dad that she'd taken her nappy off in the car.

'We've missed you,' Grandma Bett said, pouring tea from her thermos into two plastic mugs.

'Are you coming home?' I asked. He could always pick up his bag later, I'd decided.

Dad lifted Grub up and threw him in the air. 'Little rascal!' he said. Grub squealed.

'Are you, Dad?' I asked.

Dad looked at Grandma Bett, who shook her head. 'Nell's standing firm. And you're not doing yourself any favours by staying at that woman's house.'

'Cost a fortune to stay in the pub.' Dad put Grub down on the grass and scooped Lucky out from under the blanket. 'Come on out, possum.'

'What are you doing, son?' Grandma Bett said. 'You belong with your family.'

'I know. I want to be with 'em, I really do. It's just I get, I dunno, distracted. It's stupid, I know.'

'Distracted?'

'Well y'know, Nell's always so angry an' on my case all day. She's forgotten how to laugh – hardly even smiles any more. It gets a bloke down after a while. Then some woman comes along, happy as pie, without a worry in the world. I think Jesus'd understand my torment.'

'Jesus? Fiddlesticks! If that's a joke, even your humour's gone to the pits! Have you asked yourself why Nell's so angry? First that Nurse Audrey and now Frannie or whatever her name is. Nell wants a faithful husband. If that's too much for her to hope for, son, I'm very disappointed. But think of the children, think about–'

'Dad! What's that on your neck?' Elijah asked. 'Eeew yuck – looks like lipstick.'

I poured my lemon drink onto the dry brown grass, upsetting a family of ants, which stumbled and tripped over each other as they fled from the sticky juice.

Dad rubbed his neck and looked down at the rug. Grandma Bett shook her head and said something that sounded a lot like 'you bloody fool', although it couldn't have been because she never swore. Dad gave us goodbye kisses soon after that. He hadn't had anything to eat, and neither had I.

'Bye, Dad,' I called after him. I pressed my fingers into my eyes to stop the tears from flowing. All the things I wanted to say would have to wait. I wished, for probably the hundredth time, that Fat Frannie would drop dead.

As much as I desperately wanted Dad to come home, things were better after Mum became normal. I started half-liking the Believers with their tea towels and beards, though I'd never admit that at school. At school they were called the Bleeders (I asked Nathan Taylor why and he said ''cause they're bleedin' idiots') and sat by themselves at the end of the playground that was mostly dirt, where no one else wanted to play. It didn't matter that most of the girls stuffed their veils in their school cases as soon as their parents drove off in the morning. You could spot a Bleeder a mile off. The girls wore their school uniform almost down to the ground and the boys wore trousers instead of shorts, even in summer. All of them stank of church.

FROM EVERY TELEGRAPH POLE on Main Road, Nigel's face looked down at us. His brown hair was bleached by the November sun and the sticky-taped 'Missing' posters were crinkled and curling.

Sometimes, when I was on my own, I'd whisper hello to him. I'd stare into the little grey dots that made up his eyes, as if the harder I looked, the better I'd understand what was behind them. I thought it was sad that he was much more popular now that he was missing, but I knew why.

Up there on the telegraph pole, Nigel was elevated to a new status. He was no longer part of our ordinary world. I felt guilty, but I found myself wishing that I'd paid more attention to him before he went missing – not for his sake but so that I could claim his disappearance as my loss. I knew it was wrong to feel this, but I couldn't help it. The truth was I'd never even bothered to speak to him when he was around.

Then, one hot December morning, I wandered into the kitchen, still rubbing the sleep out of my eyes, to discover that my world had been turned upside down.

'Why didn't I ask him in, Nell?' Grandma Bett was sobbing. 'He was all on his own.' Her face was blotchy and she was squeezing Mum's hand. I'd never seen Grandma Bett cry before. She sniffed loudly – the kind of sniff that, if it'd come from one of our noses, would've made her say, 'You've got a perfectly good handkerchief, why don't you use it.'

'They found Nigel?' I whispered, though I didn't really want to hear the answer. It's what we'd all been waiting for, but dreading. I was only eleven then, but I was clued up enough to know that he hadn't just run away.

'Last night,' Mum said. 'Near the river.'

'Did he – did he drown?' Though we were warned never to go near the Bagooli River, I'd heard it was a good place to swim if you were brave enough and didn't think too much about the lady who drowned in it.

'No, pet. He was killed. His body was found near the River Picnic site. In the, the lantana by the water. Someone – someone killed him.'

CHAPTER FOUR

IT WAS SOMETHING THAT NORMALLY ONLY HAPPENED IN THE MOVIES. School closed early for the Christmas holidays and we were dragged along to 'Community Care' meetings in the town hall for group counselling. I got stuck in a group with Elijah's best friend, Michael. I usually liked Michael – he was pretty like a girl with long eyelashes and shoulder-length brown hair – but he kept crying because he used to play marbles with Nigel, so Mrs J the school counsellor made each of us give him a hug. I was trying to think of something to say that'd cheer him up, but then I noticed that he'd rubbed snot on my T-shirt so the only thing I said was 'yuck'.

On the day of Nigel's funeral, all the shops closed and practically the whole town turned up at St Mary's in their good clothes. Even a few of the Believers were there, despite people saying that they shouldn't be allowed in a Catholic church. Probably the only Coongahoolians who didn't make it were Constable Stewy and the sergeant. Father Scott passed on their respects: he said that they would've liked to attend the service, but couldn't afford to take the time off. In their place were four policemen who must've been borrowed from some other town. You couldn't miss them with their blue uniforms and sombre frowns. No doubt they were checking us all out, to decide who looked most like a murderer.

Elijah spotted Dad sitting in the back row with Mr Irwin from next door, Mr Lothum in his silly cowboy hat, and the other men who worked with him at the steelworks. It was the first time we'd seen Dad since the picnic at Hartley Park so we turned around and waved. I barely recognised him dressed up smartly in our dead grandad's suit. I wanted to run down the aisle and sit next to him so everyone'd know he belonged to me. But he gave us a salute and a half-serious smile that reminded us we were at a funeral, so I stayed put.

I scanned the seats for Fat Frannie and spied her in a black and white dress on the edge of the third to back row, just behind Nana and the Butcherer. Her hands were spread on the back of the pew in front and she seemed to be studying her nail polish. In the row behind her was Mrs Lothum; you could spot her hair a mile off, and it could've just been the angle of her head, but she seemed to be watching Fat Frannie too. Then Nigel's mother, Mrs Holmes, started walking up the aisle, leaning on Dr Child's shoulder, and Mrs Buchen stopped chatting to Mrs Valentine and began playing the organ. I caught a whiff of Grandma Bett's flowery perfume and felt guilty for looking around. After that, I tried to keep my eyes on the altar.

Sometime during Father Scott's sermon about caring for our neighbours, I started to feel a horrible twisting pain in my stomach.

I waited until everyone was singing 'The Lord is my Shepherd' in sad, flat voices, then I leant over and whispered to Mum, 'My tummy hurts.'

'Oh, poor pet. Try not to think about it.'

'It's *really* sore.'

'Try and ignore it. It's just grief. It'll go away soon.'

Grief? Grief was turning my stomach inside out? But it didn't go away. It was worse, not better, by the time Grandma Bett parked the Hillman under a gum tree across the road from Nigel's house.

Noticing my tears, Grandma Bett rubbed my knee. 'Oh, Gracie. It's a terribly sad time, isn't it? But we'll get through it.'

I nodded, clinging to my seatbelt as my stomach tightened. Did everyone else feel as sick as me? I sniffed back my tears and tried to be brave.

'What are we waiting for?' Elijah asked. The weather that day was grey and unusually still. It was warm, but not stinking hot like it normally was. It was like God'd put the weather on hold for Nigel's funeral.

'It's a *wake*, Elijah,' Grandma Bett replied, reapplying her lipstick in the mirror. It was just Grandma Bett and us.

Mum'd left the church with Bethany and a man wearing a dress and carrying a walking stick. He was bald and had a little beard so I guessed he was Saint Bede. Mum said they were going to the river, near the old picnic site where Nigel's body was found (in the lantana by the water), for a prayer session dedicated to releasing Nigel's soul. I frowned at Mum when she told us that – shouldn't she be with her family? – but she didn't notice.

'What's a wake?'

'A celebration. We're celebrating Nigel's life. Now, any other questions before we go inside and be on our best behaviour?' Grandma Bett craned her neck to scan the three in the back seat.

'Celebrating Nigel's life – without Nigel?'

'Yes. It's what we do when people leave this world.' Grandma Bett reached over and touched the knee of Elijah's brown corduroy trousers. 'We remember all the good times we've had with Nigel.'

Elijah thought for a moment. 'What if I can only remember bad times?' he asked, undoing his seat belt.

'Oh, Elijah, don't be silly. Nigel was a lovely, lovely boy. He was at your birthday party last year – remember? He won pin-the-tail-on-the-donkey.'

'That was Todd.'

'Really? Well, that doesn't really matter. Nigel was there anyway and he was a polite boy.'

'He pinched Melissa Stubbs's marshmallows. Put them all in his mouth at once so she couldn't eat any,' Elijah said. Grub giggled.

'Well, I didn't know anything about that.' Grandma Bett pushed the car door open. 'Gracie, please, can you get Grub?'

As Grandma Bett lifted Lucky out of her seat, she glanced at Elijah and said, 'Nigel was a good, polite boy. That's all you need to remember today. This is for his mother really, this wake. So please remember your manners.'

A skeleton of a woman, all bones under her navy blue dress, leant against the Holmes's front door, blowing smoke like one of the steelworks chimneys. She looked as though it should've been her funeral we'd just been to, not Nigel's. She introduced herself as Jean, Nigel's aunty from Newcastle, as she opened the screen door.

'Make yourselves at home. I'm just keeping watch for the old guy,' Jean said. 'Tried to get in earlier.'

'Old guy?' Grandma Bett looked around.

'Buckley? With the dog.'

'Oh, Gerald!' Grandma Bett said. 'He's harmless enough.'

'Yeah, well he was probably just here for the free food, but he gives me the creeps,' Jean said. 'And I'm hardly going to trust everyone in *this* town … You okay, love?'

I nodded, wiping my eyes. Grandma Bett put her hand on my shoulder and said, 'She's finding the whole thing terribly upsetting.'

Was I? Was my body really grieving for the boy I'd never even spoken to? I didn't really know what grief was; perhaps it happened without you knowing about it. Did I miss Nigel Holmes more than I realised?

'Yeah, her and all,' Jean said, before taking a deep drag on her cigarette. 'My sister hasn't eaten a crumb since she heard about … about what happened to him. Not a crumb.'

Eager to see how we'd celebrate Nigel's life, Elijah stepped inside first. We'd had nothing to eat since our rice bubbles that morning and Grandma Bett had promised us there'd be afternoon tea. The thought of food made me want to throw up, but Elijah complained that he was starving.

The house stank of cigarettes and sweaty adults. My stomach churned and I prayed that the toilet would be easy to find if I needed it. Toby Irwin was perched on a chair behind his little brother, Jonathan, reading *The Lord of the Rings*. He was in Year Seven at Coongahoola Central, two years above me. He was wearing dark denim jeans and a red flannelette shirt over a black Midnight Oil T-shirt, and his hair'd just been cut. I'd always liked his messy curls, but a shorter cut showed off more of his face. My heart did a quick dance and for a moment I forgot about the agony in my stomach. I looked down, not wanting him to see me with wet, swollen eyes.

Michael Sanders waved at us through the window. Behind him a barbecue was smoking. Mr Lothum, still wearing his cowboy hat, was looking at the photos of Nigel that covered the wall. A few kids from school were sitting against the wall, but no one from my class, luckily, since they'd know I'd been crying, plus I was stuck with Grub and snot was dripping from his nose faster than I could catch it. Most of the adults were standing, drinking from plastic cups, some talking and laughing too loudly, others sniffing and hugging each other. I spied a table stacked high with little sandwiches without crusts, slices, and what looked like muffins, and elbowed Elijah. He raised his eyebrows when I shook my head at the caramel slice he was handing me, but rather than dwell on it he shoved it in his mouth.

Nigel's Aunty Jean poured each of us kids a lemonade and told a man with a big orange beard to put the kettle on for Grandma Bett's cup of tea. People trickled in through the front door, and some made their way back out again, but we still couldn't see Nigel's mum. Elijah said he could hear her crying from behind a door along the hall, but Grandma Bett frowned and fingered the little cross around her neck when he asked if he could investigate. She made us promise to be good while she took Lucky to find Father Scott.

Mrs Irwin stood leaning on a bookshelf with a glass of red something in her hand. She was a short woman with sometimes blonde, sometimes brown hair, small dark eyes and a long skinny nose like a beak. One night when she was screaming at Toby in their backyard, Dad said she sounded like a bloody cockatoo. Ever since then I couldn't talk to her without thinking of cockatoos.

I noticed her watching Elijah, looking at him like he was a piece of chewing gum stuck to the bottom of her shoe. He'd tackled Michael and was now lying on top of him, laughing. I wondered whether she'd ever forgive him for killing Sebastian and making Toby lose his first pet-minding job.

Mrs Irwin saw me looking at her and called out in her horrible bird voice, 'Gracie, what's wrong with you? You look like dea– You don't look so well.'

'I'm okay.' I sniffed, looking around for someone else to talk to. I could hear an album Shelley's parents liked, Cat Stevens's *Tea for the Tillerman*, playing softly.

But Mrs Irwin wasn't finished with me. 'Haven't seen your mum around. Where'd she get to this afternoon?'

It was one of those moments when suddenly everyone is quiet and they all look at you and wait to hear what you have to say.

'I'm not really sure,' I mumbled finally, not a complete lie since I didn't know where exactly along the river she and the Believers were praying. It was us she should've been with, not them. Especially since I was half dead with grief. But I wasn't going to tell Mrs Irwin that.

Thankfully Mrs Irwin then turned the attention away from Mum to the Purple People Eater. 'You know Martha's cut down her shifts at Woolies?' she squawked. 'She was employee of the year *five* times in a row, before she started wearing that silly veil to work. Now she's spending all her time praying with that Bede fellow.'

'Does she fancy him?' Mrs Anderson asked with a mouthful of muffin.

'I don't think fancy's the right word, but she's definitely under his spell. You know, Dorrie who does the wages told me that Martha gives half her pay to him? They all do it. People in cults.'

Thankfully, before Mrs Irwin could say any more, the front door swung open and in walked Mr Irwin carrying an armful of beer, followed by Gary Burns and Dad. Dad's tie was loose and his white shirt untucked; he looked like a senior from Coongahoola Central. He headed straight to the food table, picked up a sandwich and stuffed the whole thing in his mouth. He didn't see me sitting on the orange beanbag in front of the TV, arms wrapped around my sore stomach and Grub sliding down my legs.

Mrs Lothum dashed out from the kitchen and handed Dad a can of KB and a paper plate piled high with sausages and onion. He nodded thanks and held the gold can up to his lips, looking around the room. I stared at him, willing him to notice me, but his eyes skirted over my head.

'Daddy daddy daddy,' Grub babbled. Mr Irwin gave us a nod but Dad hadn't heard.

Soon after that, someone changed the record and suddenly Dad's favourite band burst into the living room in a frenzy of guitars, causing everyone to stop talking and cover their ears. I thought AC/DC was good as far as Dad's music went, and I welcomed the fact that it was so loud I wouldn't have to talk to anyone. But we'd only heard half of the song before Grandma Bett announced that 'Hells Bells' was 'dreadfully inappropriate' and replaced it with something that sounded like a church choir.

Then I saw who Dad'd been looking for. Fat Frannie waltzed in the back door, her black and white chequered dress swishing around her legs. She wasn't as fat as Mum made out and her face was pretty, even if it was rounder than most. Her hair was silky blonde, thick and shiny like hair in magazines, and she had big blood-red lips. If she didn't eat anything for a year she'd probably be beautiful, I decided. I didn't want her to be beautiful because Dad would stay with her forever, but I didn't want her to be ugly either because that would make Mum look even worse. She smiled at Dad and he smiled back and gave her one of his special winks, the kind he gave us when Mum wasn't looking.

My nose tingled with tears; what was he doing? Then she pushed past Mr Irwin and stood between Dad and the sandwiches and Dad squeezed the top of her leg – just quickly – then put his hand back in his pocket. It suddenly felt about 100 degrees and I knew my cheeks were glowing red. I felt a stab of sadness for Mum. He was supposed to be her husband. He was supposed to do that to her. How could he betray her like this? Betray *us?* And, what if someone else saw?

Someone else had seen. I knew because just then Grandma Bett, with Grub squirming under one arm, was helping me stand up with the other.

'Let's get you lot home! Where's Eli?'

When I came back with Elijah, Dad was holding Lucky by her sandalled feet and tickling her tummy. Mrs Lothum was eyeing us from where she sat talking to Mrs Anderson on the couch, but I couldn't see Fat Frannie.

'Kiss for yer old man?' Dad asked. He didn't deserve it, but I didn't know when I'd next get the chance, so I pecked his sandpaper cheek. He didn't notice that I was angry with him, nor that I was nearly dead with pain. Elijah was jumping on his back, trying to tackle him to the ground. My brother wasn't much of a kisser.

Then Lucky started screaming so Dad handed her wriggling little body to me and Grandma Bett tightened up Dad's tie. She handed him a package she'd stashed in her handbag, which smelt cinnamony, like Johnny cakes. 'Come and visit us soon, son,' she said.

'See! It *was* her crying,' Elijah whispered when we got to the bottom of the steps. He pointed at a window at the other end of the house. Inside it was a short, round shape that could only have been Nigel's mum.

The twisting in my stomach had gone away by the time I got home. I was feeling hot and tired, but no more than usual. I was even starting to think I'd imagined it all – until, just before bed, when I was getting ready for my shower. I was climbing out of my jeans and frowning at my too-bony body in the mirror, when I looked down and saw it. Blood. *My* blood. Girls at school talked about periods and everyone knew that Hannah Mosely got hers when she was ten, but I'd never been able to imagine something so horrible happening to me. But there it was. Blood. My life would never be the same again.

'Gracie!' Elijah was banging on the door. 'Hurry up. My turn!'

'Go away!' I didn't want him to know.

'Pet.' Mum knocked on the door, a few minutes later. 'Pet, you've been in here for ages. Elijah had to wee on your gran's petunias. Please let me in.'

'No.' I grabbed the closest towel, Grandma Bett's Ten Commandments one, and wrapped it around myself.

'Please. I know something's up.'

'I can't.'

'Please, just let me in. I want to help you.'

It's too late for that, I thought. Besides, when did you last help me? You could've helped by being at the wake. Or by asking Dad to move back home so he wouldn't still be with Fat Frannie. But I said nothing as I unlocked the door.

Mum scanned the bathroom, hands on her hips. 'What is it? What's wrong?'

I shook my head, not even trying to stop the tears from streaming down my face.

'You look a bit pale.' Mum chewed her little finger. 'But it's been a hard day for everyone. Look, I feel like crying too. I feel so sad and angry. I'm scared. I want to find the person who did this.'

'It's not that.'

'No? Then what is it, pet?' Mum dropped on one knee and grabbed my hand. 'Look. I'm not going to let anyone get you. Nothing will happen to you. I promise. They're going to catch who–'

'No. Mum. It's not that. I've got my...you know...I'm bleeding.'

'What?' Mum smiled like I'd just told a joke that was only slightly funny. She stood, letting go of my hand, stepped towards the pile of clothes and peered down at the pair of *Monday* underpants I'd been wearing even though it was Thursday, because they were the only ones I could find in my drawer that morning.

Why Grandma Bett had given me stupid days of the week underwear I never understood. Perhaps she thought I needed reminding to change them, like Dad probably did.

'Oh, Gracie!' Mum wrapped her arms around me, held me so tight her fingers dug into my arms, but in a nice way. It was the first time in ages she'd hugged me, and I loved the smell of her hair, her sweet lavender shampoo. 'Don't cry. There's nothing to cry about. You're growing up!'

I lay in bed with my book, *After the First Death*, but the words blurred as thoughts raced around my head. I was relieved I wasn't dying of grief for poor Nigel Holmes, but the thought of bleeding every month until I was old was too awful to comprehend. So was the thought of wearing a pad the size of a Malibu surfboard. How would the kids at school not notice it? And all so I could have babies I didn't even want. What other horrible changes was I in for?

To take my mind away from my own problems, I thought about Nigel's mum, about her hiding in the bedroom while the rest of the town was celebrating Nigel's life. She hadn't eaten a crumb since she'd heard about Nigel, his Aunty Jean'd said. Not a crumb. I tried to imagine someone offering Mrs Holmes a crumb on a plate, and her shaking her head, *no, it's too much – I can't possibly*. The wake was for her, Grandma Bett'd said, but she wasn't really even there. She certainly wasn't enjoying the food.

What would Mum do, I wondered, if something happened to one of us? She'd been an absolute wreck when Dad left. What would she do if something really bad happened? Then I made myself stop thinking about that, too. If I imagined it too clearly it might come true.

'What was wrong with you before?' Elijah asked, after Mum'd turned the light off.

'Nothing.' I didn't normally keep secrets from him, but what could I say?

'But you wouldn't let me in and I was busting.'

'I need privacy, Elijah. I'm not just a girl anymore.'

'Huh?' Elijah thought for a moment. 'What are you, then?'

'I'm a, well, still a girl, but I'm nearly a woman.'

Woman? The word seemed wrong. It didn't seem like the right word to describe me.

Elijah laughed. 'You are not!'

'Not yet, but I will be.'

'In a million years.'

'We'll be dead in a million years.'

'I know. Reckon the murderer will come and get us?'

'Don't be silly. I'm not scared of any murderer.' I wasn't. Just as long as Mum left the hall light on. In the dark the owl clock on the bookshelf looked like a head peeking through the window.

'Me neither. The only things I'm scared of are dinosaurs and Satan,' he replied, yawning. I could hear him moving around in bed for the next hour, though, so I wasn't sure whether to believe him.

CHAPTER FIVE

AFTER NIGEL'S FUNERAL I STARTED TO GET A FEEL FOR WHAT IT'D BE LIKE to be in jail. I wasn't allowed to go anywhere without asking Grandma Bett or Mum, and most of the time when I did ask they told me not to be so ridiculous. But it wasn't only like that in our house. None of the other kids were allowed to go anywhere either. Shelley's dad made her and her brother Billy pack all their best things into two bags before he drove them to Dubbo where their nana lived. Shelley didn't even know if she'd be back in time for school. 'Depends when they catch the bastard,' was all her dad would say. Mrs Lothum told Mum about three families that'd moved away from town. They'd put their houses on the market and fled without even waiting for them to sell.

'They're acting like victims,' Grandma Bett said, playing with her gold cross. 'We're not giving in – we've got God on our side.'

So the day Dad stuck his head over our fence I couldn't have been more excited. We were in the backyard playing Commonwealth Games: Tracey Wickham (me) racing Neil Brooks (Elijah), back and forth across our paddling pool, while the twins cheered us on. Dad watched for a while, squinting through a cloud of a cigarette smoke, before yelling out, 'Wanna go to the pictures?' Elijah and I hadn't been to the Picture House for ages, and the only pictures the twins'd heard of were the ones they'd scribbled themselves with their broken crayons. We jumped out of the pool and ran inside to get dressed, our wet feet slipping and sliding on the lino.

'Good thing they haven't bought the Picture House,' Dad said as we walked along Main Road in a chain: Dad in the middle, the twins on either side of him, and Elijah and me on the edges. 'Imagine what crap they'd put on.'

'Who, Dad?' Elijah and I asked together.

'Huh? Oh, those religious freaks. They own practically everythin' else now – petrol station, junk shop, both cafes, Benji's Bakery – they now do all the baking at the camp, god knows where, in a caravan? Ted sold 'em his butchers the other day. Now the poor bugger doesn't know what to do with himself, just sits on the bench out front and looks through the glass. Makes me sick with pity to look at him.'

'What are they buying everything for, Dad?' I didn't really want another thing to worry about, what with Nigel being murdered, Dad living with Fat Frannie, Mum liking St Bede, and the angry red spots starting to appear on my chin, but I couldn't stop myself from asking. I also wanted Dad to keep talking; I'd missed hearing his voice.

'I dunno. So they can get rid of all us non-believers? Ask your mum.'

The movie was *Jaws* and the creepy music that warned us whenever the shark was coming made the hairs on my arms stand up. I stuffed too much popcorn into my mouth and watched most of the movie from between my salty fingers. Elijah and Grub wriggled around in their seats, not used to sitting still for so long, and Lucky cried the whole way through. I told Dad I thought it was great, but really I'd been praying for the credits to roll since the moment it started.

There were only seven other people in the cinema – a group of pimple-faced spiky-haired boys I recognised as seniors from school – and the bus home was empty except for old Mr Buckley and his dog Noodle (people said that once old Mr Buckley got his pension card he spent all day making the most of the cheap bus rides). It felt like that time Mum and Grandma Bett forgot it was the Queen's birthday and sent Elijah and me to school. There were no sounds of kids laughing and playing that day – only the crunch of our school shoes on the gravel road.

When we got home, Mum called out to Dad would he like a cup of coffee and Grandma Bett whispered at us to go off and watch TV even though there was only *Countdown* or the cricket, both too boring to bear. Elijah and I hid in the secret room just in case, but after hearing no yelling or smashing we crept back out. Elijah snuck two glasses from the dining room cabinet and gave me one. We held them to the kitchen door, our ears squished against the cold glass, and listened to Mum and Dad talk.

'Her name's Bethany,' Mum was saying. 'Funny, she doesn't have a last name. It's because they're all members of the same family, she told me.'

'No way! That's sick, Nell.'

'No, silly!' Mum laughed, 'I mean God's family.'

'Course,' Dad said, then, 'I like it when you laugh.'

'Any other questions?' Mum sounded nervous. 'You want to know who the bloke is, I suppose?'

'Yeah, now you're askin', I heard about some Bede fella that you were goin' round with. I was waitin' for you to tell me it was all bullshit.'

'It's *Saint* Bede in actual fact,' Mum replied. 'He's just the holiest person in the state, not some fella.'

'Is he the little bald bloke with a beard? Holds a stick, wears a dress?'

'Robe. I think he looks a bit like Gandhi.'

'What's he doing carrying that stick round? Does he think he's a bloody shepherd?

'His staff? I don't know. I thought he'd stuffed his leg, but now you mention it...' She started laughing.

'Staff?' Dad was laughing too. 'He calls it a staff?'

It was so nice to hear Mum and Dad laughing. Together, not at each other. I couldn't stop myself from smiling.

When we went into the kitchen to get something to eat, Mum was smiling at Dad, one of those warm smiles she often gave us when we got home from school. Elijah looked at me to check whether I'd seen. I was so happy, I had to blink to stop myself from crying. I started to think that Dad'd stay, but he rolled another one of his little cigarettes with his dirty yellow fingers and said he'd better be on his way. No one said anything after that, not even Mum. I couldn't believe it. Couldn't she see what power she had? All she had to do was say 'stay' but she couldn't even do that.

On his way out, Dad left his Blundstone boots next to the old worn mat that used to say 'WELCOME' but now just said 'WE ME'. It was Grandma Bett's idea; she'd even given Dad the money to buy a new pair. She wanted it to look like there was a man in our house.

Elijah lined up his Lightfoot sneakers next to Dad's boots.

'There!' he said. 'No one'll dare come near us now.'

'Elijah, your shoes are size four,' I said.

'Yeah, so?'

'So, they wouldn't scare a flea.'

'Gracie,' Mum said. 'He's just trying to help. Don't lose your rag.'

'Actually,' Elijah was saying, 'they're twenty thousand times bigger than a flea, so they–'

'But it's stupid!' I turned to Mum. 'Half the town knows Dad doesn't live here.'

'What's that got to do with anything?' Mum said.

'Well, who do you think you're tricking?' Why do we have to settle for his bloody boots? I was thinking. Why can't we have Dad?

No one answered and I felt bad as we watched Dad slowly walk down the front path and out the gate. I'd ruined everything; he probably couldn't wait to get away. But I was still angry at Mum.

She was so stupid sometimes. Why couldn't she have just given him one of her warm smiles and said, 'Please stay'?

A few days later I found a pale green notice stuck to the fridge:

KEEP YOUR CHILDREN SAFE
Please ensure that your children are out of harm's way by following these simple rules.

1. Know where your child is at all times.
2. Do NOT leave your child at the school gate – walk with them to their classroom.
3. Provide your child with a loud whistle and give them instructions on when to use it.
4. NEVER in any circumstances let your child go near the river.
5. Make sure your child is home before dark. 5pm is recommended.
6. Talk to your child about strangers and what they should do if approached. (Running and blowing a loud whistle is recommended.)
7. Do not leave your child at home alone. If you must go somewhere, leave them with a friend or neighbour.
8. Put this on your fridge where your child can see it.

> This list was put together by the Catholic church and Constable Stewart J. Thompson for the safety of the children of the Coongahoola community.

As I read the list my chest tightened until I could barely breathe. What was happening to Coongahoola? What was happening to us? Would we have to live like this, stuck in our homes, forever?

That night, Grandma Bett gave Elijah and me each a shiny silver whistle. Mine was threaded on a red ribbon and Elijah's on a blue ribbon so we could wear them around our necks. She then read the safety rules in a slow, clear voice, as if the slower she read, the more we'd hear. She and Father Scott'd been working on the list for the past week and I knew she was proud of it. They'd cut it down from fourteen rules to eight because they needed to fit them all on one page and they had to be in large type for the people who couldn't read very well. Grandma Bett cocked her head and studied the page. 'Is that grammatically correct?' she asked herself, 'to have a comma after "somewhere"?' She spent another ten minutes worrying about the comma, before shaking her head, wiping her glasses with her apron and then putting the kettle on.

It was seeing those rules on our fridge, under the Robinson & Son Plumbers magnet, the magnet that usually held school newsletters or church fête flyers, that made the whole thing seem real to me. Until then it had seemed like watching a movie: bad things were happening, but they had nothing to do with us.

However, this wasn't a story about something imaginary, it was about something terrifyingly real: a murderer. Somewhere out there in Coongahoola was the person who killed Nigel Holmes. I looked out the kitchen window into the blackness of the night and shivered.

CHAPTER SIX

WHEN I WAS YOUNGER, CHRISTMAS WAS THE THIRD-BEST DAY OF THE year, after my birthday and the last day of school. But the year Mum'd kicked Dad out and Nigel was murdered, I would've happily gone without Christmas altogether, just skipped right over it to Boxing Day. That way we wouldn't have tried to pretend that everything was okay, only to realise that things were actually worse than we thought.

Our un-merry Christmas started on Christmas Eve with Elijah and I singing carols to anyone on our street unlucky enough not to have their TVs turned up loud. After bribing us with a ten-dollar note each, Grandma Bett'd tied gold tinsel bows around our necks before leading us to a small stage she'd assembled out of Dad's old beer crates at the end of our cul-de-sac. She then handed us a list of her favourite carols and instructed us to 'sing with all your might'. She reckoned that because of Nigel dying, people'd forgotten about the festive season; she hoped our songs'd help them get into the spirit of Christmas.

I felt ridiculous. I was nearly in Year Six. I wasn't Grandma Bett's 'little angel' any more. The tinsel scratched my neck, and mozzies whined in my ears and feasted on my arms and legs. I prayed that no one from school was within earshot. It was bad enough being the girl who wore a second-hand school uniform without also being the girl who sang Christmas carols on the side of the road. Both Elijah and I knew better than to say no, though, because Grandma Bett would take back her ten-dollar bribe. She was our conductor, her Christmas bell earrings jangling as she waved her arms about. We tried to sing softly but whenever she detected a drop in volume, she raised her arms and mouthed, 'Sing up!' Elijah's legs jiggled as if he was dancing, but more likely he was fighting the urge to run away. My only blessing was that the Irwins had gone to Sydney for the week so there was no chance of Toby spotting me.

If Grandma Bett expected our singing to lure people out of their houses, she would've been disappointed. The only person who joined in was Mr Anderson on his way home from the Coongahoola Hotel. We sang 'Rudolph the Red-Nosed Reindeer' at his request (even though it wasn't on Grandma Bett's list), but he sang the wrong words and he was even more out of tune than we were. I was relieved when Mrs Anderson appeared in her nightie and yelled at him to get home. Almost as relieved as I was when Mrs Buchen poked her head out her kitchen window and asked if we minded finishing up because she had to get some sleep before playing the organ at midnight mass.

Things didn't improve much the next day. When Grandma Bett answered the front door, she made a high-pitched sound that reminded me of Sebastian's final cry.

'Merry Christmas yourself!' she said at last. 'Robbie, what have you done?'

Elijah and I dropped our spoons and raced out to see Dad standing on the WE ME mat with his head bowed. When he looked up I saw that his left eye was red, purple and yellow all at once. It was like he'd tried to copy Mrs Lothum's make-up, but only remembered to do one eye. His bottom lip looked like a fat slug, and there was a cut on his chin, like a tiny sideways smile. Poor Dad. I reached out to touch him, but felt too embarrassed at the last minute, so pretended I needed to lean against the doorframe. Surely Mum will let him come back now, I thought. He obviously needs us.

'Merry Christmas, kids.' His real mouth wasn't smiling.

'Did the murderer try and get you, Dad?' Elijah asked. 'Did you kill him?'

'Nothin' so excitin', son. Let's forget about it, eh? It's Christmas.'

Mum came up behind us, the bells tinkling on the Santa slippers Grandma Bett'd given her. She'd taken an hour to get ready that morning, blow-drying her ringlets and ironing her dress, a new red one with sewn-in shoulder pads. She looked a million times better than Fat Frannie, until close up you saw that her face was red and sweaty from leaning over boiling saucepans.

'What's going on? Frannie come to her senses and clout you?'

'Go easy, Nell. Thought you of all people'd be more Christian-like,' Dad said, pushing past her into the hallway.

'But look at you! Are you trying to scare them more than they already have been?'

As if on cue, Lucky started howling. She ran and clung to Mum's leg, wearing a saggy nappy and dragging Teddy by the foot.

I'm not scared of Dad, I was thinking. The only thing that scared me was the fact that Mum was angry with him instead of feeling sorry for him. It meant that we were no closer to getting him back.

'She's already having nightmares you know, and what is she?' Mum almost yelled (since meeting the Believers she'd given up yelling). 'She's two! She doesn't even know what a nightmare is.'

'Shark!' Lucky cried. 'Shark!' She let go of Mum and squeezed Teddy so tight his stuffing nearly came out of the hole Grub'd dug into his fur with a pick-up-stick.

'See! That's another thing. Why did you take them to a bloody horror film? Grub hasn't had a bath since last Monday.'

'I told them when to close their eyes,' Dad said, pouting and lowering his own Jersey cow eyes. 'When do I ever get to the pictures? Thought I'd pick one we'd all like.'

'All right, all right.' Grandma Bett flapped her arms as if she was shooing away a fly. 'Nell, your parents will be here soon. Shouldn't we finish the lunch? Gracie, perhaps you could organise a quiet game for the littlies. Robbie, I wouldn't normally say this, but I think you need a drink. And a shower. But please have the shower first.'

'You kids are going to have a good Christmas,' Mum'd told us the week before. 'No one can stop our family from having a good Christmas!' And she and Grandma Bett did their best to make sure of it by buying us more presents than they could probably afford, including a digital watch for me. I'd begged Mum for one about three years before when Shelley got one for her birthday. But now Shelley had a multi-coloured one and the watch I unwrapped was black with a wide wristband, like a boy's. I was so disappointed that I had to think about Nigel to stop myself from crying. He probably would've liked getting a new watch. He probably would've liked getting anything. Just being alive would've been enough. Instead, he was lying inside a shiny brown wooden box next to some ancient man called George or Arnold in the Coongahoola cemetery. And here I was, alive as anything, and ready to bawl like a baby because of a stupid present.

Elijah got a BMX bike that Mum'd bought second-hand, but he was only allowed to ride it as far as the Andersons' and back and he was bored with that after the tenth time. Grub and Lucky got a talking Big Bird and a talking Grover, which they carried around for a while before burying them under the couch cushions. Grub didn't even try to break my watch; he and Lucky lay singing 'Way in a Manger' while patting the Sebastian rug. (Even after Grandma Bett had covered the Sebastian patch in salt and soaked it in hot water, he was always there. In a way, he became our kitten. Because of Grandma Bett's constant scrubbing, the Sebastian patch became softer than the rest of the rug and Lucky would spend hours lying on it whispering and making a noise that sounded a lot like a meow.)

Nana and the Butcherer arrived to the smell of burning turkey, with armfuls of presents, including the best present we'd ever got and the only good thing to come out of that Christmas Day: a brand-new cassette player and two tapes. The player was the same size as our *Oxford Dictionary*, black with a shiny silver speaker. I put on

ABBA's *Arrival* and pretended I was one of the ABBA singers, the girl with the long, blonde hair, not the fuzzy-brown-haired one, until Grandma Bett asked me to turn it off for a while to give everyone's ears a rest.

Most of the other presents were for Elijah and Grub. Just as the Butcherer made no secret of his dislike for Dad, Nana made no secret of her preference for grandsons. But she didn't comment once that day about my messy hair or Lucky's sulky ways. A Christmas card had arrived from Mum's brother in Queensland. It was the first time they'd heard from him in months. Nana talked about nothing but Boyd. He had his own building company, his wife was a dentist and their two children were similar in age to Elijah and me, blah blah blah.

As usual, Nana and the Butcherer left much faster than they arrived and slammed the front door behind them. It started with the Butcherer asking Dad what his 'lady friend' was up to while he was 'playing happy families', and ended with Dad saying, 'I'm a grown man and you retired years ago, so why do I always feel like I'm on detention when you're around?'

I was sick of hearing about an uncle I'd never even met, but wished Nana and the Butcherer hadn't left. Mum and Dad sat slumped on opposite sides of the living room. They were both so determined not to ruin our Christmas by arguing that neither of them was game to say a word. Grandma Bett filled the silence with an even longer than usual explanation of the meaning of Christmas, which confused the twins and which Elijah and I'd heard before.

When the phone rang, we all jumped. Elijah tripped on the Tonka truck Nana'd given him, so Mum got to it first. She said, 'Yes', 'Uh-uh' and 'I'll see what I can do' for about five minutes before hanging up.

'Bethany,' she said, chewing her little finger. 'She's asked me to join them for a Christmas prayer session. Just an hour or so. You don't mind, do you?' She asked us in the posh, slightly American voice she always used after talking to Bethany.

'You're free to do what you like,' Dad said. 'Said so yourself.'

'It wasn't you I was asking. It was your mother and children.'

'Please yourself, Nell,' Grandma Bett said. 'Robbie needs to spend some time with the kids – and his old mum.'

Dad left soon after Mum without explaining what happened to his face. I didn't find out until Matty Thorpe told me on the first day back at school. He said that his dad was at the Coongahoola Hotel on Christmas Eve and saw my dad get into a fight with Andrew Hitchcock, the Captain of Coongahoola's Masters Rugby team. Apparently, Dad'd tried to kiss Heather Childs, not realising that her fiancé was Andrew Hitchcock, nor that Andrew was at the bar ordering a pie and chips. Matty's dad reckoned that if Andrew hadn't been in the pub drinking all day, Dad wouldn't have lived to see Christmas morning.

The next time I saw Dad, his face was normal again, except for the yellow around one eye if you looked closely. I'd been back at school for two weeks. I was in Year Six, my last year of primary school. Not that it was a big deal. In any other town I'd be changing schools at the end of the year, but in Coongahoola moving up to Year Seven just meant going into the prefab classrooms on the other side of the toilet block.

The only things keeping me awake at night were the thought of learning long division in term two and worrying that I'd never be as grown-up as the other girls in my class (my chest still didn't look much different to Elijah's). The green paper with the list of rules was still on our fridge and we still ran our lives by them, but they'd lost all meaning. It was as if what happened to Nigel was just a nightmare. I wondered if the whole town could have had the same nightmare and if maybe we all dreamt up Nigel too.

But then on the last day of February, I realised it hadn't been a dream and that life had changed for good. That was the day Anthea Bryce didn't turn up at school.

CHAPTER SEVEN

I WAS LYING ON THE FLOOR PAINTING A PICTURE OF A FAERY — A DARK ONE, not the babyish kind – when I spotted Constable Stewy clomping past our classroom. His normally shiny, black leather boots were caked with pale grey mud.

Josh Napper saw him too. 'Copper!'

Before Mr Friend could tell us to be quiet, the classroom phone rang. Its loud, sharp ring shut us up quicker than he could've; we'd never heard it ring before. Mr Friend stared at it for a moment before picking it up.

'Hello? Yes. Really? Sure. Yes. Certainly.' Mr Friend's grey eyes were staring over our heads. He was new to Coongahoola, sent to our school straight out of teachers' college. Mrs Lothum said he'd come in the hope of finding a wife, but the only woman desperate enough to look at him twice was Suzy Armstrong and she was already married. There was chalk dust on his elbow and a few crumbs in his shaggy beard from playtime. Twisties, it looked like.

'Okay, 6B. Carry on...' He cleared his throat. 'Carry on painting, please. I'll be out for five minutes and I don't, I repeat *don't*, want to hear your voices down the corridor.' He straightened his thin, navy blue tie and licked his lips before quietly closing the door behind him.

'Cops've hunted you down, Josh,' Baby Pete said. He'd been

called Baby Pete since the first day of school when his mum pushed him into Room One in a squeaky old pram. He said he was only riding in a pram because he'd hurt his ankle falling off a swing, but no one believed him.

'You more like,' Josh replied. 'Playin' with your willy too much. You're done for.'

'Nah!' Even standing on tiptoes, Baby Pete still only came up to Josh's dimpled chin. 'You are, I saw you havin' a wank under your desk.'

'Some other kid's been murdered,' Sharon Andrews announced. 'Most probably.' She rubbed her eye, leaving a dollop of green paint on her nose and cheek.

Everyone was quiet. My faery's wings looked like two black clouds and she glared at me from two green blobs. I tried to cheer her up with a red smile but it made her even scarier. Her lips looked like they were bleeding.

'Who d'you reckon? Someone else from Mrs Hill's class?' Matty Thorpe asked from behind the bookshelf where the new encyclopaedias were kept.

'Jason Ellis, I hope,' someone said.

'Please don't let it be Elijah,' Samantha Cook cried, playing with her curly red hair. 'I'd go mental.'

'It's not him!' I answered. 'It'd never be him. He's too fast.' I couldn't stand Samantha. I hadn't spoken to her much, but I knew that she was obsessed with royal weddings and was dead set on marrying Elijah. I just wished she'd forget about him and go after someone her own age. Elijah was way too young to think about getting married, and the idea of Samantha, always sickeningly neat with ribbons in her hair, becoming part of my family made me want to throw up.

'Didn't he kill a cat once?' someone with a blocked nose asked from down the back.

'It was an accident!' Samantha and I said at the same time. As if *she* was there.

'I reckon it's Esther – the Bleeder who wears the nana dress covered with lace like a doily,' Michelle Livingston said.

'Yeah, she's weird.' That was Penny. 'I can imagine her being murdered.'

'You know what I'm going to paint next?' Baby Pete called out, 'I'm going to paint one of youse gettin–'

The door squeaked open. Mr Friend closed it and leant against it. His face looked small and pink behind his rusty beard.

'Is Esther the Believer girl dead?' Reagan asked.

'Or Jason Ellis?'

Mr Friend opened his mouth, but said nothing as he walked across the platform and lowered himself down into his desk chair. I noticed that the crumbs were gone from his beard. Perhaps another teacher'd told him they were there.

'I've just been talking to the constable.' Mr Friend tapped his silver pen on a textbook. 'No one is dead, so I don't want to hear any more of this speculation. But Constable Stewart is concerned about someone – a girl in Year Four who didn't turn up at school this morning. Anthea. Anthea Bryce. As far as her parents knew she was on her way to school. If anyone knows anything that could help Constable Stewart find Anthea, please tell me.'

Anthea. Not Elijah. Not that I'd really thought that. Well, maybe I'd thought it for a minute.

Anthea was the prettiest girl in Year Four and when Mrs Winters told the girls to choose a boy to sit next to for the year, Anthea'd picked Elijah. The only other thing I remembered about her was that she had a little sister called Vera May, a silly name according to Elijah. (Being the only 'Elijah' in Coongahoola and maybe even in the world, he was conscious of other people's unusual names.)

'She's a River Child,' Baby Pete said. That was something I'd forgotten. 'Like Nigel.' And Elijah.

'Yes,' Mr Friend said. 'That has been noted. This river stuff, hmmm, I don't really follow–'

'It was when all the adults had an orchy,' Matty Thorpe said. 'At the River Picnic when we were babies. The River Children were born to different dads from their real ones.'

'Not all of them,' I said. I was sick of people saying that all the time. Just as well Elijah looked more like Dad than any of us. Except maybe Grub. Grub was a blonde version of Elijah, though instead of brown, his big cow eyes were a deep sea-blue (I could easily imagine Mrs Lothum saying that the males got all the looks in our family).

'I get the general idea, thank you, Matthew. Anyway, the constable had made that connection,' Mr Friend said.

The newspaper'd made the connection too. 'SECOND RIVER CHILD ABDUCTED,' yelled the front page of *The Coongahoola Times*. Grandma Bett tried to hide it from us, but Elijah spotted the word 'River' underneath her fluffy pink cardigan.

We also heard them talk about the River Children on Radio Coolio and on TV. 'Who will be next?' the TV and radio voices asked. The paper even had photos of all the River Children with big crosses drawn over Nigel's and Anthea's faces. Elijah was poking his tongue out; it was his school photo from the year before and he thought it was funny that it'd made it into the paper, but I didn't. The photos blurred together as I stared at them. My head felt hot and my throat was dry. There may not have been a connection before, but seeing all the photos of the River Children lined up, the murderer would know who to look for next. There were only two photos between Anthea Bryce's and Elijah's.

On Thursday, three days later, there was still no news of Anthea. The steelworks closed at 4pm so all the men could join in the search. Dad tapped on our door on his way past. I knew better than to get my hopes up, but seeing him cheered me up. I felt that nothing could go wrong when Dad was around.

'Just wanted to make sure youse kids were all right.' His grey overalls looked as though they hadn't been washed since Mum kicked him out. Fat Frannie mustn't have soaked them overnight in Wonder Soap like Grandma Bett did. He picked up Lucky and Grub and spun them around until Lucky screamed at him to stop.

'I also wanted to say somethin' to you,' Dad said to Mum, lowering his Jersey cow eyes. 'Um, not sure how to say it really, but um, well, that crowd you're in with, I'm not sure they're so good.'

'You're not, are you? And why'd that be?' Mum crouched down and held her hanky over Lucky's dripping nose.

'You know, people talk, these missin' kids, nothin' like this happened before this crowd showed up.' Dad stared at Elijah's rusting bike lying on the front lawn. 'I dunno myself, but some say it's more than a coincidence.'

Mum laughed, shooing a fly away from her face. 'Oh, so they're murderers, I get it! Of course, silly me. These people who are so full of love and kindness and – things you'd know nothing about!'

'Jus' be careful. You joined 'em for a bit of fun, that's what you said. But I think that Bede bloke – I think you're being taken for a ride.'

'And I s'pose your sudden concern about me has nothing to do with Frannie giving you the boot?'

Dad's eyebrows went up in a V. 'What?'

Two kookaburras laughed from the wattle tree that marked where our lawn ended and the Irwins' began. Was Mum deliberately pushing Dad out of our lives? I wondered. Every time he visited, the possibility of him coming home grew further away.

'I hear everything,' Mum was saying. 'I don't even want to, but someone told me you tried to hit on Heather Childs at the pub. Heather Childs! Didn't know she was engaged, did you? Thought she still had her schoolgirl crush on you? Well, good on her for telling Frannie! And good on Fat Frannie for turfing you for good.'

'That's not how it was!'

'No, I'm sure I only got the edited version – fit for the wife's ears! Anyway, if you're looking for somewhere to live, why not shack up with Shirley Lothum? It'd make all her dreams come true, and James wouldn't even notice.'

'I've got my standards! I know they dropped a little the day I met you, but–'

Mum slammed the door, then quickly opened it again. 'Come on, kids, come inside.'

'See you another time, eh?' Dad pulled out his falling-apart brown leather wallet and handed Elijah and me a five-dollar note each. That was more than he'd ever given us, but I couldn't get excited. It was only a piece of paper. 'You kids stick together, all right?'

CHAPTER EIGHT

MASS ATTENDANCE HAD ALMOST DOUBLED SINCE NIGEL'S DEATH, Grandma Bett was pleased to tell us, and with it the amount of work she had to do at the church. One of her new jobs was thinking of important things for Father Scott to say in his sermons, so they'd be powerful enough 'to keep the newcomers at mass and stop them from straying towards the crowd down by the river'. She usually dragged us kids to mass on weekends, but one Sunday morning I asked Mum if I could go to the Believers' meeting with her instead. I think the only reason she said yes was because of the look on Grandma Bett's face.

Before Mum and I left, Grandma Bett summoned me into her room.

'When they start talking their nonsense, put your fingers in your ears. That's the best advice I can give,' she said in a quiet, serious voice. Her room smelt of incense and made me think of God.

I nodded before walking out to find my shoes. I didn't say that a lot of the stuff Father Scott said at mass sounded like nonsense too. Or that God didn't make much sense to me anyway. I didn't understand how someone so good could let so much bad stuff happen. What had Nigel and Anthea ever done to him?

'Don't listen to a word,' Grandma Bett whispered after me.

There was a whole church full of them, a massive church, much bigger than our school hall. It'd taken them four months to build, working day and night, the Believer kids slaving along with their mums and dads, turning up to school with dirty faces and dusty uniforms. Dad'd watched on from the steelworks. He told us that he and Mr Irwin were having a smoko in the tearoom when two bearded men erected the cross on the steeple. Less than two minutes later, the sky turned an angry black and the tearoom shook with thunder. 'See, even God's pissed with 'em!' Dad said.

Walking up the aisle was like walking into something out of a movie, but I couldn't think what movie. *Star Wars*, maybe. It was quiet except for the squeaking of Mum's and my shoes. All the women and girls wore powder-blue veils like Bethany's and all the men and boys wore long white cloaks like priests. The statues were twice as big as the ones in the Catholic church and all were painted a shiny gold that hurt my eyes. I wrapped my goosebumpy arms around myself. Even though I'd been sticky with sweat from the hot drive in our car, I felt cold.

When we'd sat down on one of the hard wooden benches, Mum dug around in her handbag, pulling out her round make-up mirror and a long piece of light blue material. A veil! She stuck the veil on her head and adjusted it over her newly permed curls without looking at me, without even joking about it. Then she tucked the mirror back into her bag and held her hands together like Grandma Bett did before picking up her knife and fork at dinner. I didn't know what to do, where to look. Mum was one of them!

At last someone started talking. The Purple People Eater from Woolworths, the one who'd seen the vision of Mary, stood at the altar waving her big sausage arms in the air. Even though I didn't think much of the Believers, and she'd always given me a funny feeling, I felt sort of proud of her. She wasn't bent over the '10 Items or Less' counter wearing a plastic name badge with the 'a' worn off so people sometimes called her 'Marth', and asking if we'd noticed that lettuce was on special – she was standing in front of everyone at an altar. She was obviously very important. She stood with her head held high, every now and then passing a gold cup to the obviously even more important, purple-cloaked Saint Bede. It might have been the way her veil hung or the black clothes underneath, but the Purple People Eater even looked as if she'd lost a bit of weight. I knew the Believers were against fun things like watching TV – maybe they'd banned eating custard tarts as well.

'Do you think you're ready?' Mum asked after the last prayer had been said and the last song sung. Her veil was crooked but I wasn't going to tell her. If the kids at school found out that my mum wore a Believer's veil I'd be as good as dead.

'Ready for what?' At mass the last song meant that we could go home. That's why everyone sang it so loudly and happily.

'To meet our leader? Saint Bede.' She pointed at him kissing a giant gold foot belonging to Jesus.

'Oh, I suppose.' I waved a fly away.

'Well, you could try sounding a bit more enthusiastic.' Mum lowered her voice. 'Saint Bede has come all the way from the USA to teach the Lord's prophecies. God himself – well, it was Mary, really, Jesus's mum, that Martha saw and the newspapers talked about, but you know what I'm saying – sent him to Coongahoola. We're blessed. So please try and smile or something.'

'Yes, Mum.' I hoped he wasn't going to hug me like he seemed to be doing to everyone else.

God obviously didn't hear my hope, or chose to ignore it. The first thing Saint Bede did after Mum introduced me was to wrap his arms around me, squeeze me so tightly that I got another taste of breakfast, and say in his funny accent, 'Welcome my dear, dear child.'

He was small, too small for the long, scruffy steel-wool beard and oversized black-framed glasses he hid behind, and his breath was worse than his BO. I wanted to get out of there. If God had bothered to give me fast legs like Elijah's, I would've fled.

'Thank you,' I said in my politest voice, my eyes watering from his smell. Not even the Butcherer smelt that bad, even after playing tennis.

Saint Bede then lifted one arm off my shoulder and spread it around Mum so that the three of us were joined together by his purple wings. He started praying to God for me and my soul, even though the service was over and everyone else seemed to be having normal conversations.

I thought of Elijah, Grub and Lucky kneeling down at mass. The worst thing they'd have to do was shake people's sweaty hands and say 'Peace be with you'. As soon as it was over, Elijah and Michael and some of the other kids'd be playing chase all around the churchyard. I decided that if anyone ever bothered to ask me, I'd prefer to be a Catholic.

Eventually Saint Bede ran out of things to ask God for and he nodded for Mum and me to sit back down.

He hadn't finished with us though. He took my hand and squeezed it in his warm, slippery one, fixed his dark brown eyes on mine and said, 'My child, I want you to know that I've been in communication with God about your precious brother. I cannot promise you anything, for I am merely God's servant, but I can assure you, I've asked that your brother be spared.'

He was probably trying to make me feel better, but I felt scared, more scared than I'd ever felt for Elijah. This wasn't helped by the way Saint Bede's coke-bottle glasses magnified his eyes to double normal size.

'Gracie?' Mum nudged my shoulder with her elbow.

'Thank you,' I said again, but probably not as politely as before, because I'd decided I didn't like Saint Bede one bit and didn't think that Mum should either.

'So you heard the election result, then?' Mum was asking Saint Bede.

He nodded, looking away.

'So, you're not happy? About Bob Hawke winning?' Mum asked.

'I'd rather we didn't discuss it. Not in the Lord's temple.'

'Oh, I just thought, he is, well Bob's one of us. You know, more of an ordinary bloke, not like that Malcolm fellow. Holds the world record for drinking beer! I know you don't approve of beer or any other kind of drinking, but, sorry. Yes, this is a church.'

'Thank you, Nell. I wouldn't want anything so insignificant to come between us.'

'Yes, of course.' Mum said, blushing like a little kid.

For the next half hour Saint Bede talked only to Mum, calling her Nelly and touching her hair, winding her curls around his fingers. He told her that she was one of God's angels and that her soul was as pure as heaven itself. Mum hardly said a word, but her eyes twinkled, her cheeks glowed and she chewed her little finger. She reminded me of Samantha Cook, the annoying girl in my class with a crush on Elijah. It made me want to cover my ears or scream 'Stop!' or both, but I could see that Mum liked the attention Saint Bede was giving her. Dad hardly ever said nice things to her, and he'd only touch her hair if there was something stuck in it, like a beetle or spider web.

I started to get pins and needles in my bum and I thought about making myself throw up – that way, Mum and I'd be able to leave without getting any more hugs. But Mum'd guess that I did it on purpose and all hell'd break loose when we got in the car. Looking around, I recognised some kids from school. Lucky for me, no one talked to the Believer kids, otherwise everyone'd know what I'd been up to on my Sunday morning. There were a few boys – I counted twelve teenagers – but none anywhere near as cute as Toby, not that I'd bother liking any of them anyway. Bleeder boys weren't like real boys. They wore robes, for starters. Then Bethany's daughter, the girl with the zits who was actually named Heavenly (Heavenly!), gave me a little wave and a shy smile. I pretended not to see her, hoping that'd stop her from coming over.

It didn't.

'Hi,' she said. 'I'm Heavenly.' Her voice was deeper than I would've expected and kind of gravelly, but she didn't have her mum's annoying accent. I thought she might've had a cold, but later learnt that it was just the way she spoke.

'Hello.' I looked away, up at the statues then down at the shiny wooden floor, but she didn't take the hint.

'You're Gracie Barrett. I see you at school. In the library mostly. That's where I go at lunchtime.'

I'd read a lot since Shelley went away. Finding a best friend to replace her would've been more trouble than it was worth, and reading in the library was better than wandering the playground on my own.

Heavenly was waiting for me to say something, so I said, 'I like reading.' It was short, to the point and, I hoped, boring enough to put an end to the conversation.

'Me too,' she said quietly. 'But I'm not meant to.'

'Not *meant* to?'

Heavenly looked around before whispering, 'I'm not allowed to... read.'

'What? Who says?' I'd never heard of such a thing. Our class had half an hour of Silent Reading every afternoon at two thirty. I loved it, but some kids used it as an excuse to muck around. Mr Friend was always saying, '*Open* your books and *close* your mouths!' I couldn't imagine him telling us *not* to read.

'My father. He says books poison the mind. Except the Bible, of course.'

'That's...so...wrong!' I suddenly felt really sorry for this strange Believer girl. I'd never seen my dad read anything other than the *TV Guide* or a magazine that was mostly pictures, but he'd never tell me not to read myself. And the Bible? Who, apart from Grandma Bett and priests, could be bothered reading that?

'So you haven't read any of the Narnia books, then?' I asked, trying to imagine what a life without books would be like. 'Or Robert Cormier?'

Heavenly stepped closer and whispered, 'I've read lots. I borrowed *The Outsiders* last week.'

'I loved that! Same man who wrote *Rumble Fish*.'

She nodded, and smiled in a way that actually made her look quite pretty. 'S. E. Hinton. But it's really a lady. S. E. stands for Susan Eloise. This is the first book I've read of hers though.'

'Like it?'

She nodded again, her cheeks pink with what must've been guilt. *The Outsiders* made even me feel guilty, especially when Grandma Bett was sitting nearby. I knew she wouldn't think it was 'suitable'. I was surprised to hear that it was written by a woman.

'Don't tell anyone though,' Heavenly said. 'Father'd burn it.'

'*Burn* it?'

'It's happened before. Friday nights are bonfire night. My father's always looking for "sinful material" to burn.'

I hoped I'd never meet her dad, her *Father*. 'I won't. Promise.'

'Anyway, I like you, Gracie Barrett. I'm glad we talked. But I've got to go, I've got to polish the chalices.'

'Okay.' I wondered what chalices were, but was too shocked to ask. I watched Heavenly walk up the aisle, taking little steps so as not to trip over her ridiculously long blue dress. I couldn't believe that we had something in common. That she was a tiny bit like me. She was smart and I kind of liked her. Even so, I hoped my skin never got as bad as hers and wondered whether that was something I could pray about or whether God'd think it too trivial.

'So you know Heavenly, then?' Saint Bede asked, once he'd finished whispering – I didn't want to imagine what – into Mum's ear.

'I've seen her around.' What was it to him? I wondered.

'That's lovely, Gracie.' Mum said. That's *lovely?* What was happening to my mum?

Then Bethany walked up to us, smiling as always. To me, her teeth always looked too white and her smile too big, reminding me of the giant clown face at Luna Park in Sydney. It wasn't the first time I'd found myself wanting something bad to happen to her, for something big to fall out of the sky and land on her head or something, just so I could see a different look on her face. I feel terrible about that now, especially after what happened later.

She put her icy-cold fingers on my shoulder and kissed Mum's cheek, her clown smile frozen on her moon-shaped face. I could smell soap, sickly sweet.

'There you are, my love.' Saint Bede reached for Bethany's hand.

'See you soon, angel,' he said to Mum, kissing her on the forehead.

'Lovely to meet you, child.' He squeezed my arm as he stood up. *Child?* I'd just turned twelve. He wasn't only creepy. He was stupid.

He and Bethany walked off arm-in-arm like little kindergarten girls in the playground.

'Gracie, don't stare,' Mum said.

'Does he do that with everyone?' I couldn't believe it. I shook my head. This was wrong. The whole day had been wrong.

'What, pet? Bethany's his wife.'

'Wife? He's married?' I couldn't believe it, not after the way he'd been looking at Mum, the things he'd been saying.

'Of course. Bethany is his third wife. He has two others.'

'Three! At the same time?'

'Yes, Gracie, at the same time. It may sound strange to you, but you are quite young and need to open your mind a bit. This man is Saint Bede. He's not really a man, like your dad's a man – well, kind of a man. He's a saint! He's got so much love to give and it's God's wish that he touches as many people as he can.'

'So, *he* is Heavenly's dad?' I asked. I now hated him even more. He burned books!

'That's right,' Mum said. 'It's nice that you're friends.'

'Can we go home now?' I stood and tried to shake off my pins and needles. Grandma Bett was right. I should've stuck my fingers in my ears the moment I got into the church. The whole world'd gone completely nuts. Now even Mum was speaking nonsense.

CHAPTER NINE

I DON'T KNOW WHEN THE POSTERS OF NIGEL WERE TAKEN DOWN, BUT I remember the day Anthea's face appeared instead of his. I counted thirty-three-and-a-half Antheas (one'd been ripped in half under her chin) and that was only on one side of Main Road. Nigel's posters'd been written by hand, whereas Anthea's were typed and twice as big. Also, rather than being a school photo of just another dorky kid, Anthea's was professional and made her look like a movie star. Like with Nigel, I wished I'd known Anthea, so I could actually feel something about her now she was gone. I knew I shouldn't, but I also wished Mum'd pay to have our photos taken properly, just in case. She probably would've too if she'd known that Elijah's face was about to be on the front cover of every newspaper in Australia.

As with Nigel, *The Coongahoola Times* devoted a whole page to Anthea every day (except the day after Bob Hawke became Prime Minister), until it ran out of things to say. We found out that her parents came from Cornwall, England, then lived in Sydney until Dr Bryce got a job in Coongahoola, a year before Anthea was born.

'I believed that a move to the country would be a safe bet,' Dr Bryce'd said. 'Things like this aren't supposed to happen here. Australia is meant to be the *Lucky* Country, a *peaceful* society.' We learnt that Anthea had a peanut allergy, didn't have any pets (she was allergic to cat fur, too), but had a special doll called Roly Poly (there was a photo of a short, fat doll with sticking-up hair). She also loved cross-country running and had a good ear for piano.

A few men, including Dad, took turns going on patrol at night. 'The cops obviously can't solve this alone,' Dad'd said. 'Someone's gotta protect us.' Apparently, Sergeant Colby was angry when he heard what they were up to, and accused them of trying to do his job. But Constable Stewy was relieved. 'Every extra set of ears and eyes is a great help,' he'd reportedly said.

Elijah wanted to take action too. He must've liked sitting next to Anthea more than he ever admitted. I don't remember him saying much about her when she was alive, but after she'd been missing for three days he conned Michael into going on an Anthea Rescue Mission with him. At first I thought they were crazy, but at the last minute I decided to join them to get out of the house. I didn't want to waste any more time writing letters to Shelley since she was having too much fun with the 'Dubbo girls' to bother writing back. Besides, I thought the chance of us finding Anthea was pretty small.

The plan was simple: Michael told his mum he was going to our house after school, and we told our mum we were going to Michael's. We'd walk the back way to the river, hiding in the bush whenever we heard a car coming. We didn't talk about what we'd do if we found Anthea.

It was a hot, sticky afternoon with the sky such a bright blue you couldn't have painted a better one. It wasn't the kind of day bad things happen on, but that didn't stop me from feeling sick. I'd only been to the river twice since the River Picnic and both times I'd been so scared I'd nearly wet my pants. Nothing'd actually happened, but the thought that something could was terrifying.

In the nightmares that'd haunted me since I was two, about the River Picnic, the river was black. That's mostly what I remembered when I woke up – the black-as-night river. That, and the deafening noise. The smashing of glass, the moaning, the shrieking. It was the shrieking that made me cry. I always woke up crying and sweating from those nightmares. I shivered just thinking about them.

We walked up past Sarah Mosely's huge mansion, past the Childs's and the Halls's. Then we walked, ran, skipped down the bumpy dirt road that snaked around the river. About halfway down

River Road, we started clawing our way through the bush towards the river, the big statue of the Virgin Mary watching over us through the trees.

'Anthea!' Elijah called. 'Anthea!' He wanted to believe that she was still alive, that she was just tied to a tree or something. I don't know what he would've done if we found her body. I don't know what any of us would've done.

'Hey!' Elijah lifted his hand, signalling us to stop.

'What?' Please God, I thought, don't let him have found anything. Please God, I'll help Mum change Lucky's nappy for a week. I'll even help change Grub's.

'Over there!' Elijah said hoarsely. He pointed through the bush to a clearing, to the blue base of the enormous fibreglass Virgin Mary.

'Maybe she'll show us where Anthea is,' Elijah whispered.

'What?' Michael flicked hair out of his eyes, a habit I'd only just noticed that was already driving me nuts. 'It's a statue.'

'Not that, deadhead! The real Mary. She appears to them and tells them stuff.'

'Worth a try,' I said. Anything to avoid stepping on a dead body.

We swept away the pine cones, dried kangaroo poo and sticks with our hands, and made three cushions of dead leaves. Then we knelt and clasped our hands together like Grandma Bett did when praying for the children in Ethiopia or for the washing to dry. We focused on the statue of Mary and moved our lips like Grandma Bett did. I was pretty certain nothing'd happen, but a tiny part of me hoped something would, if only to see Grandma Bett tremble with excitement when we told her. I squinted and saw a kaleidoscope of colours, but none of them belonged to the blue veil of the Believers' Virgin Mary.

'It's not working,' Michael said.

'Shut up!' Elijah elbowed Michael. 'Might take her a while to warm up.'

The sun seeped through the trees and the slight breeze did little to relieve the heat. After kneeling with my back straight and sweaty palms held together for a few minutes, the only apparition I had was of white spots. I had felt the exact same way in Year Three when our class was singing to some half-dead people in the Coongahoola Retirement Village's stuffy dining room, moments before I fainted onto the sticky lino floor. I still feel uneasy when I hear the words, 'Australian sons, let us rejoice–'

'Let's go,' I said, crawling into the shade of a gum tree. 'It's nearly five-thirty.'

'Maybe Anthea just ran away.' Elijah stood up, brushing twigs and leaves off his grey shorts. 'Last one to the road's a rotten egg.'

I didn't mind being the rotten egg. In fact, I loved being the rotten egg. I was so happy to be out of the bush and on my way home again. No one saw us sneak around the back way, brushing the sticky grass seeds off our legs. We didn't even have to lie when we got home because Mum just asked if we were hungry.

In a way it was too easy. Two days later Elijah wanted to go on another Anthea Rescue Mission. I decided I'd rather stay home and play mindless games of duck, duck, goose with Lucky and Grub than go out looking for a dead girl. I was relieved I had when Michael later told me what happened.

A few metres from the edge of the river, they found a dead baby possum, a tiny one that can't have lived long enough to grow fur. It was probably the first time Elijah realised that Anthea was most likely dead, Michael reckoned. He said that Elijah wanted to bury it, wouldn't go home until it'd had a proper send-off. Michael told him not to be a weirdo and made a Damien Omen joke, but Elijah ignored him and started digging with his hands. Michael ended up helping – he just wanted to go home – and they buried the baby possum, but the smell of it made him throw up all over his school shoes.

The thing is, that didn't stop Elijah from wanting to look for Anthea. It just meant that Michael wouldn't go with him again, so Elijah had to go on his own.

The next time Elijah planned to search the reserve instead of the river. He announced this with a mouthful of Anzac biscuit. It was

73

after school and Mum'd just disappeared into her room for a nap. I told Elijah that he could keep my five-dollar note if he promised not to go, but he shook his head and said that Anthea needed him. I was determined not to let him go and was wondering what else I could offer him, when I heard a voice yell out from the front lawn. A voice I instantly recognised as belonging to Toby Irwin.

I reached the front verandah just as Toby leaped out of Grandma Bett's petunia bed, clutching a dirty soccer ball.

'Toby?' I said.

'Yeah?'

'You yelled something.'

'Yeah. I yelled, *Shit, you retard!*'

'Huh?' My nose stung with tears.

'Jono kicked the ball into your flowers. He's so unco.'

'Jonathan?' I looked across to the Irwins' and saw Jonathan, still in school uniform, hiding behind the bottlebrush. Phew. Jonathan was the retard, not me.

That was when Elijah made his getaway. 'See you!' He skipped past me and down the steps.

'But Elijah, no!' I yelled.

'Just remember, Michael's mum picked me up!'

'But. Wait. Mum?'

'Dead to the world!' he called out.

I raced to the gate. 'Elijah, come back!'

'What's the problem?' Toby said.

'He's going to the reserve,' I said. 'On his own.'

Toby shrugged. 'Heaps of kids do.'

'But the murderer!'

'Yeah. He's the bald geek near the river. Keep clear of him and he'll be fine.' Suddenly Toby was standing next to me, tossing and catching his ball.

Toby doesn't know about Mum and Saint Bede, I thought. Or if he does, he doesn't care.

'Yeah, I know, but–' I couldn't think straight. Toby was standing right next to me. We were standing *together*. It would've been a magical moment – if we were watching anything except my younger brother running away from the safety of our house.

'Don't worry about him,' Toby said.

'Nah. I won't,' I lied. 'And don't you worry about Grandma Bett's petunias.'

'Grandma Bett's whatsits?' Toby threw his ball up and headbutted it, leaving a smear of dirt on his forehead.

'Her flowers. It's okay. I'll just tell her I accidentally squashed them.'

'Yeah? Cool. Jono owes you one.'

Jono owes me one. But I wanted Toby to know I was doing it for him.

'So, what are you up to anyway?' I asked.

'What's it look like?' Toby kicked the ball at the bottlebrush Jonathan was still hovering behind, before running after it.

'Bye, Toby,' I called out, trying not to sound too deflated.

'See ya round.'

I slunk back inside, trying to assure myself that Toby was right. Heaps of kids went to the reserve. I didn't know whether to believe that Saint Bede was the murderer, but Nigel was murdered near the river so it did make sense that that was where the murderer hung out. I told myself, over and over, that Elijah was the toughest boy I knew, just like Dad was the toughest man – and for a while I managed to forget about him.

But then I realised that the only light I could see out our living room window was the light inside the Baileys' kitchen window. Everything else was bluey-black. I was playing Mum's *1983 On Fire* compilation tape, but the music drifted into the background. I didn't notice when one song finished and another began. I couldn't stop thinking about Elijah outside, alone, in the dark.

'Doesn't Elijah see Michael all day at school?' Grandma Bett asked from behind her prayer book. 'Why does he need to stay for tea at his house as well?'

'They're inseparable these days, him and Michael,' Mum said.

'Probably driving Helen mad too. I'll give her a call. Can you turn that thing down please, Gracie?'

I pressed the red button and the tape player stopped with a loud click. When Mum reached the doorway I couldn't hold it in any longer. 'He's not there!'

'What?' Mum spun around.

'Beg pardon!' Lucky corrected her.

'He's not at Michael's. He's looking for Anthea.'

'*Anthea*? He's at Michael's.'

'No, he's not. Not now. He's at the reserve.'

'What? What's he doing there?'

'I just said. Looking for Anthea.'

'Why on earth?' Mum said.

'But anything could– It's dark!' Grandma Bett dropped her prayer book.

'I'm calling your dad!'

She's just panicking, I told myself. It's Elijah. He'll be fine. He's smart and he's fast. But he's on his own. He's a River Child! I should've stopped him! Why did I listen to Toby? I should've told Mum earlier. What if something's happened? I ran to the window and pressed my face against the cool glass. Where was he?

Mum yelled into the phone (forgetting that she didn't yell anymore), first at Gary to get Dad, then at Dad to go and find his son.

'Robbie's going to the reserve with Gary,' she said, frantically forcing her feet into her thongs. 'Graham's on patrol tonight. But Robbie reckons he's probably down by the river.'

'And you?' Grandma Bett asked. 'What are you doing?'

'I don't know. But I can't bloody sit here!' She grabbed her keys and ran along the hall.

'But where will you go? How will you know–'

The door slammed so loudly that the windows shook. Then the house was dead quiet except for the *tick tock* of the Virgin Mary clock. Lucky started to cry. What had I done?

CHAPTER TEN

'IT'S ALL RIGHT, LUCKY LUCE,' GRANDA BETT WHISPERED, BUT HER VOICE was wobbling so I knew she had doubts. 'We're all going to pray. Gracie, Grub, come over here next to me. Let's pray for your brother.'

Dear God, I prayed in my head. Please bring Elijah back to us. Don't let anything bad happen to him. You can't let him get murdered! Not Elijah! He's only nine and he's a pretty good person most of the time. (An image of Elijah giving Grub a Chinese burn flashed in my mind, but I quickly pushed it away in case God could see it too.) Please, please, please.

'Why do we pray?' Lucky asked. She was holding her baby Mary-Anne doll by the foot and bouncing its head on Sebastian's rug.

'We're asking for God's help.' Grandma Bett's hands were squeezed together so tightly that her fingers were turning white. 'Our Father who art in heaven–'

'Where's God gone?' Grub asked. He smelt like wet soil.

'What do you mean?' Grandma Bett sounded impatient.

'He aren't in heaven. Where's he?'

'He *art* in heaven. It's an old-fashioned way of saying he *is* in heaven. Now, please let me get on with it. This is *extremely* important.'

Grandma Bett, Lucky and I were still on our knees (Grub had

slid under the couch and was talking to his sock puppets) when the front door burst open. I knelt up straight, straining my ears for the sound of Elijah's feet in the hall, but all I could hear was the *swish swish* of Mum's thongs. I sank back down.

Mum's face was so puffy that her eyes'd practically disappeared. I quickly looked away before I started crying too.

'He's not back?' Mum's voice was too high, like a crazy woman's. 'Has Robbie called?'

Grandma Bett shook her head. 'Not yet. We're praying, Nell. You can join us.'

'Praying? *Praying* won't tell me where Elijah is. I want my little boy. I want him home with me – right now! Gracie, how could you let him go? You know the rules. What the hell were you thinking?'

'I told him not to. He didn't listen.'

'You should've told me!' She was yelling now, the kind of yelling she only normally did at Dad. 'I am your mother, for Christ's sakes!'

'You were asleep,' I said, tears sailing down my cheeks. I knew it was a weak excuse. 'And Toby said not to worry.'

'Toby? Toby Irwin? What'd he know? If he's anything like his old lady, he's a stuck-up little shit!'

'Nell! Listen to yourself,' Grandma Bett said. 'Here, Gracie love. A tissue.'

'Oh, give over, Bett.' Mum frowned at both of us as she paced around the room. 'I don't know what to do! Where to go! I can't...I can't just wait here, while he's out there – alone.'

'Why isn't Eli here?' Lucky asked.

Just then the phone rang. We all froze. Then Mum screamed, 'Answer it! Answer it!' even though she was the one running towards it.

'Hello! Robbie?' she yelled into the phone.

I could hear breathing, fast breathing. I wasn't sure whether it was mine, or Grandma Bett's or Lucky's. Maybe it was all of our breathing combined.

'Who?' Mum yelled. 'What do you want? No, I don't want to win a trip to Los Angeles! Fuck the 1984 Olympics! Yeah, I'm sorry you bothered me too. Now get off my phone line and don't you ever call here again!' She dropped the receiver so hard that Lucky covered her ears.

'Bugger it!' Mum said. 'I'll go to the reserve too. Those bloody men are useless.'

She'd just picked up her keys when someone tapped on the front door.

Mum burst into tears when she saw who was standing on the WE ME mat. 'Oh, thank Christ,' she sobbed. The rest of us crowded behind her, the twins squeezing in between her and the door.

Elijah's face was covered in scratches and dirt, and shiny patches made by tears. Next to him stood Mr Hall the bus driver, holding a dirty blue ribbon with a whistle hanging off it. The whistle Grandma Bett'd given Elijah.

'Why's Eli crying?' Lucky asked.

'He's fine,' Mr Hall said. 'Just scratched; and scared, I expect.'

'What happened? Eli?' Mum grabbed his hands.

'He chased me! I ran and ran, and he ran and I ran faster and faster.' Elijah started bawling.

'Yeah, and you blew *this*, kid.' Mr Hall handed Elijah the whistle. 'Reckon that scared him off.'

'My go!' Grub yelled, pulling the whistle out of Elijah's hand.

'Who is *he*?' Mum was hugging Elijah and kissing the scratches on his face. 'I'll kill him!'

'Don't know.' Elijah sniffed. His long black lashes were plastered together with tears, like a wet paintbrush. 'It was dark.'

'You must've seen something. Grub, stop blowing that!'

'It was dark. Boots. Boots, that's all. Black. Maybe.'

'Boots! Every man at the steelworks wears boots,' Grandma Bett said. Then she pointed at Mr Hall's dirty black ones. '*And* men who drive buses.'

'Sorry,' Elijah said. 'I was just going to save Anthea.'

'*Save* Anthea? Oh, of course you were, pet. Let's go and fix you up.' Mum took Elijah's hand and he stepped inside.

79

'I heard that from my yard.' Mr Hall nodded at the whistle in Grub's hand. 'Then found the lad running down the middle of the road. Took a while to get any sense out of him, to calm him down. Soon as I knew he hadn't been attacked or anything, I thought I'd drop him home.'

'Thank you so much, Andy. I'll call Constable Stewy now,' Grandma Bett said and she practically ran along the hall.

I stood in the doorway, relieved at seeing Elijah but horrified by the thought of what could've happened to him, what'd nearly happened.

'You're real lucky, kid,' Mr Hall said.

I looked up. I'd forgotten he was standing there.

'Could've been much worse. *Much* worse.' He shook his head. 'Your brother's the one that got away.'

CHAPTER ELEVEN

THIS TIME ELIJAH WAS FAMOUS FOR A GOOD REASON. *THE COONGAHOOLA Times* called him 'Superboy', and the article on the front page said:

The boy who shocked the town at age five by killing a cat has stunned Coongahoola again, this time evading a murderer.

Under his favourite school photo (of him sticking his tongue out), it said, 'The unbeatable Elijah Barrett aka Damien Omen.' The photo even made it into *The Sydney Morning Herald*.

Mum ripped the phone out of the wall socket, saying that the sound of it ringing gave her a stinking headache. Constable Stewy and another policeman dropped in three times, with more and more questions for Elijah, desperate for him to remember something that'd help them. Elijah had never been so popular. People sent him stuff in the mail: mainly congratulations cards, but also a lotto ticket, a fluffy koala holding a love heart, two Bibles, a *Dr Who* book and a bag of marbles. On his first day back at school, everyone from the little snotty kindergarten kids to the big hairy-legged Year Twelves, lined up in a guard of honour, and Elijah walked through it with his hands stuffed in his pockets like it was nothing special. He spent that first lunchtime autographing things for other kids: their pencil cases, homework diaries, school bags, even their arms. Michael acted as his assistant telling kids to line up and, when the line got too long, signing Elijah's name for him.

Elijah's story of his escape changed depending on who was listening and how much he thought they'd believe. In one version, the murderer was accompanied by two pit bulls; in another, bullets from the murderer's rifle zoomed past Elijah's ears. One night when we were lying in our beds I asked him what really happened.

I thought he'd fallen asleep because it was a while before he said, 'It was real dark. But I told myself I wasn't going to leave till I found her, even though the mozzies were biting me – and it was spooky on my own. I was looking for that hollow tree we made a cubby in once. If I ever ran away, that's where I'd hide. Then I heard something. I called out her name, but no one said anything. I started running, and someone else started running too. I could hear footsteps and breathing. The breathing got louder and louder, and then a voice – a man's voice – said, "Elijaaaaah," sort of in a whisper, but in a scary way.'

'He knew your name!' I said, shivering.

'Yeah. That was the scariest thing of all. I kept running and branches scratched my face and poked me in the eyes but I hardly even felt them. Then I remembered my whistle. You know how we felt dumb wearing them round our necks?'

'They looked stupid,' I said.

'Yeah, but if I didn't have the whistle I dunno what would've happened. I was still running and hardly had any breath, so at first it was too soft like when Lucky tries to blow it, but then I blew it real hard. I dunno what happened then. Somehow I made it to the road and Mr Hall was there.'

'Elijah.' I felt cold and goosebumpy under my blankets. 'That's awful.'

'Yeah.'

'Are you crying?' I sat up.

'I thought I was dead meat,' he said and sniffed. 'But don't tell anyone.'

NEWS OF ELIJAH'S ESCAPE even reached Shelley because she finally decided to write me another letter. She was back to her old self, saying she missed me and Elijah (even though she hardly knew him), and sparing me all the gossip about her many new Dubbo friends. She even wrote a secret message inside the envelope ('Hey, Lothum! You're a nosy bitch.') in case Mrs Lothum snooped when sorting the mail. No one could prove that Mrs Lothum peeked at the mail while doing her shift at the post office, but back when she was the telephone operator we used to hear her wheezy breath down the phone line. One time when I was talking to Shelley, Mrs Lothum sneezed. From then on Dad'd finish phone calls with 'Over and out, Shirl' before hanging up.

Sergeant Colby said on the *ABC News* (the 'real' news according to Grandma Bett) that it wasn't certain that the offender was targeting children born in October 1974 (he didn't say 'the River Children', Mum reckoned, because the rest of Australia wouldn't know what he was on about). But the sergeant also said that he and Constable Stewy had few other leads, so this was one that they were exploring. This wasn't news to us because their police car'd been spotted outside the house Ken Knowles lived in with his mother, and Ken was the one who'd called meetings at the Baptist church to discuss what should be done with the 'abominable' River Children after Elijah ran over Sebastian and Tristan Kelly tampered with his neighbour's car muffler. Grandma Bett'd also heard that Stewy had a word with old Mr Buckley at least twice and everyone knew that he hated Aborigines, homos, cat owners (and their cats) and River Children.

'The River Children are a reminder of what went on at the River Picnic and, as such, are a symbol of immorality,' said a woman who sounded like she had a peg on her nose, on Radio Coolio. 'Murdering them,' she went on, 'while being terribly drastic, could be seen as one way of eradicating the problem.'

Back then I still didn't really understand what went on at the River Picnic and why it mattered that a percentage of Coongahoola's population was born as a result. I knew that something terrible had happened. Even though I'd only been two at the time, I still had nightmares about that night. I'd heard kids at school talk about an orchy, but to me that was just a sickly-sweet orange drink you bought from the tuck shop. All Grandma Bett'd say was, 'I can't vouch for the others, but Elijah's got your father's eyes – there's no denying that he's ours.'

Three days after Elijah's escape, Mum invited Dad over 'for a talk'. I knew what it was about. After the newspaper, TV and radio made the River Child connection, no one talked about anything else.

'G'day,' Dad said as he plonked himself down in his old seat. 'Now where are those little rascals, eh?' Lucky and Grub giggled from under the kitchen table as Dad lifted the tablecloth. On hot days, under the table was the coolest spot in the house, or so the twins believed. 'Ah huh! Who's hidin' down here?'

'You're looking... well,' Dad said to Mum. I noticed that the whole time he was tickling the twins he kept his eyes on her. She was just wearing cut-off jeans and a faded 'Sydney Hard Rock Café' T-shirt, but they were clean and her hair sat neatly on her shoulders (one good thing about her veil was that it tamed and smoothed her curls – she'd been to a prayer session that morning) and she smelt of her lavender shampoo.

'Yeah, thanks.' She surveyed Dad's holey black INXS T-shirt, dirty jeans and unshaven face and sniffed up his cigarette and old-sock smell. 'You've seen better days. Frannie not taken you back in?'

'Who? Fat Fran? Nah! That woman was way too serious. Flattin' with Gaz these days. Up by the BP.'

'Well, good for you, I s'pose,' Mum said. 'But we're not here to talk about you.'

'I always liked Gary,' Grandma Bett said. 'Does he own a washing machine?'

Dad looked down at his jeans. They were almost green with grime. 'Not that I know of.'

'We're talking about me!' Elijah sang out from under the table where he'd joined the twins.

'Why don't you children go and play out the back,' Grandma Bett said. 'I don't think they need to hear this, do they?' She looked at Mum.

'Don't want to!' Lucky whined, wrapping herself around the metal table leg. I untangled her and shoved her thumb in her mouth, and she quietly followed us along the hall. When I'd let the others out the door, I snuck back inside to find out what was going to happen to Elijah.

'Nell, I think it's okay,' Dad was saying. 'No bloke'd be game to jump our fence.'

'Gracie has her whistle too,' Grandma Bett said.

'See! It's just... stuff like this. I really can't handle it. I'm scared for him, *really* scared. That's why I called you, Robbie. I've had an idea. I've talked it through with Mum and Dad and they've talked to Boyd about it. Bett's all for it too—'

'Boyd? But he buggered off years back,' Dad said.

'Look, he and his wife have two kids and are doing all right by the sound of it. I want to send Elijah to him until it's safe.'

'But he lives up north!'

'Yes. A few hours away. Don't make it sound like we're sending him to the moon!'

'Seems a bit drastic, Nell. Cost a fortune too. Where'd we get the money?'

'Mum's going to pay for it. She always has a bit put aside for emergencies. And you know how much she loves Elijah.'

'But how long for?' Dad asked. 'Could take them ages to catch the mongrel.'

'I hope it won't be long. But at least he'll be safe! And we might be able to sleep again.'

Elijah was going away! To Queensland. I felt sad that he'd be leaving me here, that I'd have no one, apart from the twins who didn't really count, to hang out with at home. But I was annoyed too. I'd never even been to Sydney and my nine-year-old brother was going to live in a whole different state. Queensland was sunny

and full of beaches and Dreamworld and other places with roller
coasters. If he had to be sent away, why couldn't they send him
somewhere boring?

The next day when Mum told Elijah what they'd decided, he did
a good job of pretending he didn't already know.

'But I've got two matches left before the end of the season!' he
said.

'I'm planning to book a ticket for the twenty-ninth, when it's a
bit cheaper. That's a week away. You'll only miss one game.'

'The last match!'

'I'm sure they play cricket in Queensland. Maybe you could play
on Evan's team.'

'Who's Evan?'

'Your cousin. Have you been listening to anything I've said?
He's only a year older than you. Should be fun.'

'What's his batting average?'

'Elijah, I've got no idea.'

'But he plays cricket?'

'Look, he could play the bagpipes for all I know. But he's a boy.
I'm sure you'll have a few things in common. The main thing is
you'll be safe.'

The adults'd also decided that until Elijah boarded his plane,
he'd never be left alone outside our yard. It was my job to watch
him at school. I even ate my lunch with him and Michael next to the
handball courts, something I didn't mind doing with Shelley away.
It saved me from looking as lonely and pathetic as Heavenly, the
spotty Believer girl, and it reminded everyone that I was the sister
of the bravest boy at school. Michael joked about going to
Queensland too, and he and Elijah imagined what life would be like
there for both of them.

'We could change our names. You could be Damien and I'll be
Luke Skywalker,' Michael said with a mouthful of honey sandwich,
making me realise how much Michael would miss his friend. 'Or
would you rather be Darth Vader? You'd be a pretty good dark lord.'

Dad spent his days off at our place and Grandma Bett washed his clothes and hung them on our clothesline, so that the murderer would think Dad lived with us (and also so we could sit in the same room as Dad without feeling sick from his stink). On the way to and from school, Elijah wore our dead grandad's navy-blue fishing hat pulled down to his eyes and his shirt collar standing upright.

It was Mrs Irwin who brought the news about Anthea.

'Nell!' She banged on the door, making Mum jump and spill her coffee. 'Nell!'

Mum struggled with the new lock on our door, still slippery with grease, before it clicked and the door swung open.

'News!' Mrs Irwin screeched. 'The Bryce girl.' She had half a cigarette in the corner of her mouth and a full cigarette in her hand ready to replace it. On the end of her fingers, horrible long shiny nails were filed like claws and painted the same deep red as her lips.

'Come in, Jane,' Mum said.

Mrs Irwin burst into our hallway in a puff of smoke. Jonathan followed quietly in his too-white Dunlop Volley sneakers. I hadn't even noticed him behind her. I wished Toby'd come instead. Even if he ignored me most of the time, he was the only one who could make everything seem less of a nightmare. I'd only seen him once since the day Elijah went to the reserve, when I walked past the hall during a Year Eight assembly.

'It's not good, Nell, kids. Not good!' She walked across our living room and back again, a row of gold bangles on her arm tinkling, while Jonathan folded himself into the corner near the TV. I wanted to stamp on his white sneakers. I waited for Mum to ask Mrs Irwin to kindly put her cigarette out (Grandma Bett never let Dad smoke in the house), but she didn't. Instead she sank into Grandma Bett's armchair and started chewing on her little finger. Jonathan stared at Sebastian's rug as his mum's feet stomped over it. No doubt Toby'd filled him in on what'd taken place on it all those years ago. Jonathan opened his mouth, but changed his mind before any words got out.

Mrs Irwin pointed a red claw at Elijah. 'Oh you lucky, lucky boy.'

'What is it, Jane?' Mum said.

'Same story, pretty much.' Mrs Irwin bowed her head. 'I don't know the details, but very similar to little Nigel.' She sucked loudly on her cigarette and let the smoke slowly pour out of her mouth and nose. She was so revolting. How could she have given birth to someone as perfect as Toby? The air in the living room already felt hot and sticky. The smoke made it worse and I started coughing. White flecks of ash floated onto Sebastian's rug and still Mum said nothing.

'Near the river, the site of the River Picnic.' Mrs Irwin glanced at Mum. 'If I were you, I wouldn't let your boy out of this house.'

CHAPTER TWELVE

ELIJAH KICKED OPEN THE DOOR TO THE SECRET ROOM SO WE COULD HEAR what Dad was saying.

'I'm now askin' you to please stay away.'

'And I've said before, it's none of your business what I do!' Mum yelled.

'But Nell, they're suspects. He's a suspect. For murder!'

'Come on, Robbie, half the bloody town's a suspect! Ken Knowles's been questioned at the station, not once but twice, and you know how much he hates the River Children – the spawn of sin and all that bullshit. Constable Stewy's been following Gerald Buckley round since the minute Nigel went missing. Gerald may be about to kick the bucket but you never know what he's capable of! Even Andy was questioned – nice-as-pie Andy! So why pick on Saint Bede? Just 'cause he's different, he's American and he's trying to do some bloody good.'

'Well, you're stuck in your own world, but what people are sayin' is that the Believers don't like what happened at the River Picnic any more than those Baptist idiots. And the picnic happened smack bang where their church is, where the Virgin Mary apparently showed up. God, Nell, maybe she told 'em to kill the kids! These people are nutters! Did you hear they light big bloody fires to burn anythin' that's not as mental as they are? They'll burn the whole town down if we don't do something about 'em! An' d'you know the money they earn goes to this Yankee Bede bloke? And he's started buyin' up the town? First the bakery, then Bob's joint, now the shop on Jenkins Road. They're takin' over, doin' people out of jobs and probably killin' our kids. How can you sit around and sing songs with them?'

'God, I'm sick of hearing this, Robbie. What I think is you can't handle me finally having friends, enjoying myself. You had your chance and you blew it and now you want to ruin everything.'

Elijah pulled the door shut. 'Here we go again.'

Because the day of Nigel's funeral had been made a holiday, the council did the same for Anthea's. All of us kids were happy to have a day off, but not everyone was. Dad's boss, Mr Watson, was on Radio Coolio complaining about how much the day was costing him.

'It's Dr Bryce's daughter for crying out loud!' Grandma Bett said, turning off the radio. 'And after all he's done for this community.'

Warm raindrops pelted down as we ran up the path towards the Anglican church, as if the whole world was crying for Anthea. Even Constable Stewy and Sergeant Colby took time off to come to this funeral. They stood in the back row of the church with five other policemen who weren't from Coongahoola. All wore matching serious faces. Old Mr Buckley was also in the back row, his dog Noodle curled up asleep against him. Mr Hall sat a few rows in front with his arm around a crying Mrs Hall. I looked around for weird old Ken Knowles from the Baptist church, but I couldn't see his thick black glasses or the big blue eyes that stared through them.

It was Nigel's funeral all over again. Practically everyone who lived in Coongahoola was there, dressed in the same good clothes they'd worn to Nigel's, the men squeezed into old suits and the women in long fancy dresses. I was wearing a blue-and-white-striped drop-waist dress, a dress I loved because it made me feel like I belonged in a magazine. Mum'd bought it just before Nigel's funeral.

She must've been psychic and sensed I'd be needing something decent to wear.

Apart from the fact that we were sitting in the Anglican church instead of the Catholic one, the only difference I could see was that, instead of smiling, Fat Frannie was pulling mean faces at Dad, her lip twisted up like Billy Idol's.

When the last hymn was finally over, Anthea's parents and sister made it down the aisle, past the giant wooden cross, and outside. The rest of us lined up to shake Constable Stewy and Sergeant Colby's hands. Then, when the sergeant said they'd better be off and the two of them headed down the aisle, people cheered, waved and even saluted them.

'Keep up the good work, men!' Arty Jones called, his voice echoing around the church.

'Only a matter of time,' Graham Anderson said.

'Go get the bastard!' someone else said.

Grandma Bett frowned and quickly crossed herself. Even though the Anglican church wasn't God's real house, he might've been standing outside the door.

'It's a sign,' Grandma Bett whispered to me as we stepped out of the church, nodding towards the sky. 'From above. Anthea has His blessing.' The rain had stopped and the sun was burning through the clouds. Steam floated off the path and the air smelt like worms.

I watched from behind a banksia tree as Mrs and Mr Lothum walked down the church path, Mr Lothum's moustache drooping and cheeks sagging like one of those puppies that never grow into their skin. I wanted to avoid Mrs Lothum in case she'd read the message Shelley'd written to her on my letter and thought I'd had something to do with it. Shelley reckoned Mrs Lothum looked like she belonged on the Saturday morning cartoons, along with Bugs Bunny and Porky Pig. She was big in the middle with a tiny head and sticks for legs, as if she was made of plasticine and'd been squeezed at both ends. Her hair, which she regularly dyed different shades of brightest orange and red, was a shiny orange that day. I remember because it clashed with her red tartan jacket.

The wake was in our school hall, two blocks away. The Bryces were too upset to organise anything, so the school's Parents & Citizens Association did it all, baking biscuits, cakes and scones and asking everyone they knew to do the same. The tables were crammed with food, food of all kinds, more food than I'd ever seen, even at a birthday party. The adults stood around the tables dropping crumbs and sipping tea from white paper cups. They weren't talking as much as they did at Nigel's wake. Even us kids were quiet, drinking watery red cordial and stuffing our mouths full of cake. I wondered whether we were all on our best behaviour because we were in the school hall and all the teachers were there. It felt like they were watching, waiting for an excuse to yell at us.

The Bryces only stayed for half an hour and they didn't say much or go near the food. Not even Anthea's sister, Vera May, ate one of the lamingtons, cupcakes, buns or slices and you could tell by the size of her cheeks that she would've tried more than one if it wasn't her sister who'd died. She waited while her parents shook hands with the same people who'd lined up to shake Constable Stewy and Sergeant Colby's hands, as if hand-shaking made things better. Then she slowly followed them back outside, dragging her feet as she walked.

I saw Toby stuffing a handful of chips into his mouth. He noticed me looking, brushed a few stray chips off his stripy shirt and walked towards me. I wiped my mouth in case any cake crumbs were lingering.

'Gracie.' Toby stood so close that I observed, for the first time, a light layer of fluff along his top lip. I wondered when he'd start shaving. Did fourteen-year-olds shave?

'Hi, Toby.' My cup of lemonade was shaking in my hand.

'That thing about Elijah,' he said.

'What?' I took a step back, realising that if I could analyse his face, he could do the same to mine.

'You know.'

'In the reserve?'

'Yeah.'

'It was scary.'

'I know. I'm glad he's okay.'

'Thanks, Toby.'

'Yeah. I felt a bit. Bad.'

'Me too.' My mouth was dry. I lifted the foam cup to my lips, realising too late that it was empty and pretending to take a sip anyway. Luckily, though, by the time I'd taken the cup away from my still-parched mouth, Toby'd walked off.

I spent the next few minutes reliving the conversation with Toby in my head, making the bits I said much more articulate and assuring Toby that he played no part in Elijah's near-capture. It wasn't until old Mr Buckley started yelling that everything went wrong.

'What's this then?' His dirty fingers held up a soft white bun with pale blue icing. Where his little finger should've been was a knob like a tree stump.

He crushed an empty can of Fosters under his muddy boot. All the other adults were just drinking tea or coffee, but old Mr Buckley had brought beer in a green canvas bag, which he'd left where Noodle was tied up outside the hall.

When no one said anything, he kept talking. 'I'll tell ya's what it is. It's a bloody picture of that Virgin Mary on a bloody iced bun!'

'Yes, Gerald.' Grandma Bett stepped out from behind the urn. 'A very generous donation from Benji's Bakery, along with the caramel slices. Fresh this morning!'

'From the bakery those nutters bought from our Mike? And what for? So they could put their religious bullshit on buns?' Old Mr Buckley waved the bun in Grandma Bett's face.

'It is a little unusual,' Grandma Bett said. 'And I can't say I'd eat the apparition myself, but I'm sure it's harmless enough. Gracie ate one, didn't you?'

'Um-mmmm,' I said, my mouth full of a creamy ginger kiss and my face burning. I'd thought the picture on the bun was of a Russian doll, like the ones Shelley's uncle'd sent her from England.

'Harmless? These freaks aren't harmless, they're destroying the town.' Old Mr Buckley breathed his sour beer breath towards me.

'Hear, hear!' Deep voices cheered. Adults stood around the buns, staring and poking them before picking them up and looking closely.

'You're damned right, Joe,' Mr Irwin yelled, dropping a bun and squashing it under his shiny, black pointy-toed shoe.

Others dropped the buns and stamped them into the wooden floor. *Plop, plop, plop. Squish, squish, squish.*

'What an insult! Kill one of our children, then send iced buns to her funeral!' The normally polite Mrs Flannigan chucked an iced bun at the wall. It hit the clock, and left a big blue splodge on 9 before sliding to the floor.

'They're killing this town!' Mrs Irwin screeched, grabbing three buns at once.

'Please! Everyone. This is an emotional time.' Sweat filled the lines in Grandma Bett's forehead. 'We're all upset. We're all feeling angry. But, please, this is the school hall. Treat it with respect.'

'Your boy's woman is one of them!' old Mr Buckley said. 'No wonder you're defendin' their poncy buns. Your own grandson nearly copped it an' you're still defending the fuckers! You must be as screwed in the head as they are.'

The hall was quiet except for the rain on the roof and the sound of a bun dropping beside Jonathan Irwin's Dunlop Volley. Where were Stewy and the sergeant? Didn't they think to keep an eye on the wake? Toby was watching me, his mouth full of something, and squinting as if he was seeing me in a new light. My cheeks burned and I felt like throwing up all the sweet stuff I'd just eaten. Nurse Audrey turned around to face Grandma Bett, her dark eyes wide open, waiting. Elijah and Michael stepped closer to me and I squeezed Lucky's chocolatey hand. I looked around for Grub. I wanted to grab them all and run, get them out of there. But where could we go? There was nowhere.

'My daughter-in-law is not one of them,' Grandma Bett said at last.

'No? Well, where is she now then?' That was Mrs Irwin. The cow.

Grandma Bett touched the cross that hung around her neck and looked at her feet. She reminded me of a little bird that'd been hit by a car and couldn't fly. My eyes stung with tears.

'Enough! Please!' Father Scott shouted, and wiped jam from his lips onto his sleeve, something we always got in trouble for doing. 'That really is enough. I don't want to waste the sergeant's time by calling him in here, do I?'

Then Grandma Bett gasped at something on the floor behind me. I spun around. Grub lay flat on his back, giggling. His face, his hair, his striped funeral shirt and the navy shorts Mum got half price at Best & Less were covered with shiny pale-blue icing. He kept giggling and used his sticky blue hands to slide his body along the floor, a blue smear following him like a snail's trail.

Lucky pointed at him and squealed, 'Dirty Grub! Dirty Grub!'

'Where's your dad?' Father Scott asked Elijah and me. We looked at each other and shook our heads. I didn't care where Dad was. Toby had seen everything! I didn't dare look up. I kept my eyes on the floor, the floor smeared with Grub's mess. Now Toby'd know about Mum and Saint Bede. He'd think that I was a complete retard, that I came from a family of retards. He'd never want to speak to me again! Then there was everyone else: what was everyone at school going to say about Grandma Bett defending the Believers? And about my mental baby brother turning himself blue? I wanted to disappear. Why couldn't I be the one going away to Queensland? I'd make sure they never let me come back.

'I'll have a look outside.' Father Scott stepped over Grub and around the blue mess. 'Stay here and mind your grandma.'

I was standing next to Grandma Bett, my hand resting awkwardly on the sleeve of her cardigan, my attempt at *minding* her, when I heard a man's gravelly voice: 'That was a bit rough.'

I turned and saw Mr Lothum frowning. 'Some people have no respect,' he said.

'She helped organise the food.' I nodded at Grandma Bett, who was staring across the hall. 'She's done nothing wrong.'

'No, I'm sure she hasn't.' He touched Grandma Bett's elbow. 'Sorry about that, Mrs Barrett. They were way out of line.'

Grandma Bett forced her face into a smile, but after a few seconds, despair dragged it down again. 'Thank you, James. There's no need for you to apologise. It's difficult; for everyone.'

'Doesn't excuse bad behaviour, though. You take care of yourself. You too, Gracie.'

'Thanks,' I said. The kindness in Mr Lothum's voice, in his sad, scarred face, made me want to cry.

Dad followed Father Scott inside like a naughty boy following a teacher, his hands behind his back. His hair was wet and the white shirt Grandma Bett'd ironed for him that morning was splotched with rain. Dad's friend Gary followed Dad, and three girls in matching denim mini-skirts, probably seniors from Coongahoola Central, followed Gary. They were wet too. Dad didn't even turn around to say goodbye to them. He walked with Father Scott straight over to us.

'Bloody hell! Sorry, Father, but what a ber-leeding mess! Are you okay, Mum?' Dad grabbed Grandma Bett's hand, but she didn't look up or say anything.

'Okay, let's go.' Dad picked up Lucky, brushed the coconut icing off her chin and the front of her corduroy pinafore, and took Grub's sticky blue hand. My feet slipped and slid on the blue icing as I followed Dad out of the hall, keeping my eyes on the floor. The rain had started again, heavier than before, the drops stinging my bare arms. Another sign from above? I wondered, as we ran towards the school gate.

When we got home we found Mum filing her nails and singing a hymn I remembered from the Believers' prayer meeting, something about a waterfall that never stopped flowing. She stopped singing when a blue Grub sprinted along the hallway.

'What on earth?' she said, stretching her neck to see. Grandma Bett walked into her room, closing the door behind her. We didn't see her again until the morning.

'Should've called the cops!' Mum said when we told her what happened. We stood around the bath watching the water turn blue and Grub turn back to his normal pinky colour.

'Yeah? What good'd that do?' Dad flicked his tie against the bathroom mirror. 'Besides, they're not exactly twiddling their thumbs.'

'The cops've already talked to Gerald Buckley, your mother said so. He's probably trying to turn the attention away from him.'

'Nell, are you thick? Can't you see this is out of control now?'

'It's everyone else that's out of control. The Believers weren't even there.'

'Come on, be reasonable. Stay away from them. From him!'

'I can't do that.' Mum was pulling a comb through Grub's gooey blue hair.

'Why? Cause you like him?'

'Because he's asked me to marry him,' she whispered.

Chapter Thirteen

NANA AND THE BUTCHERER WERE THE FIRST ONES TO WALK DOWN OUR hall; their wrinkly faces poking over the top of the presents they hugged in their arms, and Nana's flowery smell stinking the place out. Two of the neatly wrapped parcels were for the cousins Elijah was going to live with, Sasha and Evan. One was for Uncle Boyd and Aunty Helen, and the other three were for Elijah. There was a yellow Rip Curl T-shirt (soft and new, not stained and second-hand), a pair of blue-and-yellow board shorts, and a bumper bag of licorice Allsorts to eat on the plane.

Mum and Dad'd decided to have a party for Elijah the day before he went to Queensland. Mum said it was a 'thank God you're still alive' party as well as a farewell. I thought he was lucky enough to be going on an aeroplane on his own without also having a party, but I knew to keep my mouth shut.

Nana'd dressed as if she was the one about to go somewhere, her face powdered pale pink and her turkey neck dripping with plastic pearls. She dragged Grandma Bett's armchair to the middle of the living room and sat herself down, ready to tell anyone who squeezed past that she was the one who'd paid for Elijah's tickets. When the Butcherer heard that Dad was outside manning the barbecue, he let out a long, loud whistle of relief. He sank into the old couch in the sunny corner of the room with Gibbon's *Decline and Fall of the Roman Empire*.

The Andersons were next to show up. 'Yummy!' Grub said when he saw their green station wagon pull up across the road in the shade of the gum tree. He followed them along the hallway and into the kitchen, before returning with stuffed cheeks and fists full of Mrs Anderson's famous lamingtons.

Michael and a few of Elijah's other school friends, Jamie, Scott, Jo and Melissa, arrived with their parents. Michael carried a stack of his favourite comic books, a gift that Elijah'd never fit into his luggage. Then the six of them played races in bare feet – along the hallway, round the living room (careful not to bump into the half-reading, half-dozing Butcherer), along the hallway again, and to the front door, Elijah getting there first every time.

The Lothums arrived with the Irwins, Mr Lothum and Mr Irwin joining the men out the back, and Mrs Lothum and Mrs Irwin heading straight for the kitchen. (I was surprised that Mrs Irwin could bring herself to come. At Anthea's wake she'd been acting like Mum was more evil than Satan.) Toby and Jonathan Irwin trudged along the hall, past my bedroom, and disappeared out the back door without even bothering to say hello.

I'd taken special care in getting ready that morning, even borrowing some of Mum's 'Pink Pearl' nail polish, but Toby'd rather kick his stupid soccer ball outside. I didn't know whether it was because of what happened at the wake, or just because he really liked football. At least he was playing in my backyard, I told myself. I sat at the living room window and watched as he dribbled the ball past his clumsy little brother. It was obvious that Toby hadn't taken as much trouble in getting ready as I had. He was wearing blue trackies with a Parramatta Eels jersey. But then again, he was a boy, I supposed.

'Whatever are you so engrossed in, Gracie?' Mrs Lothum'd snuck up behind me.

'Nothing.'

'Ah, I see,' she said in her posh voice. Mum once said that Mrs Lothum talked with a plum in her mouth, and I used to look for it when she spoke, but her lips moved too fast.

'Just watching them play soccer,' I said, wishing she'd go away.

'Of course. Tobias in particular?' Mrs Lothum winked at me.

'Toby? No. Just. There's not much else to do.' I looked away. She could talk! Everyone in Coongahoola knew she liked my dad. She'd even moved to our street because of him. After her baby'd died, she and Mr Lothum'd sold their house out of the blue to Mr Kingsly and moved into the small red-brick house on the corner.

Dad said it was no coincidence. 'That sheila's obsessed with me,' he'd said. 'She'd move right into our bed if I hung a To Let sign on it.'

The only people we were surprised to see at Elijah's party were Mrs Muller and her twins, Sammy and Abigail, two more of the fourteen River Children who hadn't been murdered yet. Mrs Muller was tall, skinny as a stick insect and covered in freckles. She hid behind a crinkly brown hanky and blew her nose when Lucky and I answered the door, but anyone could see she was crying.

'Hello,' Sammy and Abigail whispered at the same time, like perfect twins (the only thing Grub and Lucky did together was bawl their eyes out), then they both looked down at their matching dirty grey sneakers, wishing their mum was more normal, I bet.

Since there was a No Smoking sign up in our living room (Grandma Bett'd made it out of the inside of an empty fish fingers box), the Mullers spent most of the time standing on the verandah. Mrs Muller puffed away, poking her head in the window to breathe her smoky air all over us. She said that she'd never even touched a 'fag' until the Bryce girl went missing and that now, as if she didn't have enough to worry about, she was probably going to drop dead from lung cancer. She said that if she had the money she'd send Abigail and Sammy on a one-way ticket to Antarctica because it was the furthest place away from Coongahoola she could think of.

'But I can't even cough up enough for the electricity,' she said.

Mum shook her head. 'Sorry we can't help. Elijah'd be staying here too if it wasn't for my mum.'

The Mullers made me nervous, not because Mrs Muller looked like a monster when she cried (and a scarecrow when she didn't), or even because she wanted us to give her our money. But because of the twins' eyes. Things were bad enough already without Mum noticing that Abigail and Sammy had the same brown, Jersey cow eyes as Elijah. And Dad. Nathan'd explained it to me at school. He said it meant that our dad was their dad too, that Dad'd been with their mum at the River Picnic (as well as ours!). Their hair was yellowy like their mum's and their faces were splattered with freckles like hers, but the more I looked at their eyes, the more I thought of Elijah and Dad. I was glad that Dad was busy with the barbecue in case he noticed it too (and didn't know already).

When Dad and the other men came inside carrying plates full of barbecued meat, and calling out 'Grub's up!' (meaning the meat was ready, not that my brother was hanging from the ceiling, which was my initial thought), I had an idea.

I opened the screen door to the backyard, then closed it behind me in case Mrs Lothum was prying again.

The sun had disappeared behind the dirty grey clouds and a cool breeze was blowing the towels on the clothesline. I thanked God that Grandma Bett hadn't left any of our undies hanging out.

'Lunch is ready,' I announced. Toby's Parramatta jersey lay on the grass. Stepping over it, I spotted a black book, a notebook. What could it be for? I wondered. What was Toby writing? His and Jonathan's soccer scores? Or something more interesting? 'Come and help yourself!'

'Not hungry, thanks,' Toby answered, without taking his eyes off the ball.

'But there's heaps of sausages. Even steak if you're quick,' I said.

'We don't have to.' Jonathan turned to face me with his hands on his hips. He was freckly, with flappy ears that stuck out like pink flags. He didn't look remotely like his older brother, which made me wonder if Toby was adopted (Toby also bore little resemblance to Mrs Irwin – thankfully).

'Mum said we only had to come 'cause Elijah's our neighbour and it's polite,' Jonathan went on. 'But we don't have to go inside your house and we don't have to talk to you.' It was the most I'd ever heard Jonathan say and it confirmed that he was a mummy's boy.

Toby kicked the ball against the fence, angrily, like the ball had done something to annoy him.

'But, why wouldn't you want to?' I asked. What a stupid question. Mum, of course. Mum and Saint Bede.

'Cause you're freaks!' Toby kicked the ball against the fence so hard that I squeezed my eyes shut. When I opened them, I was surprised to see the fence still standing.

He may as well have kicked the ball right in my face. *Freaks!* I might've made a small noise of shock – 'oh!' or 'ah!' – I'm not sure. All I remember is quickly walking inside (fighting the impulse to run) so the boys couldn't see my tears.

It was mid afternoon and I hadn't eaten since breakfast. I'd been looking forward to lunch, but the sausages, steak, onions and potato salad suddenly lost their appeal. The smell of greasy meat made my stomach churn. I opened the door to my room, but found Grub, Lucky and little William Naples jumping on the beds. The secret room was busy too: Elijah and his friends were playing truth or dare. Had I been in a better mood I would've stuck around to watch (Elijah'd just been dared to kiss Jo!), but I couldn't get Toby's venomous voice out of my head. I needed to be on my own.

With nowhere else to go, I returned to the chair at the living room window. Not wanting to look, but unable to stop myself, I spied Toby sitting under the clothesline, stuffing his face with bread and sausages, his black notebook resting on his knee. Jonathan sat on the grass, also eating a sausage, Mrs Irwin standing next to him, cigarette in one claw, an empty paper plate in the other. *Not hungry, thanks.* Liar!

I was relieved when the party came to an abrupt end. Lucky'd found her baby doll behind the couch the Butcherer was snoring in with teeth marks on its arm. She let out a scream that made the Butcherer jump and everyone else stop talking. She then threw herself on the ground, banged her legs and arms against the floorboards and cried, 'Grub ate Mary-Anne!' her tiny face screwed up in anger. Everyone, including Nana and the Butcherer, left soon after that. Toby and Jonathan must've climbed over the fence. If they'd braved walking through our house, I would've seen them.

Except for Elijah's face being covered in lipstick kisses and the sick feeling in my stomach whenever I thought about Toby, that night could've been any old normal night. We ate grilled cheese with tomato sauce on toast for tea, Grub cried because Mum said there was no ice cream left, Lucky screamed after getting a splinter in her knee from the wobbly chair, Grandma Bett said, 'Excuse me, please,' and went to her room (she was still in a bad mood from Anthea's wake), Dad drove back to his flat to watch the footy with Gary, and Mum lay on the couch, her head facing the TV, but her eyes looking at the wall. Elijah and I snuck off to the secret room where we sat on the lumpy old cushions Grandma Bett'd given us, eating licorice Allsorts.

'What's wrong?' Elijah asked. 'Didn't you like the party?'

'Yeah. It was good. Until someone said we were freaks.'

Elijah laughed. 'Freaks? Who?'

'Toby Irwin.'

Elijah dug deep into the bag of Allsorts. 'Is he *still* mad about Sebastian?'

'That was years ago! I don't think he gives a toss about that. No, it's Mum, I reckon, and what happened at the wake.'

'Well, *his* mum's a freak. One thing I won't miss is her ugly face looking at me out the window.'

That was the first I'd heard of Mrs Irwin watching Elijah, but it didn't surprise me. '*She's* the one who never got over the kitten. But, I'm sick of thinking about the stupid Irwins. Wonder what Sasha and Evan are like.' I tried to imagine how I'd feel if it was me going away on my own. Happy to get away from here, undoubtedly. But also – scared, probably. Elijah never seemed to be scared about much, except nearly getting murdered, and that would've terrified anyone.

'Doesn't matter. I'll just run away if I don't like them.'

'You can't run away! We don't have enough money to come and look for you.' As I popped another licorice in my mouth, I noticed my fingernails. I'd chewed them so much that day that most of the 'Pink Pearl' was gone, and the skin around them was red raw.

'I could go in the Los Angeles Olympics,' Elijah said, scraping the pink, white and yellow layers off his Allsort with his teeth. 'Then, when I win, I'll sell my gold medals and fly back here.'

'Don't sell your gold medals, or no one'll believe that you ever won. But anyway, the Olympics aren't till next year. If you run away, call me from a phone box. But please don't.'

'I won't before the end of term.' Elijah's lips and tongue were purpley black. 'I told everyone I was going for ages, till high school even.'

'That's stupid! It won't be that long. Wouldn't you miss us?'

'Yeah. I'd prob'ly miss you and Grub and Lucky and Grandma Bett and Mum and Dad and Michael. Not really many others though.'

'Well, make sure you write to me. You're lucky going to Queensland. You have to at least tell me what it's like.'

'Write letters?'

'Yes!' I pushed another Allsort into my mouth even though I had a sickly sugary feeling in my throat and my stomach was ready to burst. I'd never shared a bumper bag of anything before.

'Sounds boring, but I might.'

'YOU WON'T BE NEEDING that in the Sunshine State,' Grandma Bett said to Elijah as we waited in the kitchen for Dad to pick us up. Grandma Bett smiled for the first time since before old Mr Buckley'd yelled at her. She probably didn't want Elijah to remember her as a grumpy grandma. She removed the whistle that hung around his neck.

'But you can always do with this, wherever you go.' She held up a silver chain, shiny like it'd cost lots of money. Hanging from the chain was a small silver cross with a tiny little dead Jesus on it. She did the chain up at the back of Elijah's neck and gave him a big hug. Elijah made a face as if she was squeezing him so much he couldn't breathe. I laughed.

'Can't a boy hug his grandma?' she asked me, making a tutting sound with her tongue.

Elijah tried to wriggle out of her arms but Grandma Bett said, 'You have to sit still on the plane, Elijah. This is good practice.'

I heard a car rattle up the driveway, then a screech of brakes, and ran to let Dad in the front door. He carried a bunch of dark red roses wrapped in green tissue paper. He saw Grandma Bett look at them and quickly said, 'They're for Nell.'

Grandma Bett nodded as if she'd known that already and went back to twirling Elijah's hair with her fingers. He should've bought Grandma Bett flowers too. She needed more cheering up than Mum did.

'Gracie, Elijah will need to take this as well.' Mum stood in the doorway holding the brown school case I'd got for my birthday, my name written in sparkly silver pen across the top.

'But what will I use?'

'I don't know, there's plenty of plastic bags. It won't be for long.'

I shrugged, imagining the teasing I'd have to endure turning up to school with my lunch and sports gear in a plastic bag. It was bad enough having a second-hand school uniform. Even though the dress was from the Andersons and Heidi'd grown out of it after only one year, Sarah K and the other popular girls announced to the whole class that it came from St Vinnies, which was the worst possible place for something to come from, according to them. Even Shelley gave me a funny look when they said my mum shopped at St Vinnies, and she'd always told me she didn't mind having a poor friend.

'Roses?' Mum asked when Dad handed her the flowers.

'Yep. Seven of them.'

'First time for everything.' Mum put my school case down on the table. 'They look a bit past it – half price?'

Dad sighed. 'Nah, bit of a discount maybe. Whatever happened to the thought that counts, eh?'

'That's a load of codswallop that gives you an excuse to be more of a cheapskate than you usually are. Is it 'cause of what Saint Bede asked me?'

'Don't be daft,' Dad said. 'It's 'cause of nothin', it's 'cause you're Nell and I wanted to give you roses.'

Mum looked at Dad, then held the roses up to her nose and breathed in their smell. 'Okay, thanks. Thank you.'

We couldn't all fit in the station wagon, so we had to leave Grandma Bett at home. Elijah and I'd sometimes hidden in the back while we drove to places around Coongahoola, but Dad'd said we couldn't do that in Sydney or we'd get busted by the cops.

Dad drove and Mum sat in the front seat pointing out all the turn-offs he'd missed, swearing at him to slow down, and then saying she shouldn't be swearing because the Believers don't use that kind of language.

'Keep yer hair on, I'm not goin' to dob on you,' Dad said.

'I don't care about them knowing. It's God that bothers me.'

'I won't say a word to 'im neither.' Dad lit one of the cigarettes he'd rolled on our kitchen table before we left, and I quickly wound down my window, concealing the 'T.I. sux' I'd absent-mindedly smeared into the dirty glass. The smell of smoke in our hot, stuffy car made it hard to breathe.

'Oh, shut up, he can hear us!'

'You really reckon? You reckon God would bother to listen to you talkin' about the cheapest place to stop for petrol and you sayin', "Look there's a big tree, let's pull over here so Grub can take a piss."? Wouldn't he have better things to do?'

Mum blew a raspberry, something she normally told Lucky off for doing, and sank back into her seat.

I looked out the window at the dry brown grass, gangly grey gum trees, falling-down fences, rusty yellow tractor and a few cows standing around looking bored. Grandma Bett was always talking to God – how could he hear what Mum was saying at the same time? And what about everyone else in the world? How could he hear them all at once?

'So when will you make up yer mind, d'you reckon?' Dad asked a few minutes later as we drove past a bent sign that told us that Sydney was still another 134 kilometres away.

'About what?' Mum said.

'You know. Him.'

'Oh, I don't know. No hurry, I guess.'

'No, there's not,' Dad said. 'Course you're still married anyway. That could be a problem.'

'Divorces are easy enough to get. Sally Evans got one.'

'Yeah? Well, Sally Evans is ugly. I'd divorce her any day.'

'Frannie Larson's fat as a pig!'

'Yeah! And Saint Bede's a bloody dwarf with four eyes and one of them yankee-doodle voices.'

'You're a shocker, you are!' Mum said, but she smiled and they started laughing. I elbowed Elijah and he looked up and grinned before staring back down at the Rubik's Cube Mrs Lothum had given him. Mum and Dad were almost starting to act like normal parents.

Cars were all around us: behind, in front, and on either side. There was hardly enough room on the road for so many cars, so sometimes we didn't move at all. Elijah, the twins and I wriggled around trying to get comfortable, our legs sticking to the warm car seat. People beeped their horns, mostly at us, and Dad said, 'Bugger me! Wrong lane,' more than once. I worried about him getting busted by the cops and going to jail for driving so badly. Then nothing would stop Mum from marrying Saint Bede and where would we live?

Would Grandma Bett ever consider letting him stay in our house? His 'crackpot ideas' would drive her crazy. And what about his other wives? You could probably fit one small bed in the secret room, but you'd never get three in there. Eljah's bunk was spare – might I end up sharing a room with Heavenly? What would the kids at school say? And what if Saint Bede's other wives had kids at our school? They could take over our house completely. My life would be over for sure.

'BLIMEY!' MUM SAID AS we walked through the sliding doors to the airport. There were people everywhere and signs pointing in all directions. 'Everyone hold hands until I figure out where the hell we're meant to go.'

Standing in the long, winding line of people, we listened to the family behind us talk in a funny accent about what they were going to eat when they got home. They must have been Americans. They sounded like people right off the TV, only louder, like Saint Bede. Even the fat red-haired girl who was only about four years old spoke in the funny accent. I wondered what flapjacks were.

Finally it was our turn and Mum handed Elijah's ticket over to a smiling lady wearing an Ansett badge. Mum smiled back at the lady and asked her if she'd be so kind as to look after Elijah on the plane, to show him where the toilet was and make sure he got something to eat.

The lady stopped smiling, looked from Mum to Dad, then at Elijah, me, Grub and Lucky, then she smiled again.

'I won't actually be on the plane, but I will see that your little boy is well looked after.' She glanced down at Elijah's ticket. 'So, where are you people from?'

'Quite a few hours from here. Place called Coongahoola,' Mum said.

The woman's smile disappeared again. 'You're kidding!' she said. 'I've heard about the dreadful things going on there with those crazy religious people.'

'He's got two suitcases,' Mum said. 'My mother's fault, she gave him so much stuff to take. Couldn't say no since she paid for his ticket. But they're small – school cases, really.'

'What are those people called again?' the Ansett lady asked, leaning forward.

'The Believers,' Dad answered.

Mum lifted the suitcases onto the black belt that took people's cases away.

'Yes, yes, the Believers! I'm surprised you're not all boarding the plane.'

'Thanks for looking after Elijah,' Mum said, without looking at the Ansett lady. 'A load off my mind. Come on, kids.' I watched as Elijah's and my school cases were swallowed up.

Dad said airport food is a bloody rip-off so we sat on some hard plastic seats near a shop that sold a million kinds of lollies and ate the sausage and tomato sauce sandwiches Grandma Bett'd made us. We were tired from being stuck in a car for so long and from walking all over the airport. Even Grub and Lucky ate without saying the sandwiches were too soggy or that the sausages looked like they were bleeding all over the bread.

Then it was time. We walked Elijah to his boarding gate, which didn't look like a gate at all. My legs felt all shaky and I forced my mouth to smile to stop myself from crying. This was it. Elijah was leaving us. He screwed up his face as Mum and I kissed his cheeks, then he shook Dad's hand and waved at the twins.

'See yas!' he said, swinging the plastic bag with his boarding pass, Rubik's Cube and leftover licorice Allsorts.

'Bye,' I said. It came out as a whisper.

Elijah then turned around and walked through the gate as if it was the most normal thing to do in the world.

CHAPTER FOURTEEN

AFTER ELIJAH'S ESCAPE, A LOT OF PEOPLE RECKONED THAT THE MURDERER wouldn't be game to strike again. 'That Bleeder nutter knows the cops are on to him,' I heard a man with a ginger Afro say at the supermarket checkout. I started believing it too. That's why on the first day of April, just three days after Elijah'd left, when Nathan Taylor said that another River Child'd disappeared, I thought it was an April Fool's joke. The year before I'd believed Shelley when she told me that Mr Kingsly'd been run over by the school bus. I was determined not to be fooled again. So it wasn't until I went back into the classroom after lunch that I knew something was wrong.

Mr Friend sat at his desk with his arms crossed and his head down. He kicked his shiny brown shoe at the swirly pattern on the carpet and let out long noisy breaths like Grandma Bett did when people swore on TV. After we'd all sat down and stopped talking, he looked up at us with tired eyes. He waited for Josh to turn around, then he told us in a flat, quiet voice that Michael Sanders'd left Scott Oliver's house in Bottlebrush Crescent on his BMX bike around teatime the night before. I was listening, but it took me a while to understand what he was saying. *Michael Sanders. Michael!*

Mr Friend said that Michael's family was still waiting for him at nine o'clock, and at nine-fifteen his dad'd called Constable Stewy. That's all he said and no one put their hand up to ask a question. We already knew the story.

This time the victim was someone I knew. It was my turn to be really sad. So, in a terrible way I'd actually got what I'd wanted. But the weird thing was, I didn't even cry. For the first few hours I felt absolutely nothing.

All I remember about the rest of that afternoon is seeing Mum at the school gate, her eyes wet and bloodshot, and her ringing Uncle Boyd to ask him to break the news to Elijah before he heard it on the TV. Dad had tea with us at our house that night, but Grub was the only person who ate anything.

'This just can't be happening.' Mum pushed away her plate of sausages and mashed potato. 'I keep thinking about how Helen and Bruce must feel. It's just a bloody nightmare.'

'Yeah, I let them down big-time,' Dad said, angrily stabbing his fork into a sausage. 'I told Bruce to take the night off since he'd done patrol the night before. Promised him I'd do a good job, but I stuffed up.'

'Nonsense, Robbie,' Grandma Bett said. 'The river's a huge area. You did your best.'

'But I wasn't even at the river! I thought, 'cause of what happened to Elijah, the reserve was a better bet. Only thing I saw was a couple of possums doin' the business; and a limping kangaroo. I was bloody useless.'

'Robbie, you tried. This is not your fault.' Grandma Bett patted Dad's arm.

MY TEARS CAME LATER that night, in the dark of my bedroom. I started thinking about Michael, about how yesterday he was as alive as I was, and now he was probably dead. How was that possible? I tried to remember all the things we'd done together or that he'd said to me. One time, when we were playing in the reserve, he asked if I'd mind marrying him when we were older. I said I'd think about it, but he'd have to get his hair cut or else he'd have to wear the white dress because he'd look prettier than me. Secretly though, I was happy that he'd asked. I'd never appreciated him enough. For a little brother's best friend, or someone to marry, there were many worse boys. I now knew that Toby would never want to marry me, so I could've made do with Michael. But not any more. Michael was gone.

This time it didn't take the sergeant and Constable Stewy long to find the body. There wasn't even time for anyone to stick up posters of Michael with his floppy long hair. His body'd been buried under some lantana bushes near the Bagooli River, not far from where Nigel'd been discovered (apparently, Anthea'd been buried with more care on the opposite side of the old picnic site). They found Michael's BMX too, inside a hollow tree.

'The sucker is getting lazier,' I heard Mr Irwin say to Dad over the back fence, the fence Toby'd nearly obliterated with his soccer ball. 'He's gonna be behind bars before he can say alleluia.'

I didn't know then how Michael was killed because Grandma Bett kept turning the TV off whenever he was mentioned, and sneaking the newspaper into her bedroom. Owen Beattie said that Michael'd been chopped up into little pieces and fed to old Mr Buckley's dog, Noodle, but we knew that his body'd been found so it couldn't have been eaten. Besides, someone'd said that Anthea was baked in an oven for ten minutes. When Samantha Cook asked Mr Friend if that was true, he told Mr Kingsly and we had to stay after school for a special assembly where Mr Kingsly said that the oven story was a nasty rumour and only to believe what was reported in the school newsletter.

Apart from all the people standing round with cameras and microphones outside the church, Michael's funeral was a lot like Anthea's (and Nigel's). We said the same prayers and sang the same sad songs. Grandma Bett said that no one'd felt like organising another funeral so they just followed the same programme as

Anthea's. The only real change was that this time it was Michael inside the small brown coffin, and it was Michael's dad and two brothers carrying it up the aisle. I tried to picture Michael inside the coffin, the expression on his face now that he was dead, but it just made me cry. The only good thing about him dying – and I felt awful for even thinking this because it certainly wasn't a good thing for Michael – was that it made the incident with Toby – Toby calling us 'freaks' – seem trivial.

Mum didn't let Elijah come home. She told him there were other ways of saying goodbye to Michael without putting his own life in danger. Mrs Lothum obviously hadn't made it to the funeral either. When I snuck a look around in the church, I saw poor Mr Lothum sitting on his own, under his floppy cowboy hat, in the row behind Dad and Gary. Ken Knowles from the Baptist church hadn't turned up again – his mum was sitting by herself near the organ. As I was turning back around, Mrs Irwin caught my eye and stared at me. Even when I was facing the front I could feel her eyes on the back of my head. I guessed Toby was sitting next to her, but I didn't really care.

We'd finished singing *Abide With Me*, and Michael's mum blew her nose for the hundredth time. I thought we were about to leave, when the sergeant stood and squeezed past Constable Stewy and the Mullers. He walked all the way up the aisle to the altar where only holy people are meant to go. He whispered in Reverend Gregory's ear and the Reverend nodded at the microphone.

'Sorry to keep you, but since you're all here together I'd like to say a few words.' Sergeant Colby cleared his throat. He had a big bald head like an egg and eyes that looked like they'd easily pop out of their sockets. Everyone was scared of the sergeant. Dad said people even hung up when the sergeant answered the phone at the police station because they were more scared of him than of the burglar or whoever they were calling about. He was always complaining of prank calls – he had no idea that it was just people hoping to get Constable Stewy. It was only since the murderer struck that people were glad that the sergeant was around. Constable Stewy was all right for catching boys who exploded your letterbox with fireworks or put eggs in your car muffler, but for dealing with a murderer, someone more like Sergeant Colby was needed. That's what Dad reckoned anyway.

'First, my condolences to Helen and Bruce and to Andrew and Timothy. Michael's loss is an absolute tragedy. As were the losses of Nigel and Anthea before him. I just want to reassure you that Constable Stewart Thompson and myself are working around the clock on this case. As you're probably aware, we've had a few extra police join our team and some of the local blokes have been doing their bit, too. But we're stepping up the investigation. From tomorrow, a special force will arrive from Sydney and we will not rest until whoever's terrorising this town is brought to justice.'

'Why don't you just bang 'im up now then?' a man called out from behind us. We all spun around to see who it was. Even Grandma Bett turned her head.

The sergeant's face was glowing red in the candlelight. 'We are questioning a number of people, and I can assure you that as soon as we know for certain who's responsible for these crimes, we'll be making an arrest.'

'A Yank! Yay-high. Calls himself a saint.' The voice was Graham Anderson's. Next to him, Heidi and her mum were looking down, embarrassed. Next to them, Andy Hall and his wife were also looking down.

'If you've got some proof, Mr Anderson, by all means share it with me. That goes for everyone else, too. If you know anything, *anything* at all, talk to Constable Stewart or myself. Just don't spill your guts to those reporter mugs outside. Their speculations aren't making our job any easier.'

The wake was in the school hall, just like Anthea's was, and Michael's mum and dad stayed the whole time even though they looked like they wanted to be somewhere else. I didn't see Anthea's parents, but Nigel's mum crept into the hall and hugged Michael's parents, then snuck back out before anyone tried to talk to her. The tables were filled with food, but this time I didn't feel like eating any of it. I didn't feel like talking to anyone either, especially not Toby, so I stayed in a quiet corner with Grandma Bett who was also trying to avoid talking to people. Constable Stewy turned up in his shiny black boots and neatly ironed blue uniform, his gun sticking out of his belt just in case. But old Mr Buckley didn't try anything this time. He fed Noodle a handful of cheerios and then left.

Though I was relieved Mrs Lothum wasn't there (would she be upset about the message Shelley had written to her in my letter?), I wondered why not. When I asked Grandma Bett, she said, 'She's not well. A bundle of nerves, so they're saying.'

'A bundle of nerves?'

'A nervous wreck. She's just not herself. In fact, on Tuesday morning, Nurse Audrey saw her with a bucket and sponge cleaning her letterbox! I mean, she does work in the post office, but I've never heard of anyone cleaning their letterbox.'

'But why?' Surely it had nothing to do with the message.

'I think it's stress. All the worrying has got to her.'

'Because of the murders?'

'That's probably a large part of it. And the Believers. You know, they've just bought Julia's salon and they own the chemist now, too – the hide of them! – and Mrs Lothum doesn't like change. Working in the Post Office she's always been the eyes and ears of the town. But now she doesn't know who's who or what's what, and knowing these kind of things is everything to a woman like her.'

'What's a woman like her?'

'Shallow, if you ask me, Gracie, but that's not something I'd like you to repeat. She wouldn't be your godmother if I'd had any say in the matter – she's hardly a good role model! – but she was there for your mum during your birth. Gracie, please stop chewing your nails. They look terrible!'

I looked down at my blunt, bleeding nails. My hands no longer looked like they belonged to me. I used to be proud of my long pink fingernails, but now they were as short and ugly as old Mr Buckley's. I shoved my hands in my pockets.

The not-so-secret message probably hadn't helped, but I was glad to hear that something else was wrong with Mrs Lothum. Shelley was the one who'd written it anyway, not me, and she was coming back to Coongahoola in eight days! Her parents had decided it was safe enough for her and Billy to come back since the murderer was only going for River Children. They hadn't lived in Coongahoola when the River Picnic happened anyway, so they had nothing to worry about.

CHAPTER FIFTEEN

THE DAY BEFORE SHELLEY CAME BACK, WE WERE ON OUR WAY HOME from Woolworths when Mum said out of the blue that we were going to stop by and visit Saint Bede. I realised then why she'd worn a new blouse, white with a red flower on the pocket and big padded shoulders, to do the grocery shopping.

'No! We can't go there!' It wasn't only the thought of what the kids'd say to me at school if they found out. I was scared of Saint Bede. I'd heard what people said about him, what Dad said about him. I thought about him before I went to sleep and his small round face and hot breath turned my dreams into nightmares.

'You can see your friend,' Mum said.

I liked the idea of seeing Heavenly again. I'd thought about lending her my copy of *Tex* but never got a chance to talk to her at school with all the other kids around. But no! Saint Bede was too creepy, and what if he'd killed Michael? I didn't want to go anywhere near him.

'I don't have any friends,' I said. 'Not there.'

'What about Heavenly? You seemed to get on well.'

'Didn't have much choice.' How could Heavenly bear having Saint Bede as a dad? She was against him burning books, but did she love him anyway?

'Oh, you can be so difficult sometimes! Your grandma's cleaning the church. I can't leave you at home alone.'

'Home'd be safer than there!'

'Don't tell me you're listening to that nonsense.'

'Can we go to Dad's?'

'Dad's? Well, I s'pose, if he's there, but, Gracie, I thought you'd have more sense. You've even met His Holiness.'

'His what?'

'Saint Bede!'

Mum parked outside the small red-brick flat next to the BP station, the one with the falling-down letterbox that said '24/1' in black felt pen. Gary's rusty old brown car sat slumped on flat tyres in the driveway and Dad's worn-out thongs lay with two other pairs where a doormat should be.

'Hello?' Mum called through the ripped wire in the screen door. 'Robbie, your kids are here to visit.'

Dad walked along the hallway in just a pair of black footy shorts. 'Phone call'd be nice, but come in.' The door squeaked as he opened it.

'I'll pick them up in an hour.' Mum passed Lucky to Dad.

'Oh, I see,' Dad said. 'Where're you goin'?'

'I don't see how that's any of your business.' Mum backed away from the door.

'B'lievers!' Grub said.

'Jeeezus! You're *still* seein' him? After what happened to Michael? You've been brainwashed, Nell. It's the only possible explanation,' Dad called out. 'The guy's a freak! He's bloody dangerous!'

We followed Dad along the hallway, past the pieces of metal covered in grease – 'Gazza's fixin' me motorbike,' Dad explained – to the living room. Gary lay on the couch with a car magazine on his hairy tummy and Mr Irwin sat in a chair with a gold can of beer in his hand.

It was dark and damp, and a few degrees colder than outside, but the men were acting like it was the middle of summer. I wondered whose feet I could smell.

'G'day!' They nodded at us as Dad plonked himself back down in an old green chair that groaned under his weight.

'That bloody woman, I tell ya! She's a hopeless case. She's gone to see that Believer fella!'

'Bloody woman!' Grub giggled, hoisting himself up onto Dad's knee, and the men laughed.

'Reckon she'll say yes to him?' Gary asked.

'Yes?' Dad scratched his leg.

'You said he asked her to marry him.'

'Oh, that. Well, she can't, mate. She's still my Mrs.'

'Yeah, but if he's married to three women, you think he'd give a toss if Nell's married already?'

Dad thought for a moment. 'Bloody hell. I could kill him.'

'Yeah, why not?' Mr Irwin said.

Dad laughed, looking at us. 'Come on, Dez, I'm a family man.'

'You don't have to *kill* him, just sort him out. I'll help you if you like. Fact half the town'd be keen to help make him pay.'

'Yeah, you're probably onto somethin' but can we talk about it later? Gracie, you might find somethin' to eat in the kitchen, bikkies or whatever,' Dad said. 'Along the hall, second on the left. Bring somethin' out for the ankle-biters, will you?'

'I just can't believe you didn't stop her,' Mr Irwin was saying as I left the room.

The kitchen sink and surrounding lime-green benches were buried in dirty dishes, beer cans and an ice cream container half-filled with cigarette butts. The fridge was empty except for some rotten-smelling thing wrapped in a tea towel. I closed it quickly and tried the cupboard. I grabbed the opened packet of milk arrowroot biscuits. My feet almost stuck to the dirty floor.

Walking along the hall, I heard Gary say, '...snapped her neck – with his hands.'

I stopped still. Anthea?

'Shit! Poor girl.'

'Yeah, well, she got off better than the last kid. Must've put up a fight. Beaten to a pulp. Stewy reckons he struggled for at least an hour–'

Gary stopped when I walked in. My hands and face were sweating, and images of Anthea were spinning around in my head.

'Geez, you managed to find food!' Gary said when I sat down. 'You did well.'

The biscuits were soggy and tasted over a hundred years old. Lucky spat hers out into her hand and Grub hid his inside the *TV Guide* and asked Dad if we could play outside.

Out in the front yard, Dad kicked at an empty can of KB. 'I haven't got a ball or anythin' but youse can boot one of these around.' He showed the twins how to score a goal by kicking the gold can between the bin and the rusted wheelbarrow that looked like it was growing out of the ground.

The clouds were smothering the sun and I sat on the cold concrete fence, picking bindi-eyes out of my bare feet and wanting every car that drove past to be Mum's. The dry wind blew leaves, dirt and rubbish up the street and dust stung my eyes. I could hear Gary's words: 'snapped her neck'.

What if Saint Bede wanted to murder Mum all along? Nigel, Anthea and Michael could've just been practice. Maybe he wanted everyone to think he was only murdering River Children so he could get Mum without anyone suspecting. What would I do if Mum was killed? I wouldn't be able to handle it. I'd want to be dead, too. Then I spotted a little blue car, like the one Elijah and I used to see parked outside our house when he and I got home from school on Friday afternoons back when Mrs Lothum visited Mum for a weekly gossip. It was Mrs Lothum behind the steering wheel. Her hair was everywhere, even hanging over her face. I thought she might stop and say hello, especially since Dad was there. But when I waved, she looked away quickly without smiling.

Another nine cars passed before our dirty white station wagon turned the corner. I nearly cried seeing Mum, I was so relieved.

'Mum!' I said, diving into the front seat.

'Yes?'

'Mind if I get a lift?' Dad poked his head in Mum's window as the twins climbed into the back, Grub clutching the empty KB can.

'Where to?'

'Yours. I'd like a chat.'

'Get in then, but don't start on me now. I've got a headache.'

WHEN MUM AND DAD'S voices started getting louder, I slid off the couch.

'We too?' Lucky asked. She was wearing a red dress that I'd worn when I was little, but the pockets had ripped off and the hem was falling down.

'Yeah. Come on.'

Lucky and Grub toddled after me with their hands pressed tightly over their ears.

'Wait!' Lucky ran back to the living room. She returned with her Mary-Anne doll (a band-aid covering the teeth marks Grub had left on her arm) and Poor Doggy, her brown fluffy toy dog with only half an ear.

I was too old for hiding away in a stupid cupboard with a couple of babies, but it was better than listening to Mum and Dad going on and on about nothing. At least in the secret room we could pretend that our family was happy, like Shelley's and everyone else's.

'See! You can't help yourself,' Mum was yelling. 'You say you want me back but you're still a bloody–'

I slammed the door and we sang the theme song to *The Goodies* over and over until Mum knocked on the secret room door.

Dad'd had to go home, she told us, her eyes red and her nose streaming, 'Be a pet, Gracie, and set the table for tea.'

CHAPTER SIXTEEN

THE LAST PLACE I'D EXPECTED TO FIND SHELLEY ON HER FIRST DAY BACK at school was in our classroom. Usually no one'd be seen dead in the classroom before the bell rang, not even the kids without friends. She sat at the new wooden desk Mr Friend'd carried in for her on Friday afternoon, with her head bowed over a magazine. I nearly didn't recognise her. Her white-blonde hair'd been cut short at the back like a boy's, but left long on the top and hanging down over one eye. I'd seen a few senior girls with hair like that smoking outside the school gates. It made Shelley look older and watching her flick strands of silky hair away from her face made me proud to be her best friend. I pulled a clump of my blonde fringe down but my fingers slipped off it before it reached my eyebrows. Mum always cut my fringe too short.

'Shell!' I rushed over to her desk.

'Hi.' Shelley glanced up at me before returning her eyes to the magazine.

'I've been waiting for you. Under the shady tree. You haven't been away that long! Did you forget?'

'No.' Shelley looked at the new red digital watch on her skinny tanned wrist.

'I saved you a locker.'

'Thanks. I've already put my bag away.'

Shelley lifted up the magazine – a *Dolly* with Cindy Lauper on the cover – and held it in front of her face, but her neck was as red as a tomato so I knew that her face was red as well. She always turned red when she was nervous. When Nathan Taylor picked her for his softball team her face went so red that Miss Jones worried she had sunstroke and told her to sit the game out under a tree.

'Are you okay?' I asked.

'Yes,' she spoke in a whisper, but stayed hidden behind Cindy Lauper, so I took the hint.

I sat down at my old wooden desk, three rows behind, heaved up its lid and dug around for the book I'd borrowed from the library the week before: a big fat orange one called *To Kill a Mockingbird*. I was sure that Shelley'd tell me what was wrong at lunchtime. Maybe she liked a boy in Dubbo who she was never going to see again. Or perhaps her parents'd had a fight. I couldn't imagine that though. Her mum and dad were always kissing and holding hands like mums and dads in movies.

Mr Friend let Shelley out for lunch before me and she didn't wait outside. The only girls I recognised near the shady tree that used to be our hang-out were from Elijah's class. Then, as I was walking past the toilet block, I saw Heavenly limping along. As she hobbled closer, I noticed a huge red splotch on her school uniform, near her knee.

I checked to see if anyone was watching before I went over. 'What happened?'

'I'm all right, really.' She sniffed, not looking all right at all. 'I was chased.'

'By who?'

'Children in my class.'

'Looks sore,' I said. Reddish-brown blood was oozing through her dress.

'It doesn't hurt,' Heavenly said. Her face was red-raw with pimples and wet with tears.

'How come you're crying then?'

'I'm just sick of it. I'm sick of being treated like an outcast.'

'I know the feeling.'

'Do you?' She didn't say it in a mean way, but it made me think. Did I really know? Did I have any idea what it'd be like to be a Believer?

'Perhaps if you take off the veil,' I said. 'Maybe then kids'll leave you alone. It just looks a bit–'

Heavenly stared at me through her tears, and I could tell I'd hurt her feelings. But I wasn't sure if she was upset by what I'd said, or by the fact that I'd started backing away.

'*No one* knows how I feel.' She spoke quietly. 'I hate this place. One day I'm just going to – go.'

'Where? Where would you go?' She'd look even more out of place in a city like Sydney.

'Tamworth. A delivery van goes there from our camp on Saturday and Sunday mornings before church.' She'd obviously given it some thought. 'It's full of Virgin Mary Muffins and Buns, but there's room to hide in the back. I've looked in the window.'

I nodded, wanting to believe that she'd really be brave enough to escape from the camp. I wanted to say that I did kind of understand, that I also felt like an outsider, and that I sometimes hated Coongahoola, too. But I couldn't. I had to think of myself, my own reputation. I couldn't be seen talking to her.

'I'm sorry, bye.' I turned and walked away, without looking back to see if the hurt look was still in her eyes.

I eventually found Shelley leaning against the brick wall at the side of the new tuck shop, talking and laughing with Sarah K and Hannah Mosely, the prettiest girls in Year Six, girls who'd hardly paid us any attention before.

I stood still for a moment, shocked. It wasn't so much that Shelley was with Sarah K and Hannah instead of me, but that she looked like she belonged with them.

I looked down at myself, my flat chest, scrawny knees and scuffed shoes, then over at the glamorous Sarah K and Hannah Mosely. Could I blame Shelley for wanting to ditch me? I looked like a nine-year-old and not a particularly pretty one. But still, Shelley and I'd been best friends since kindergarten and we hadn't even had a fight. Surely she still liked me at least.

'There you are!' I said, trying not to be intimidated by Sarah K and Hannah.

Shelley gave me a look I couldn't understand before turning back to them and saying, 'No joke! His name was Mr Stevens and he looked just like Simon off *A Country Practice*, except he was way taller–'

'I forgot to say I like your hair,' I butted in.

Sarah K and Hannah both took a step back, as if I had nits.

'It was cut ages ago.' Shelley tossed her head, still looking at Sarah and Hannah. 'Looks foul today.' She was holding a shiny red cassette player, one that stood upright instead of lying flat like ours did, with 'Boom Box' written on it in big black letters.

'Well, anyway, I've got loads to tell you,' I said. 'Elijah's been gone for–'

'Look Gracie,' Sarah K said in the bitchy voice she used on people she didn't like. 'Much as we'd love to hear about your famous little brother, she's not allowed to talk to you. Okay?'

'What? Says who?'

'Says her parents.'

'Says *all* of our parents,' Hannah added, blowing an enormous pink bubble.

'Why?' I asked. But I already knew why.

Hannah's bubble popped. ''Cause you're one of *them*,' she said, peeling the pink gum off her lightly freckled nose. Her strawberry breath was sickeningly sweet.

'A Bleeder!' Sarah K added in case I was too stupid to follow.

'No, I'm not! Shelley, you know that!'

Shelley shrugged but still didn't look at me.

'Mum maybe, but not me,' I continued. 'Not Dad either. He hates them more than anything, more than he hates the Liberal party, even – you should hear the stuff he says. Wants to kill them! And my grandma practically lives inside the Catholic church. She calls them crackpots.'

'Sorry, but it's really up to our parents.' Sarah didn't sound sorry at all. 'Turn it back on, Shell. I want to hear The Cure.'

'Well, stuff you!' That was all I could think to say before walking off, and I wasn't sure I'd said it loud enough for them to hear over their music. I didn't care that Sarah K and Hannah weren't allowed to talk to me. They never had anything nice to say anyway. But Shelley! Her parents liked me, they let me stay at their place and eat tea with them and her mum let me flick through her *Cleo* magazines. I thought about crawling under one of the prefab classrooms, curling up in the dark and bawling my eyes out, but I was too angry. Now I *was* starting to feel like an outcast – and it was all Mum's fault.

The library was closed on Mondays so there was no chance of disappearing between the bookshelves. Why was this happening to me? It wasn't fair. I wanted to get out of there, but where could I go? If I snuck home, Grandma Bett'd just drive me straight back to school again, and probably give me extra jobs as punishment. I bit hard on my thumbnail, tasting blood. Walking past the toilets I saw another Believer girl sitting cross-legged in the dust in her ankle-length school uniform, playing jacks on her own. She looked up from under her dirty blue veil and smiled at me. She smiled as if she knew me. Could she be another of Saint Bede's children? I shivered and looked away, walking faster and blinking back my tears. Then I slipped into my classroom and pretended to read *To Kill a Mockingbird*, the noise of the playground buzzing in my ears, until the bell rang.

SHELLEY SHARED PAINTING EASELS with Sarah K and ignored me for the rest of the afternoon. When I got home and slung the plastic shoe bag that carried my lunchbox over the coat rack, I didn't think the day could get any worse. I should've known better. I ran straight to the secret room and scribbled a letter to Elijah before rereading it and ripping it into tiny pieces. If I told him how bad everything was in Coongahoola he might want to stay away forever.

I'd planned to refuse to eat that night, but by the time Mum yelled out that tea was ready my stomach was growling, so I sat at the table and sawed through two rissoles. Grandma Bett talked the whole time, complaining that she was having trouble coping at the church. She said that mothers'd started bringing their children in for confession, some of them every day, in case their lives were about to 'get cut short'. That was all well and good, she said, but poor Father Scott was now spending half his life in the confessional and had little time for anything else.

'Confession every blooming day? What's the world come to?' Mum asked with a mouth full of sloppy beans.

'It's not as crazy as it sounds, Nell,' Grandma Bett said. 'It's like insurance, a way of guaranteeing that their children have a place in heaven.' She looked at me when she said that and I guessed that it wouldn't be long before I'd find myself inside Father Scott's confessional.

Neither Mum nor Grandma Bett noticed that I hadn't said a word all evening. It didn't help that earlier that afternoon Grub'd found the giant Easter bunny Mum hadn't got around to posting to Elijah and, after gnawing his way through the body and head, had given Lucky the ears to suck on. Hours later they were still running around the house at a million miles an hour, two sticky brown faces, laughing like maniacs one minute, crying like babies the next.

I went straight to my room after washing the dishes without saying goodnight to anyone. I climbed into bed but didn't feel like reading and couldn't sleep. I listened to Grub and Lucky laughing as they slid and splashed in the bath. If only they understood that their mum was thinking about marrying a murderer. I was still awake, counting the faded roses on the yellowing wallpaper, when Mum crept in and turned out my light. She didn't look closely enough to notice the tears on my face.

It was a couple of hours later that I heard voices outside. My owl clock glowed 1.15am. The voices were whispering so I didn't recognise them or hear what they said, but it sounded like there were a few of them and at least one was female. I squeezed my eyes shut and tried to think of a prayer, but in my panic all the words escaped me. The people were in our front yard, I was sure of that, but I didn't want to look out the window. That's what people do in horror movies and something bad always happens to them. What if it was the murderer? What if the murderer wasn't just one person, but a whole group? My heart was beating so fast, I was struggling to breathe. I thought about running into Mum's room, but how could I do that and still be mad with her? Besides, Mum was no help. If people broke into our house, she'd probably just yell at them, which'd make it worse. Grandma Bett would annoy them even more by falling onto her knees and saying the rosary in that embarrassing way she does, talking really fast like she's speaking another language. So I just did what I used to do when Mum and Dad's voices forced their way through my bedroom wall – pulled my scratchy old bedspread up over my head and blocked my ears, and I stayed like that until sleep finally saved me.

I woke to the sound of the front door clicking shut. I blinked the sleep out of my eyes and saw the sun creeping through the gaps in my fraying green curtains. The owl clock said 6.45am.

I heard Grandma Bett's sensible shoes disappearing down the path, then the gate creaking open and closed. I must've dreamt the voices in the night. Nothing bad'd happened. It was a Tuesday morning and Grandma Bett was on her way to seven o'clock mass as usual.

Then I heard Grandma Bett cry out, 'Ohhhhh! Ohhhhh! Nell! Nell!'

I sat up. Mum's bedsprings squeaked, footsteps thumped along the hall, the front door opened and slippers slapped along the path. 'Fucking hell!' Mum yelled, loud enough for the whole world to hear. 'What the? Who in God's name? Jesus!'

I slid off my bed and raced out of my room, through the front door and down to the gate where Grandma Bett and Mum stood. I could smell the paint before I looked up at our dirty white fibro house and saw what they were staring at. Red paint, the colour of blood. Huge letters, dripping red. Nine letters, all capitals, together spelling out, screaming out: *MURDERERS*.

Grandma Bett's handbag lay splattered on the path, a mess of keys, lipsticks and hymn sheets. She clasped her shaking hands and whispered the 'Our Father'. I wasn't sure whether it was because of the word written on our house or the words that'd come out of Mum's mouth. I leant against the gate and shivered as cold dew ran down the back of my legs.

'Nell! It's got to stop,' Grandma Bett said, after 'deliver us from evil'. 'You've got to stop it.'

'Me? This is my fault?' Mum yelled, not seeming to care that if anyone looked out their window to see what all the fuss was about, they'd spy her holey blue underpants through her see-through pink nightie. 'The people of this town trash your joint and you blame me! I'm so sick of this. Can't you see that this is probably the work of the murderer trying to pin the crime on someone else? We'll move out if that's what you want.'

'That's not what I'm saying. I don't want you to leave.' Grandma Bett sniffed. Her mouth sagged and the wrinkles in her face seemed deeper than ever.

'We'll move in with Saint Bede,' Mum yelled even louder, as if announcing it to the street. 'See what the town says about that!'

Oh God, I thought. Toby probably heard her. He was probably watching us right now, with a sneer on his face.

'No!' I cried.

Mum and Grandma Bett both turned, as if they'd only just noticed I was there.

'Nell, I really don't think that would be wise.' Grandma Bett forced a smile through her tears. 'Gracie, why don't you go and have your breakfast?'

'No! I'm not having my breakfast and I'm not moving in with, with a – with a fucking murderer!' I kicked the cold metal gate, hurting my bare toes, and ran back up the path.

As I opened the front door, I spun around and glared at Mum. 'And next time I need a haircut, I'm going to the hairdressers!' I slammed the door behind me.

I ate my rice bubbles, even though they tasted like nothing and I felt full already. It seemed like the only thing to do. I wanted things to be normal and eating rice bubbles, listening to them spluttering away as they drowned in the milk, was normal. I didn't go to school though. No one told me to go and I was hardly about to suggest it. I knew what all the kids would be talking about.

'I'll get some paint stripper,' Dad told Grandma Bett. He'd come to our place instead of the steelworks after Mr Irwin called to tell him what'd happened. 'Some more white paint, too, cover up the damage. House could do with sprucin' up anyway.'

'Thank you, Robbie.' Grandma Bett leant to give Dad a kiss but he'd already turned away, so she patted the naked-lady tattoo on his arm instead.

'What's yer mum up to?' he asked me. We could hear swearing and thumping from her bedroom, coat hangers scraping on metal, cupboard drawers being yanked open and forced shut.

I was thinking of what to say back, of how to say that I wasn't Mum's shadow, that I had a mind of my own, when Mum burst into the kitchen, red faced and white knuckled, dragging an old brown falling-apart suitcase behind her. An ancient Band-Aid was stuck on it, which said *Nell Butcher age 12*. The messy handwriting looked a lot like mine.

'Right! I'm off! Kids can stay here, they don't need me.'

'Nell, please. I didn't mean for you to go,' Grandma Bett said. 'Please sit down and have a cup of tea.'

'That's your answer to everything isn't it? A cup of bloody tea!' She turned and heaved her suitcase along the hall. 'Robbie, you can have your bed back, might want to change the sheets –'

'Nell!' Dad rushed towards her. 'Nell, please. Wait!'

'What?' Mum stopped outside my door.

'Yer not even dressed,' Dad said.

Mum looked down at her nightie and fluffy-bunny slippers. She grunted, dropped her suitcase, pushed past Dad and tripped back along the hall towards her bedroom.

'But don't go! Please!' he called after her with a croaky voice. 'I don't want you to go.'

CHAPTER SEVENTEEN

IT WAS THE SCHOOL COUNSELLOR WHO CAME UP WITH THE IDEA OF memorial seats. She wasn't really a school counsellor, though. She was just a friend of Mr Kingsly's who'd lost her husband and three sons in a bus crash in Turkey, making her an expert on people dying. Mrs J, she'd told us to call her, and she was available in the Remedial Reading room every Tuesday if anyone wanted to talk. Anyway, she suggested that the school build special seats to dedicate to the murder victims. Notes were sent home asking dads who were builders (there were five, not counting Nathan Taylor's dad who was still in jail) to bring their toolboxes to school on the third Sunday in April.

The day after the working bee, we had a special ceremony instead of our usual assembly. We lined up on the grass near the tuck shop, squinting in the sun as we listened to Mr Kingsly thank everyone he'd ever met, before Sarah K's dad, Mayor Kirk, lifted an old pink bed sheet to reveal Nigel's seat (later just called Nige, e.g. 'meet you at Nige'). We then followed the teachers down to the basketball court and clapped as Mayor Kirk yanked off another pink bed sheet to unveil Anthea's seat. Each of the seats had a bronze plaque with a special message engraved on it, but Anthea's dad'd made an extra donation so hers included a small photo framed by an 18-carat gold heart. (Because of the photo and because she was so pretty, Anthea, as her seat was soon called, became the place where the popular girls hung out, including Sarah K, Hannah Mosely and Shelley. Even some of the seniors visited Anthea after school, leaving beer cans, wine casks and cigarette butts for us juniors to pick up when we were on litter duty.)

Our final destination was the dirt area outside the toilet block. There, we held our noses as Mayor Kirk uncovered Michael's seat, and watched Mrs Olsen smack a Year Three girl for flushing the loo while Mr Kingsly was saying the school motto. I wondered if it was luck of the draw that Michael got that spot, or was it because he was the type of person who'd be happy anywhere? Mr Kinglsy described it as a peaceful place to sit and reflect in the shade, but I couldn't imagine Anthea's parents allowing her seat within smelling distance of the loos.

It was a long, hot ceremony, not just because of the sun beating down on our foreheads. I had the extra trouble of hiding from Year Eight as the whole school traipsed from seat to seat. Toby and Heavenly were in Year Eight. I couldn't face seeing either of them.

Only once the bell rang and all the kids ran to their lockers for their lunch could I relax. I took mine to Michael's seat, thinking I'd eat my peanut butter sandwiches on it on behalf of Elijah.

This bench was erected on 17 April 1983
in memory of Michael Sanders
1974 – 1983
Much-loved classmate and friend

'Hey, no Bleeders allowed!' Sarah K said as I was reading the plaque. I turned to see her with Hannah Mosely and Shelley, all three trying to looking cool with jumpers tied around their waists, white socks rolled over their ankles like donuts and dress collars standing up. They must've followed me from the lockers.

'He was my brother's best friend. And I'm *not* a Bleeder.'

'Well, your mum is. Josh saw her with *him*. Holding hands and everything like he was your dad.'

'Saint Bede is not my dad!'

'That's what you call him? *Saint Bede! Saint Bede*, I'm going to bed – can you tuck me in?' said Sarah K, who'd been on her best behaviour all through the ceremony, until her dad'd driven off in his fancy silver car.

'*Saint Bede*, give me a kiss good night!' Hannah laughed.

Shelley was laughing too. She turned away but I could tell because her body was shaking.

'*Saint Bede*, I've wet the bed! Can I snuggle up in your b–'

'He's not my dad. I don't even like him. He's a bloody murderer and I hate him!'

Everyone was quiet. Even Sarah K was too shocked to say anything for a moment. Then she smiled.

'So, he *is* the murderer?' she asked. 'Did you watch him?'

'No.'

'You helped him!'

'No. No, I just know.'

'How can you *just know*?'

'Because – he told me.'

'He told you he was the murderer?' Sarah K said so loudly even the kindergarteners playing hopscotch could've heard.

I nodded. He might as well've, I was thinking. Everyone knows he's the murderer.

'So Constable Stewy knows?'

'Um... no. I–'

'Have you told Mr Kingsly?'

'No.'

'Come on, let's tell him!' Sarah K looked at Hannah. 'There might be a reward for catching the Bleeder. Come on, Shelley.'

Shelley looked at me and I could tell she knew I was lying. I could see in her eyes that she felt sorry for me, but obviously not sorry enough because she flicked her fringe off her face, then turned and ran after the others.

By the time lunch was over, half the school knew what I'd said. I sat at my desk and tried to pretend that kids weren't whispering about it, and that Mr Friend wasn't frowning at me from behind his maths textbook. I stared at the desk and tried to remember what my life was like before everything went wrong, back when kids actually liked me. I wished I could magically develop a fatal disease – preferably a painless kind that'd kill me in my sleep. If I was dead I wouldn't have to worry about anything. I wouldn't have to think.

Josh from my class'd told us that if you ate six tubes of toothpaste, you'd drop dead. It sounded easy, but I'd felt like throwing up after one mouthful of Colgate. I wasn't really trying to do anything, just seeing if it'd be as easy to do as it sounded.

I was almost relieved when Mr Kingsly knocked on our classroom door and said, 'Can I borrow Gracie Barrett, please?'

Mr Kingsly's office still smelt of new paper and textbooks. The only other time I'd been inside it was when I'd turned up at school in bare feet after losing my school shoes in the reserve. Mr Kingsly'd dug through the cardboard Lost Property box until he found a pair of old brown JC sandals, two sizes too big and still sticky from someone else's sweaty feet, and made me wear those until the next term when Mum finally bought me new shoes.

'Sit down please, Gracie.' Mr Kingsly pointed at one of the yellow plastic chairs in front of his desk. He then sat in his chair and carefully lined up his gold pens side by side, as if they were kids outside the staffroom on detention.

'All right, I've heard some disturbing news today and I think you and I – and probably the police, but we'll come to that – need to have a talk.'

'Yes, Mr Kingsly.'

'How are things at home?' he asked, leaning so far forward I smelt the egg on his breath.

'At my home? Um. Pretty boring.' I noticed a photo of the Butcherer smiling alongside photos of two other ex-principals on the wall above the filing cabinet.

'Boring?'

'Because Elijah's gone to Queensland. He's staying with our Uncle and Aunty who I've never even met.'

'Yes, I know Elijah's away and I'm sure you miss him. He's a good lad despite what some people say, and certainly a brave one. What about your parents? How are they going?'

'Um, Dad's okay. And Mum's okay too; I think.'

'Your dad's living at home?'

'Yep. Just moved back. He said it's great to be home because the only thing Gary cooks is chops and baked beans.'

'And your mum?'

'She can't really cook either, but Grandma Bett's okay.'

'Is your mum living at home, Gracie?'

'No.' It came out as a squeak. I looked down at the carpet, at my swinging legs, at the grey scuffed toes of my black shoes.

'Where's your mum staying, Gracie?' Mr Kingsly was still leaning forward, elbows on the desk and chin resting in his hands.

'With the, um, with the Believers,' my mousey voice said.

'Is she living with the man they called Saint Bede?'

'No!' My normal voice was back. 'She's just staying there for a few days. She had a fight with my grandma after some people painted our house with red paint that dripped like blood. They painted–'

I couldn't say the word. Tears filled my eyes and spilled down my cheeks in big fat drops.

'It's all right, Gracie. You're not in trouble.' He reached out and touched my hand. His hands were much softer than Dad's. I stared at his hairy white knuckles. 'Listen to me. I'll get to the point: some girls from your class told me that you said this Bede man confessed to you. Is that correct?'

'Yes,' I said, quiet again.

'All right. Very well. Do you think we should call the sergeant now then? Together.' He picked up the phone.

'No.'

'Why not? Can't you see that it's the right thing to do?' He gently put the phone down.

'No. Because I–' I started bawling like a baby, my face dripping with tears and snot.

Mr Kingsly tore a handful of tissues out of the box on his

windowsill and handed them to me. 'Gracie, you're obviously terribly scared of this man. Is that why you won't tell?'

'I'm scared of him, but that's not why.'

'It's perfectly understandable to be scared. I'd be concerned if you weren't! But you have my word that the sergeant and Constable Stewart won't let anything happen to you.'

'But I lied! He didn't tell me anything. Sarah K and Hannah Mosely were teasing me so I just lied.'

Mr Kingsly frowned. 'Saint Bede didn't say anything to you?'

'No.'

'You're not just saying this because you're scared?'

'No.'

'He didn't mention anything at all?'

'I haven't seen him for weeks. I don't like him.'

'So you just made the whole story up?'

I nodded. 'But it wasn't really a *whole* story. It was just *one* thing.'

'I see.' Mr Kingsly sat back in his seat, still frowning. 'Well, I won't be calling Sergeant Colby after all, but I will be calling your father. I am very disappointed in you, Gracie Barrett. *Very* disappointed. And the granddaughter of Mr Butcher too! You could've caused a great deal of trouble. One thing I can't tolerate at my school is lying.'

I nodded, not looking up.

'You might also want to have a little chat with Mrs J tomorrow.'

'Yes, Mr Kingsly.' I buried my face in tissues.

CHAPTER EIGHTEEN

Dear Gracie

Whats happening? Mum called really late and said shes staying at the Bleeders camp!! She didnt say much else cause the phone kept beeping but she was crying. Uncle Boyd talked to Nana on Monday but he made the phone cord stretch all the way into the laundry so I couldn't hear. Why did Mum go? When will she be home? Do the kids at school know?

Evan's a crap cricket player, but reckons hes a champion at rugby league. I reckon hes a liar. He can do lots of tricks with his yo-yo though, even round the world.

You better write to me now since Ive written to you twice and writing was your idea anyway.

Bye!
    from Elijah

PS: Make sure no one throws out Michael's comics from under my bed. I want to keep them to remember him when I'm old.

I HAD WRITTEN THREE letters to Elijah, but they'd all ended up ripped into small pieces and stuffed inside the mouse-hole in the secret room. I'd decided that if Elijah knew what was going on, he'd want Uncle Boyd to adopt him for sure.

I didn't want to mention what was happening at school. After Shelley's parents forbade her to talk to me, the other kids weren't allowed to either. Michelle Livingston said her mum wanted me booted out of the class because I was putting everyone's lives in danger. Whenever I was around, kids'd start whispering – just loud enough to let me know it was me they were whispering about. Also, after I lied about Saint Bede, Mr Kingsly'd decided I should see Mrs J every Tuesday until the end of term. Mrs J was a nice lady, but I had trouble thinking of anything to say to her, and on the day I did, she burst into tears (I didn't find out till later that one of her sons killed in the bus crash was also called Michael).

I didn't want to tell Elijah about the house either. Dad'd spent a windy afternoon halfway up Gary's ladder scraping the nine bleeding letters off the front and covering up the mess with white paint. But Grandma Bett said the paint cost a small fortune so she could only afford a little tin – not nearly enough to do the whole front of the house. So despite the fact that the horrible word was no longer there, a shiny white patch reminded us where it'd been.

I couldn't tell him that sometimes it felt like the whole world was against us, against me. Or, if not the whole world, at least most of Coongahoola Central. And that I wasn't handling it all that well. That I cried myself to sleep most nights – cried so much that when I woke my eyes stung and my whole face ached. And that I had to psych myself up, firstly to step inside the school gate, and then to keep my feet moving – left right left right left right – until I was inside the classroom.

And there was no way I would've told Elijah about Mum. Even though it was her fault that the kids at school would rather sit next to a kid with nits than next to me, I never wanted her to leave us. And her moving in with Saint Bede? That just made everything a million times worse.

'How is he?' Grandma Bett asked, pretending that she wasn't trying to read Elijah's letter over my shoulder while she stirred the gravy.

'Okay.' I'd tried telling her how much I missed Elijah and all the other stuff that was going on, but the worried look in her eyes and the way she frantically crossed herself made me swallow my words. She had enough to worry about. I didn't want to make her wrinkles any deeper than they already were.

'He must've said more than that.' Grandma Bett raised her thick grey eyebrows at me.

'He heard from yer mum?' Dad asked. He lay back in his chair squeezing an empty can of KB, his hairy toes curled around the edge of the kitchen table.

'Don't know.' I crossed my fingers under the envelope.

As MUCH AS I'D wanted Dad to move back home, I'd felt like crying when he turned up carrying a huge cardboard box stuffed with his greasy work clothes, car magazines and Led Zeppelin records. Mum'd only been gone for four days. It was like he was stealing her place. I knew there was no way she'd come back while he was living there. The twins knew it too. At bedtime they kicked and screamed and cried for Mum, especially Grub who wasn't used to putting up with Grandma Bett all day long. Dad wrestled them into their beds, bribed them with hot Milo and told them Mum'd be home in a few days. He said that as soon as she came to her senses, we'd be a family again. I knew better than to believe that. Way too much had changed.

Grandma Bett was happy to have Dad home though, even if she closed her eyes and prayed when he burped at the dinner table. She said that as much as she loved us kids, we were a handful and she could do with some help. When Dad was at work, she was bossier than ever. After school she sometimes made me keep the twins out of trouble by singing hymns to them in the spooky church foyer while she watered the gardens. I could tell by the bored looks on the twins' faces that they put up with even worse things while I was at school.

I kept a tally on the wall of the secret room of how many days Mum'd been away. It was fifteen on the Saturday morning Grandma Bett placed one twin on each of Dad's knees and told him that she and I were going to church. I had no trouble figuring out why. Dad'd only pretended to be angry when Mr Kingsly'd phoned him earlier that week. When I got home from school he just said, 'Don't worry girl, that Bede is goin' down.' Grandma Bett thought my trouble at school was a much more serious matter.

'You'll feel better after a little talk with Father Scott,' she said as she guided me down the church aisle by my elbow. 'And if something was to happen to you – which I'm sure it won't – I, for one, would take some comfort in knowing that your sins had been forgiven.'

As I stepped into the confessional, Grandma Bett tapped me lightly on the shoulder. 'While you're there, Gracie,' she whispered, 'it wouldn't hurt to mention your bad language. Start again with a clean slate, that's the girl.' Then she closed the curtain behind me.

The confessional was stuffy and stank of old people and sweat. I knelt on the hard wooden kneeler and bowed my head. I could hear Father Scott through the screen that separated us – the good person from the bad – sipping on the cup of tea Grandma Bett'd made him in the old chipped presbytery teapot.

'Ahhh,' Father Scott said at last after a big gulp. I heard him put the teacup back on its saucer before sliding the screen open and starting to talk to God. He then remembered I was there, led me through the 'Act of Contrition', and asked if I had anything to confess.

'Um…'

Father Scott began humming 'Come to the water' (Grandma Bett's favourite hymn) and tapped his fingers softly on the wall.

'Saying swear words – once or twice,' I said finally. 'Thinking swear words – quite a lot really; um, drinking milk straight out of the carton, copying the answers to my maths homework out of the back of the textbook, watching *Prisoner* while Grandma Bett was on the phone, thinking mean thoughts about the boy next door, wishing I could die.' Coming up with sins was easier than I thought.

'Wishing you could die?' Father Scott repeated.

'Yes. But not that often.'

'That's a dreadful thing to hear, Gracie.'

'Sorry, Father.'

'I'm shocked and saddened.'

'Sorry.'

'Can you tell me why you've had such terrible thoughts?'

'Um. A few reasons.' I swallowed hard. I didn't want to cry, I *couldn't* let myself cry. What would Grandma Bett think was going on in here? 'Mainly 'cause the kids at school... hate me and sometimes I think it'd be easier if I... wasn't alive.'

'I'm sure they don't *hate* you, Gracie. Hate is such a strong word. And, even if you think *not being alive* would be *easier*, what about the people who love you? Your parents? Your grandma? Your little siblings? How would they feel? It certainly wouldn't be *easier* for them.'

Father Scott's voice had grown louder and louder, and I realised that he was standing up. In the confessional! I hadn't known him so worked up since the time he discovered 'Mary is a slut' spray-painted on the refectory's back door after mass.

'I didn't really think about that.'

'Obviously not. You haven't actually... hurt yourself, have you?'

'Hurt myself? How?' I wasn't going to mention the mouthful of toothpaste. It hadn't actually hurt me, but it'd made me feel sick the next few times I cleaned my teeth.

'Never mind. Just think about the people who love you and erase those other thoughts from your mind.'

Father Scott lowered himself back onto his seat. 'These are truly difficult times, Gracie. But you've got a lot to be thankful for. When you feel despair, just remember everything you have to be thankful for. You *need* to be strong. Promise me you'll be strong.'

'Yes, Father. I promise.'

'Good. Thank you, Gracie. Is that all now? Or, was there something else?'

'Um. There is something else.' I tried to swallow but my mouth was dry. 'I told a lie.'

'I see. Are we talking about a serious lie or just a little white one?'

'Um, serious, I think. Not sure.'

'Well, a little white lie is just a harmless untruth and is often unavoidable. Like when a friend asks if you like their dress and, although you don't, you say "yes" to avoid hurting their feelings. We all tell little white lies from time to time. It's the big ones that are the worry. Lying is one of the worst sins.'

'I said Saint Bede was the murderer!' I blurted out, before I could change my mind. 'But I made it up.'

Father Scott said nothing and the church was so quiet I could hear the tea gurgling down into his belly.

'That's all now?' Father Scott asked.

I'd wished at least ten times a day that the murderer would kill Sarah K or Hannah Mosely, or preferably both. Chop them into tiny pieces, bake them in the oven, strangle them – I didn't care as long as I didn't have to see their perfect-looking faces laughing with Shelley all day long. But I couldn't tell anyone that, especially not a priest.

'Yes, Father.'

He sighed with what must've been relief. 'I think eight Hail Marys and seven Our Fathers shall suffice as penance – but stick to just the little white lies from now on. You don't want to get yourself into any trouble. And, *please* take care of yourself, Gracie. Remember what you have to be thankful for. Remember your promise.' I could smell the tea on his breath.

'Yes, Father. Thank you.'

I was so relieved that Father Scott hadn't told me I was going to hell that I forgot to say my penance while kneeling next to Grandma Bett in the front pew. Instead I thought about lunch – whether there'd be any hot cross buns left or if Grub'd found them hidden behind the lettuce at the back of the fridge. I didn't remember until after Grandma Bett'd dropped me off at home on her way to the hairdresser's.

I was halfway through my fourth 'Hail Mary' when we heard a car pull up in our driveway. It wasn't our car. It was much quieter, like a car on a TV ad. Grub jumped onto the couch to see who it was.

'Mummy!' He leaped onto Sebastian's rug and raced for the door. Though Mum'd phoned us every day, this was the first we knew that she was coming to see us. I was so excited my heart nearly jumped out of my chest. I stood up, dusted the carpet fluff off my jeans and watched through the window as she closed the door of a shiny blue car. On the back of the car was a sticker that said, 'Believers in Christ'.

Mum swept up Grub and Lucky and swung them around like Dad usually did, only, unlike Dad, she nearly dropped Grub and had to quickly put them both down on the steps. She then stood up slowly and rubbed her back. She wasn't wearing her veil, but her curls were squashed flat against her head and the veil poked out of her handbag as if she'd stuffed it in there moments before.

'Well, look who's here!' Mrs Irwin screeched from where she stood in a haze of smoke on her verandah.

'Can we go inside?' Mum asked me, like I was the adult. 'I really can't be bothered dealing with that.'

It felt weird to be leading Mum into our house. She'd only been gone fifteen days, but it already felt like she shouldn't be there. We sat at the kitchen table and Mum dug around in her handbag until she found three gold Easter eggs.

'How are you all doing, pet?' Mum asked me.

'When are you coming back?' I licked the melting chocolate off my wrapper.

She sighed. 'I don't know. I'm not really welcome anymore.'

Lucky laughed as she bounced on Mum's knees. I hoped what the kids were saying at school about the Believers having fleas was made up or Lucky'd soon be crawling with them.

'But you're the one who wanted to leave!' I said, pushing my chair away from the table. The last thing I needed was to turn up at school with fleas.

'Oh, it's complicated, pet. But you've got your grandma. And

143

your dad's back, too, by the looks of things.' Mum nodded at the collection of gold beer cans that'd gathered near the sink, then at Dad's grimy yellow thongs lying in front of the broom cupboard.

'Nell's that you?' Dad called out from the bedroom where he'd been watching footy on the black and white TV.

'Hello, Robbie,' Mum said. 'Don't mind me, just talking to my kids.'

Dad thumped along the hallway and poked his head into the kitchen. His hair was sticking up in all directions like he'd just woken up. 'Good to see yer all in one piece.'

'Why wouldn't I be?'

'I'm just surprised you haven't had yer head hacked off, that's all. So what's he like then? To live with?'

'I couldn't tell you, but I bet it's a damn sight better than living with you – with all your nonsense talk. Are you deliberately trying to scare the life out of the kids? I'm sharing a caravan with Bethany. Not that it's any of your business.'

Mum was living with Bethany. That meant she must also be living with Heavenly. I probably should've felt happy for Heavenly, that she had someone normal around (well, almost normal), someone who'd let her read as much as she wanted – but instead I felt jealous. Mum belonged to us. She should've been home with me.

'Well, it is my business 'cause I'm bein' made a fool of. Your olds are goin' mental, blamin' me for it an' all. But it's nice to know you're not cheatin' on me. Does that mean the weddin's off?'

'It was never on. I haven't made up my mind. When I do, you'll be the second to know.'

'The second–'

The phone started ringing. Dad grabbed it.

'Yeah? She is, yeah. Who is it?'

Dad held the phone out and winked at Mum. 'Yer girlfriend. Bethany.'

Mum dragged Grub, who was clinging to her legs, over to the phone and snatched it off Dad.

'Bethany?' She frowned and tried to untangle the twisted phone cord.

'No. What? No, I'm all right standing up. What is it? Where are you calling from? Huh?' Mum's shoulders slumped and she screwed up her face.

'When?' Her voice was cracked. 'Oh Bethany. God! Sorry – but bloody hell, that's it! They've gone too far. Look, hang in there. I'll be back soon. No, it's all right. Thanks for calling. Bye.'

Mum dropped the phone and took a deep breath. Grub wrapped his arms around her knees and buried his face in her thighs, smearing chocolate on her white jeans. 'Mummy mummy mummy,' he sang.

'What's happened, Mum?' I hadn't seen her look so worried since the night Elijah was missing. Surely another kid wasn't dead. I couldn't handle another funeral. I'd had enough of all the sadness. My mind started racing through the list of River Children. Who came after Michael?

'Some kinda trouble?' Dad asked.

'The bastards!' Mum shook her head.

'Who?'

'The sergeant, Stewart.' Mum spat out their names as if they were clumps of dirt. 'They've got him. Saint Bede. They've gone and taken Saint Bede.'

CHAPTER NINETEEN

DAD WAS BACKING THE CAR INTO A SMALL SPACE BETWEEN AN ORANGE van and another old bomb like ours, when we noticed someone waving at us from the school gate.

'Who's that?' I asked, before recognising the fire-engine hair and too much make-up that you'd only ever see on my godmother, Mrs Lothum.

'Thought I'd catch you here, Robbie,' Mrs Lothum panted when she'd hurried over, stuffing a pink hanky under a white lacy bra strap. She tried to poke her face in Dad's window, but it was only wound down halfway and her hair was too big.

'Hello, Gracie!' She gave me a big plastic smile.

I waved and gave her a pretend smile back. I looked at her with her newly coloured hair, hot pink lipstick and silvery-blue eye shadow. Even though she no longer seemed to be a 'bundle of nerves', something seemed not quite right and it wasn't just that her teeth were yellow and her lipstick'd bled onto one at the front. There was something wrong underneath her make-up, something she'd painted over.

'G'day, Shirley.' Dad chewed on a burnt matchstick. 'Been a while. You've been outta sorts, or so I've heard.'

'Yes, it's quite true Robbie. I've been a bit under the weather. But I'm better now. I feel great – after hearing the news! That's why

I was hoping to run into you. I wanted to see your face. You must be so, so relieved. It can't have been easy with Nell, and all she's put you through.'

Dad broke the match in two and stared out the windscreen. 'Nell's a bit mixed-up right now. But she'll come right. So, when did you hear about that Bede fella?'

'Yesterday. Pam Frawley saw it happen! Saturday afternoon around four. Pam was hiding Easter eggs in her dahlias – treasure hunt for the kiddies – when Sergeant Colby and Constable Stewart drove past, the evil little man in the back. In broad daylight! I delivered the mail to the station this morning, went inside to drop off a banana cake I'd baked, and saw him there with my own two eyes.' Mrs Lothum pointed at each of her small dark-ringed eyes to make it clear that these were the two she'd seen him with. 'In the cell! He looked back at me and I knew for certain – not that I'd ever had any doubt – that he was the one. If looks could kill, I certainly wouldn't be standing here now. He's the murderer! Robbie, we can relax. It's over. Little Elijah can come out of hiding now. Isn't that wonderful?'

'Yeah, it's great news, Shirl.'

'And James says that you were going to sort him out yourself! He said you turned up at his caravan ready to give him what for!'

Dad caught my eyes in the rearview mirror. 'Yeah, well, dunno what I would've done. I just checked out where he lived, but yeah, it was your James who talked me out of it. Said I would've been the one who ended up in the slammer. True too.'

'Well you've got nothing to worry about now! And what about Nell? Will she be moving back in?'

'Dunno, expect so. She's my wife still. Anyway, gotta go, bills don't pay themselves.'

But Mrs Lothum wasn't ready to say goodbye. She twisted a sparkly pink button on her white dress. 'Robbie, I just want you to know, if you'd ever like someone else to talk to, someone who isn't mixed up, hasn't been – brainwashed, you've always got me.'

'Yeah, Shirl, thanks.'

'Promise you'll call me when you need to talk? Any time.'

'Scout's Honour.' Dad held up the fingers of his left hand in a salute, something he always offered in the place of a promise. (The reason being, Dad'd explained to us one night when Mum was busy bathing the twins, that the Scout's Honour wasn't a real promise. It was just something a Scoutmaster, more than likely an American, maybe even one of those sicko paedophile Scoutmasters, came up with. And as he'd never been a Scout, it didn't bind him to anything.)

When we heard the faint ring of the school bell, Mrs Lothum opened my door. I slowly undid my seat belt and picked up my green Coongahoola Central School jumper and the plastic bag that carried my sandwiches and banana.

'Doesn't seem that long since we were slaves to that bell, does it, Robbie?' Mrs Lothum was saying.

I tried to imagine Mrs Lothum as a schoolgirl, and had to cough back a laugh. It made me think of a mufti day we had in Year Four. Since all the kids were wearing casual clothes, Miss Parson's idea of being funny was turning up in a school uniform, her belly bulging out like a bowling ball and her fat legs spilling out of her socks. Mrs Lothum was even older and uglier than Miss Parsons.

'Seems like a lifetime to me. See you later, Shirl.' Dad started winding up his window. 'Out you get, Gracie – yer gran'll pick you up.'

I waved at Dad and ran through the gate to avoid any more talk from Mrs Lothum. Then I slowed to a walk, dreading the hours of school that stretched ahead. The playground was so quiet it was spooky. A carpet of wet orange and brown leaves softened the sound of my school shoes. I tied my jumper around my waist and slung the plastic bag over my shoulder. I usually wrapped my jumper around the Comfort Shoes bag so no one'd know I was carrying it, but that day I couldn't be bothered. No proper school bag was the least of my worries. Dead leaves dropped off tree branches and the sky grew dark with angry clouds.

I was kicking at a clump of soggy leaves when I saw Baby Pete skipping towards the boys' toilets, pulling his blue shirt out of his baggy grey shorts.

'What're you doing here, Gracie Barrett?' he called out, bravely going against his dad's supposed ban on talking to me.

'Why? It's a school day, isn't it?'

'Yeah, but none of the other Bleeders are here.' He walked over, and stood on tiptoes to make himself look tougher. 'The king of all Bleeders is in jail and the rest of them are shitting themselves. Don't you know anything?' He wrinkled his freckly nose.

'I knew that, but I'm not a Bleeder.'

Poor Heavenly, I was thinking. Where was she? How did she feel about her dad being in jail? About her dad being a murderer? Now she'd be an outcast forever.

'Yeah, well they're calling you a liar. They reckon you're just protecting the saint murderer man.'

'Why would I? I don't even like him.' I flicked a wet leaf off my shoe. Baby Pete only came up to my nose, spat when he talked and stank like he pissed his pants. He'd been picked on so much I couldn't be angry with him.

'So, you're not protecting him?' he asked.

'No!'

'Really?'

'Cross my heart and hope to die.'

'Stick a needle in your eye?'

'If you insist.'

'Well, how come they say you are?'

'Because *they* hate me. I don't know why, but they do and they want everyone else to hate me too.'

Baby Pete scratched his chin. '*I* don't hate you, Gracie.'

'Thanks. I think you're the only one.'

IT WAS A WHILE before anyone noticed that I'd snuck into the classroom. It was like the last day of term. School bags'd been tossed onto the floor instead of stuffed into lockers and everyone stood at the back of the room, too excited to sit down and all talking at once. I crept over to my desk, pulled out *To Kill a Mockingbird* and tried to be invisible.

At first all the talk was jumbled together like when you bump the radio and it gets stuck between stations. Then someone said 'Shush!' and everyone shut up. I didn't have to turn around to know it was me they were looking at.

'I reckon she helped him,' Sarah K said.

'Yeah, an' they sent her brother away to make it look less suss, like they were worried about him being murdered too.'

'She could've killed us!'

'Everyone in your seats now!' Mr Friend's voice boomed from the doorway. School hadn't even started yet and he already had big dark patches of sweat under his arms. Stink-o-rama! Elijah would've said.

'But, sir. The murderer's been caught!' That was Shelley. She never used to speak out like that. She used to just do what she was told like I did. She looked like a lopsided echidna that day with her hair all gelled up on one side. Maybe wild hair makes you braver, I thought.

'That might be so, Shelley, but it doesn't change the fact that none of you have finished your Viking projects, does it? In your seats!'

'Now, before you take out your project books...' Mr Friend waited until all the groaning and banging of desk lids'd stopped. 'I'd like the artist responsible for this,' he held up a painting, 'to explain what it's about.'

It was Jesus hanging on the cross, except that instead of having long brown curly hair like the Jesus on church walls, this Jesus was bald, had a big grey bushy beard and wore black glasses almost as big as his head. A few kids laughed and a couple of girls snorted – Sarah K and Hannah Mosely, I guessed.

'That's the murderer, sir.' Baby Pete waved his arm. 'He's been killed on a cross. Y'know, for Easter and that.'

'Oh, so this is your work, Peter?'

'No, I can't paint that good.'

'Paint that *well*, Peter. Okay, so whose is it? Who stuck it on the door?'

The classroom was quiet except for the muffled sound of someone trying not to laugh.

'Okay, if the artist isn't going to own up, I've got no choice but to put you all on detention today at lunchtime. You can take twenty minutes to eat your lunch – twenty, not a minute longer – then come straight back to class.'

WHEN THE BELL RANG for lunch and everyone shoved each other to get out the door, I stayed at my desk. I tried to eat my sandwiches, but the brown bread was too dry and the peanut butter stuck in my throat. To stop myself from crying, I ripped the middle page out of my project book and started writing a list.

Things to be thankful for:

1. *The murderer's been caught.*
2. *Mum can't marry Saint Bede if he's in jail.*
3. *Elijah can come home soon.*
4. *I'm not a real outcast like Heavenly.*
5. *I won't be picked on forever.*
6. *No one in my family is dead.*
7. *Baby Pete doesn't hate me.*
8. *Dad hates Mrs Lothum.*
9. *Dad likes (loves?) Mum.*
10. *I don't think about Toby any more (much).*

Then I heard voices outside, coming closer. Out the window I saw Sarah K followed by Hannah and Shelley, then all the others. I screwed up my list, chucked it into my desk and dug out my book. The clock above the blackboard said 12.08: another twelve minutes before detention started. The kids burst into the classroom and swarmed around me.

I shut my book and looked up at ten, twenty pairs of eyes.

'Did you know that Anthea Bryce was Josh's cousin?' Sarah K

asked, with her hands on her hips. Her eyes were the evilest of the lot.

Josh nodded and said, 'Her mum cries every day still.'

'How would your mum like it if you were murdered?'

'She wouldn't,' I said.

'What about your step-dad?'

'I don't have one.'

'The one you tried to cover for – liar!'

'We're not going to murder her,' Baby Pete said, taking a step back. 'Are we?'

'Don't be daft,' Hannah replied. 'We're just going to lock her up. One, two, three – get her!'

Then they had me. My arms, my legs, my head.

'*Dirty liar! Dirty liar!* ' they chanted, dragging and pulling at me, lifting me up. '*Dirty liar! Dirty liar!* '

I closed my eyes, kicked out and swung my arms, but there were too many of them. '*Dirty liar! Dirty liar!* '

Someone had my hair and I thought they were going to rip it out of my head. '*Dirty liar! Dirty liar!* ' Someone else's sharp fingernails dug into my neck like claws.

'Take the vacuum cleaner out, and she'll fit.'

'Noooooo!' I yelled.

'What's wrong? Shelley says you live in a cupboard at home, weirdo!'

'Please leave her alone,' Baby Pete said. 'She doesn't even like the murderer.'

'Shut up, Petey, you girl!' That was Josh.

They stuffed me in the cleaning cupboard in the back corner behind the bookshelves. As Sarah K was forcing the door shut, I saw Shelley's face. She was wiping her eyes on the sleeve of her school jumper.

'While you're in there you can think about how Anthea's mum feels!' Sarah K said. 'And Michael's. And Nigel's.'

It was much smaller than the secret room and I couldn't see a thing. My nose and eyes started to run and I did nothing to stop them. I had a prickly feather duster in my face and smelt dust and paint and smelly boys' socks. I imagined all the daddy-long-legs living in that cupboard and could feel their little feet running up and down my arms and legs. What if there were funnel-webs? If a funnel-web bit me I'd be dead in five minutes. But who'd care? Definitely no one at school, not even Shelley. I wouldn't mind – that was for sure. I knew I wasn't meant to think it, but being dead would suit me fine. What would Father Scott know? Everyone treated him like he was the next best thing to God. I bet no one'd ever stuffed him in a cupboard. I felt like Heavenly and the Believer girl who played jacks in the patch of dirt near the toilets. What'd happened to me? I was never the most popular girl in the class and I'd suffered my share of teasing, but I'd never been the kid everyone hated. I'd been in there for about ten minutes when Mr Friend flung open the cupboard door and reached for me with his soft, pink hands.

'Oh Gracie, what have they done!' he cried, and I thought he was going to hug me. He blew dust out of my hair, brushed cobwebs off my dress and told me to go and wash my face.

The other kids watched on, no one daring to speak.

'Who put you in the cupboard?' Mr Friend asked when I got back from the toilets.

I looked at the carpet and shook my head. If I dobbed them in, they'd hate me more.

'All right then, sit down. But don't worry, I'll find out who's responsible.'

Mr Friend said I didn't have to stick around for detention because he was pretty certain that I wasn't the one who'd painted the picture. In the end, Josh owned up to that, but Hannah'd told him to do it, and Sarah K'd blue-tacked it to the classroom door, so all three of them were put on detention for a week. No one bothered me for the rest of the day.

That afternoon, the phone rang in the middle of *Dr Who*. I raced Grub for it, hoping it was Mum or Elijah.

'I'm so sorry.' It was Shelley. 'Gracie, I've been so horrible. I wanted to talk to you, to still be friends but Mum said I couldn't because of, you know, your mum. Gracie – are you there?'

'Yes,' I croaked, the taste of dust and cobwebs still in my mouth.

'What could I do? Sarah K and Hannah let me hang around them. You know what they're like. When they were mean to you, well, I kind of had to go along with it.'

'How come you're talking to me now?' I chewed on the remnant of a thumbnail as warm tears slid down my cheeks.

'Today – the cupboard – that was bad. I'm still not meant to talk to you, but Mum's picking up Billy from Cubs. I had to say sorry. As soon as Mum says I can be your friend again, you can come over and borrow any of my magazines. Or tapes. I'll copy you one! I got some really cool music from my friend Rosie in Dubbo.'

I didn't have the strength to do anything but agree to be friends again. It still hurt that her mum'd turned against me and I didn't think I could ever like Shelley much after what she'd done, but I took her apology as a sign of a chance that things could get back to normal.

We were eating ice cream and peaches when the seven o'clock news came on Radio Coolio. Instead of switching it off like she usually did when us kids were around, Grandma Bett turned it up.

'...arrested Kevin Jones, the man also known among the Believers' cult members as Saint Bede. US-born Jones is wanted in relation to unlawful sexual conduct with fourteen-year-old twin sisters, believed to be former members of the cult, between the years of 1979 and 1981. A Channel 9 news report on the recent Coongahoola murders, which showed footage of the cult's camp, prompted the girls to contact police. Coongahoola's Sergeant Colby said this afternoon that while Jones is being questioned about the sex allegations, there is no evidence to link him to the recent spate of murders in the area...'

'No evidence? All you gotta do is look at the bloke.' Dad was drinking peach juice straight from his bowl like Grandma Bett always told us not to. 'So he's a rapist as well. Jesus!'

'That's not how the reporter put it, Robbie. Don't jump to conclusions,' Grandma Bett said.

'He's a bloody murderer and a filthy pedo as well, and my wife prefers him to me! How d'you think that makes me feel, Mum?'

'I can understand you're upset, but Robbie, the kids! They don't want to hear this.'

'Murderer!' Grub giggled from under the table.

'Pedo!' Lucky laughed, ice cream and peach juice dribbling down her chin.

'What's a pedo?' I asked. It didn't sound like just another word for saint.

Before Grandma Bett could say anything, we heard the front door open and slam shut, the sound of wet shoes squelching and squeaking on floorboards, and something being dragged along the hallway. Then there was Mum, standing in front of her suitcase in a purple dress I'd never seen before, dripping with rain and tears. Soon tears were sliding down my own cheeks. Seeing Mum cry made me cry. I'd cried so much lately, it didn't take much to set me off.

Instead of running up to her, the twins froze, their eyes wide. I saw then that the purple colour from Mum's dress had run, weaving purple cobwebs down her arms and legs.

'Sorry, had to get out of there.' Mum sniffed. Her hair stuck to the side of her head like it'd been painted on. 'I'd go to my olds but they drive me crazy.'

'Don't be silly. You're always welcome here,' Grandma Bett said, smearing the cobwebs on Mum's arms with the Coongahoola Steelworks tea towel.

'Just in time for the washin' up.' Dad smiled and pointed to the pile of dishes on the sink. His fingers were yellow from all the cigarettes he'd smoked that day. *Stay*, Mum, *stay*, I was thinking. Don't take any notice of him.

As if she'd read my mind, Mum looked down at Dad. 'You – don't say another word.' Then she stared at the wall in front of her and said to no one in particular, 'Hell of a day, think I'll hit the sack. Anyone mind if I take Elijah's bed?'

I wiped my tears and smiled at Mum, shaking my head.

CHAPTER TWENTY

I GUESSED WHO THE LETTER IN THE BLUE ENVELOPE WAS FROM AS SOON AS I pulled it out of the rusted grey letterbox we shared with a family of redback spiders. It was my job to check the mail each day and the only letters Mum ever got came in white envelopes with 'Mrs Narelle P. Barrett' typed in their plastic windows. She usually ripped them up or swore and added them to the pile of letters pinned to the notice board next to the fridge. I checked underneath the letters for redbacks then stuffed the blue one up my jumper and ran inside.

'Anything for me?' Mum sat at the kitchen table in her worn-out pink dressing gown, a mug of black Nescafe in one hand and an old *TV Guide* in the other. Anyone would've thought it was breakfast time, not four in the afternoon.

'Only Grandma Bett,' I said, throwing a brown envelope down on the table. If Father Scott could tell little white lies, so could I.

'Nothing from Eli then?' Mum sighed.

'Nope, not today.'

I closed the door to the secret room and sat with my back against it in case Lucky tried to barge in. She'd started using it as a place to escape from Grub, running in there to sulk whenever he wanted to torture her dolls. I opened the envelope carefully in case I'd made a mistake and had to close it up again. The letter was written on thin notepad paper with a blue pen that was running out of ink. I hadn't been mistaken.

Nell,

How are you my dearest? I think of you constantly and am deeply saddened that you have not visited me during the time of my confinement — you who are destined to join me, to be my wife, my fourth and most beautiful wife.

I pray to the Lord for you. I pray that you have the strength to rise above this, to see the truth through a fog of evil and lies.

You are weak, but God will help you. He will lead you back to me — all you need to do is surrender to His will. I've done nothing but what He has instructed me to do and who am I to disobey the word of our Saviour?

Please surrender to the Lord, Nell. Come and visit me. I long to see your beautiful smile.

Yours in the love of the Almighty Father

Bede

My heart was jumping. I'd never stolen anyone's mail before. What would Saint Bede do if he found out? He wasn't a real holy man, he was a fake if he thought God told him to do what he did to those girls. And to murder kids from Coongahoola Central. And why would God tell him to marry Mum when she was already married to Dad? I couldn't give the letter to her. Saint Bede was in jail, Mum was at home – and that's where they belonged. I ripped the tissue-thin paper into tiny pieces, stuffed it as far as my fingers could reach inside the mouse hole and tried to forget it ever existed.

I'd hoped Mum'd soon move back into her room with Dad, but instead she tipped her old brown suitcase upside down on Elijah's bed. She folded her T-shirts and jeans and stuffed them, along with a pile of underwear all in a knot, into Elijah's empty drawer, hung her three dresses in the cupboard next to my school uniform and hid her wedding ring, once shiny gold but now a yucky brown, in my jewellery box on the bookshelf. At night she buried her head under Elijah's pillow, her curls spilling out the sides, or lay awake, angrily flicking through Grandma Bett's old magazines. I was glad she'd come back to us, but I hadn't forgiven her for ruining my life. And as much as I hated Saint Bede, I wondered if he'd still call her beautiful if he heard how loud she snored.

One night Mum lay on her side, facing me, and started talking about the Believers. Normally I pretended to be asleep when she talked in the dark, but this time I sat up, the squeak of my bedsprings telling her to go on. I wanted to know what'd happened when Saint Bede was caught. She didn't leave the Believers because of that, I discovered. She left because of what happened when he'd gone.

'Half of them reckon he's innocent, the other half are convinced he's guilty.' Her voice was croaky from hardly being used all day. 'Bethany's head of the innocents – she says he'll be out in a few days. The other group says he'll be locked up for good. The ones who didn't leave town right away are hanging around hell-bent on getting revenge. All the money they've earned has always gone to the church and they were quite happy for Saint Bede to be in charge of it. But now they're saying that he's a crook and they've been left with nothing.'

'So which group were you in?' I asked.

'Neither. They're acting like school kids, no offence. Two blokes threw rocks at our caravan. Grown men! Some others stole stuff from around the camp. Said it was owed to them.'

'So you're glad about Saint Bede?'

'Glad? Why would I be? Who's to say those twins didn't make it all up? Girls do that all the time. He's no rapist, he's a man of God, he's innocent.'

I thought for a while. 'Mum, have you seen Saint Bede since he was caught?'

'Me? No. I think they only let family visit. Ha! And he's got three wives. How on earth does that work?'

We both giggled. It'd been a while since Mum and I'd found the same thing funny.

'Mum, did you stay in the same caravan as Heavenly?'

'Yeah, I did. Sweet girl. Bit of a mystery to Bethany, though. Lives in her own world.'

'I feel sorry for her,' I said. 'She gets picked on at school.'

'Yeah, kids are rotten.' Mum rolled away towards the wall. She muttered, 'And adults are even worse.'

INSTEAD OF WORRYING ABOUT it being too busy at church, Grandma Bett now worried that it was too quiet. Father Scott'd only taken three people for confession that week and she was one of them. What sins could Grandma Bett possibly confess? That she'd drunk too many cups of tea? Or that she was the one, not Dad, who always forgot to replace the empty toilet paper roll?

'How shallow people are.' Grandma Bett stepped onto the table to dust the top of the fridge. 'As soon as things start to look up, they turn their backs on God.'

She lowered her voice so Mum couldn't hear from my bedroom. 'The church was half empty yesterday morning. You know why? Because there was a free sausage sizzle in the Woolworths car park! Now I'm as happy as anyone that Saint Bede's been put away and I don't mind a sausage sizzle now and then, but I still find time to go to mass.'

Before she could go on, the phone rang. It was Father Scott. Grandma Bett grunted as she climbed down from the table and I passed her the phone.

'Okay, we all need cheering up,' Grandma Bett announced after she'd untangled the phone cord and hung up the receiver. 'Let's go out for tea tonight. My treat.'

Father Scott had just told her he was cancelling the 'Catholics in the community' meeting planned for that night because Mrs Turnball had the flu. Without Mrs Turnball, it'd just be him and Grandma Bett.

When Grandma Bett told Mum she was shouting us tea, Mum laughed and said she'd rather eat a cockroach sandwich than have a meal out with Dad. She'd barely spoken to him since moving home.

I'd noticed him watching her whenever she was around, but she just pretended he wasn't there.

'Come on, Nell, it'll do the family good.' Grandma Bett said. 'Go on, get dressed up. We'll make a night of it.'

I couldn't remember ever going out for tea before, except to Nana and the Butcherer's, but that didn't count because Nana made us eat all our vegetables and her cakes had big dips in their middles and were sometimes still mushy inside.

I wore my only going-out clothes, my funeral clothes, the blue-and-white-striped drop-waist dress, white scratchy stockings with a ladder climbing all the way up one leg and black school shoes.

Lucky didn't want to get dressed. She cried, 'No cockroach sandwich!' as I pulled her red corduroy pinafore over her white skivvy. Grub would only wear his favourite T-shirt – red with a dinosaur on it, a hand-me-down from Elijah – and blue overalls, but he had shoes on and Grandma Bett'd scrubbed his face with warm soapy water and combed his hair. It felt like we were a real family, a normal family, going out for tea. All that was missing was Elijah.

Pizza Shack had only opened in Coongahoola a month before and already Sarah K had been there three times, and Hannah and Shelley twice, though Shelley's family just got takeaways. We were lucky to get a table. The man who took our order, 'Steve' I read on his name badge, told us they'd been full every night for the past two weeks. He wasn't sure if it was because people were celebrating a certain person being locked up or just that they were now brave enough to leave their homes after dark. Luckily for us, Mum wasn't listening.

Our table was squashed between Lucy Valentine's nana and pop's table and Dr Childs and his wife's table, next to the window looking out onto Main Road. I couldn't see Sarah K or Hannah, but I spotted Baby Pete and his dad at a small table near the door to the toilets.

'To us,' Grandma Bett said, lifting up her glass of orange juice with a smile.

Grub, Lucky and I looked up from our plates, our mouths stuffed with soggy garlic bread. Dad tore his eyes away from Mum, and she stopped examining her fingernails, which was her way of pretending she didn't know Dad was watching her. We were all waiting for Grandma Bett to say something else. The adults usually lifted their glasses on Christmas Day, but Christmas was ages away.

'It hasn't been an easy time,' Grandma Bett went on, dabbing at her mouth with her hanky. 'But things can, and *will*, only get better.'

We all nodded, then before Grandma Bett could say more, Grub knocked his coke over with his elbow reaching for the garlic bread. Grandma Bett got up to find Steve and ask him for a cloth.

I stared out the window, watching balloons dancing in the breeze. Three balloons – two blue and one pink – were tied to every telegraph pole on Main Road. They'd mysteriously appeared on the night Saint Bede was arrested. Even though there were three tied together on each pole, each balloon looked lonely out there in the dark, and watching them filled me with sadness.

The pizzas were bigger than I'd imagined and Steve put three of them, still steaming, in the middle of our table. They smelt better than Grandma Bett's baked dinners and tasted yummier than cheese on toast. I wanted to eat slowly to enjoy every bite, but I had to gobble fast to keep up with Grub and Dad. After I'd stuffed the last crust into my mouth, I went to the toilets, even though I didn't need to go. I walked right past Baby Pete's table and waved hello. I had to make sure the kids at school heard I'd been to Pizza Shack. Baby Pete smiled shyly and his dad winked at me.

'So can Elijah come home now?' I asked Grandma Bett as I squeezed back into my chair.

'It's not for me to say,' she said. 'But I can't see why not.'

'What? Why would he come home now?' Mum gulped down her glass of wine. 'With the murderer still on the loose?'

'But the murderer's in jail,' I said, knowing it was the wrong thing to say.

Mum tipped more wine into her glass, splashing some onto the red and white tablecloth, and drank it like water, wincing as she swallowed. 'So that's what you all think, is it? The town's safe because Saint Bede's behind bars?'

People around us stopped talking and Dr Childs was staring at Mum. Grandma Bett fiddled with her cross and looked down at the mushrooms Grub'd lined up on the tablecloth, one in each white square.

'Come on, Nell, it's pretty bloody obvious,' Dad said.

'Obvious? What would Saint Bede want with the River Children?'

'I've told you before. There are a few theories floatin' round. Main one's that the kids were born after what went on at the picnic an' the picnic was right where his church is. Some religious nutters mightn't like that idea. You know, they say it was immoral and everythin'.'

'He wears black boots,' I said. 'Remember Elijah noticed that the murderer had black boots on?'

'Every bloke at the steelwork wears black boots! Your dad has black boots!' Mum said. 'Andy Hall has black boots! He was wearing black boots the night he rescued Eli.'

'Surely you're not accusing Andy, Nell,' Grandma Bett said.

'Not really, but it was a bit of a coincidence – he just happened to *find* Elijah. Look, I grew up next to the Halls. I'm pretty certain the guy's harmless, but … the thing is, you've got to keep an open bloody mind.'

'There's one!' Lucky threw down her piece of pizza and let a mouthful of cheese slide down her chin and onto her pinafore. 'Cockroach!'

'It's an olive, lovely. Settle down,' Grandma Bett whispered. I realised I needn't have bothered walking past Baby Pete. By now, everyone in the restaurant was looking at our table. Even Steve, who'd been flat-out carrying trays all night, was leaning against the wall with his arms crossed, watching. I sat back in my chair, gnawing on what was left of my fingernails, praying for the night to be over.

'Well, I'll tell you my theory.' Mum was almost yelling as she reached for the wine carafe again. 'My theory is everyone's going to be sorry because Saint Bede is an innocent man.'

'Well, my theory is you've been brainwashed beyond a joke,' Dad said and Grub laughed. A long string of cheese joined Dad's chin to his pizza.

Just then we heard the scream of a siren. 'Ne nah ne nah ne nah,' Grub sang as the police van sped past the window.

'Could be anythin',' Dad said.

Mum raised her eyebrows and lifted her glass to her mouth. 'Wonder what Andy's doing tonight,' she said.

'My tummy hurts!' Lucky cried.

'Everybody had enough to eat?' Grandma Bett asked. 'Perhaps it's time to go.'

CHAPTER TWENTY-ONE

'TOLD YOU SO.' DAD STOOD IN FRONT OF THE TV. HE'D JUST COME home from watching football with Gary.

'What?' Mum didn't look up from the crossword she'd been working on all afternoon.

'The cops last night. It wasn't a murder. Don Bellows kicked Greg Pearce's dog – that half dingo mutt. Gaz heard it from Stewy.'

'That's good,' I said, not that I'd been particularly worried. Saint Bede was in jail. Coongahoola was safe. I was more worried about how long it'd be before Mum let Elijah come home and how much of the world'd heard about Mum losing the plot at Pizza Shack. Our family didn't need any more bad publicity.

'It's wonderful news!' Grandma Bett rested her knitting needles on her lap and turned to Mum who'd sunk deep down into the beanbag. 'Isn't it, Nell?'

'Not for Greg's dog,' Mum said, stabbing holes into her magazine with a pen.

'It means her fella isn't off the hook.' Dad was smiling like he'd just won a big prize.

'I hardly think it's something worth boasting about.' Grandma Bett picked up her needles. 'Another child's life could've been lost! And Nell, I don't think you've any reason to sulk.'

Mum nodded, but she whispered, 'Piss off,' into her coffee. Then she ripped the crossword out of the *New Idea* and screwed it into a ball before disappearing along the hallway and into my room. She spent the rest of the afternoon watching the black and white TV she'd snuck out of her old room while Dad was at work.

On Monday another letter in a pale blue envelope arrived for Mum, followed by another on Wednesday. I read them in the secret room with my back against the door. Both smelt like old man's BO, but it was what they said that made me want to throw up. The second one was the worst. The writing was all smudged with what Saint Bede said were tears for his 'angel bride'. I wished I'd opened the envelope with gloves. I didn't want to touch a murderer's tears. Just like the first letter, it begged Mum to visit him. I spat on it like I'd seen a girl on TV do to something she hated, a photo of an ex-boyfriend or something. Then I ripped it into tiny pieces and stuffed them in the mouse hole.

At school it was almost like Saint Bede'd never existed. Mr Friend made our whole class say sorry for locking me in the cupboard and they said, 'Sorry, Gracie,' all together with their heads bowed like they were praying and not one kid laughed. The teasing stopped. No one said that I stank like incense or I ate Jesus's body for breakfast and Shelley even smiled at me when no one was looking.

None of the Believer kids were brave enough to show up any more, not even the girl who used to play jacks in the dirt and seemed to live in a world of her own. To begin with I couldn't get Heavenly out of my head. I couldn't stop wondering how she was doing and what it was like having a dad in jail. I felt bad for the way I'd treated her the day she'd hurt her knee. But then again, she was a Believer and most of the town, including Grandma Bett, didn't approve of them.

So, keeping away from her was the right thing to do, wasn't it? I shouldn't have even asked her if she was okay in the first place. Then I started thinking that I didn't really know Heavenly very well anyway, and that if I'd got to know her properly we mightn't have liked each other much. We were pretty different. She wore a veil to school, for starters! After a while I just forgot about her. It was easier that way. It meant that life was almost back to normal. At school, at least.

The news that Baby Pete and I'd gone to Pizza Shack on Saturday night got around, but no one really cared because Hannah S had stopped at McDonalds in Buller on Sunday, and that was far more exciting. I was just glad that Baby Pete hadn't mentioned what'd happened while we were at Pizza Shack.

ON TUESDAY I FOLLOWED him out the classroom door at playtime. He was running after Josh and some other boys who were chasing a soccer ball.

'Peter!' I called out to him.

He stopped and turned around.

'Can I talk to you for a bit?'

'S'pose so.' His face turned pink under his freckles. 'Um, I'm sorry. It wasn't my idea.'

'What wasn't?'

'Locking you in the cupboard. Well, maybe I did say, "What about the cupboard down the back?" but I was joking. I didn't think they'd do it. I tried to make them stop.'

'Don't worry about that. I don't care about it any more. I just wanted to say thanks.'

'Thanks?'

'For not saying anything about my family, about Saturday night.'

'Oh! Saturday night!' He threw back his head and laughed, showing a mouth full of crooked teeth. 'Oh yeah, you'd be mincemeat for sure if they knew about that. But it's not your fault your family's psycho and *I* know what it's like to be picked on. Some of them,' he nodded in the direction of the soccer field, 'call me *Baby* Pete.'

I didn't say anything.

'What was your mum's problem anyway?'

'You didn't hear?'

Baby Pete looked around to see if any of his friends'd waited for him. They hadn't.

'Want to go to the tuck shop?' he asked. 'I've got twenty cents.'

I nodded. Baby Pete didn't seem as bad as everyone said. He did spit a bit when he talked, but today he smelt more like shoe polish than wee.

'Your mum yelled something about that saint murderer, but I couldn't hear much else. She was real pissed off though. Was the old lady with the rosary beads your nana?'

'Yeah, that's Grandma Bett. Silly thing is, I started the fight, asking if my brother could come home.'

'Didn't he go ages ago?'

'Yeah, before Easter, before Michael.'

Baby Pete thought for a while. 'What if he never comes back?'

'He will!'

'How do you know? What if the saint wasn't the murderer?'

The idea that the murderer could be someone else made me feel sick. Could it really have been Andy Hall the bus driver? Or old Mr Buckley. He was horrible enough, but way too ancient. My head started throbbing. If Mum was right and it wasn't Saint Bede, who could it be? And what if they never caught him?

'I don't have a brother.' Baby Pete was digging one- and two-cent pieces out of the pockets of his baggy grey shorts. 'Where'd Elijah go to? Red or green frog?'

'Green, please. He's in Queensland.'

'My cousins live there. In Brisbane. Todd and Luke. They've got a Commodore 64 computer.'

'Have you been to their house?'

'Yeah – heaps.'

'Did you fly there?'

'I wish! Nah, we're too broke. Dad or my uncle drives. And we took two buses once. Took forever, but at least we got to stop at the Big Banana. Are you going to see Elijah?'

'I don't know. I'd like to. But I don't have much money. I reckon it'd cost over a hundred dollars to fly.'

'You could hitchhike. Josh's hitchiked – twice. If he can, anyone can. Even a girl.'

Baby Pete lined up behind Jessica Andrews and I leant against the tuck shop wall, squashing ants with the toes of my black shoes and thinking about what he'd just said. I had Elijah's address. I could go and see him. I could bring him home, tell them I wasn't coming back without him.

'Here.' Baby Pete pulled a green frog out of a small white paper bag.

'Thanks.'

Over Baby Pete's shoulder I spotted Shelley, and I was about to turn away before she saw me looking when I noticed someone familiar standing next to her. Someone who, even then – after I'd convinced myself I didn't give a stuff about him – made my face feel hot and my legs go wobbly. Toby Irwin! Before I could stop myself, I glared at them both. I hate to imagine the look on my face – shock, anger, hurt, all mixed up together. I bet my mouth even dropped open, making me look like a complete freak. They were both looking back at me, nervously, as if I'd busted them. Shelley'd known I had a crush on Toby. I'd liked him since he and I were paired up for the egg and spoon race at the school fête, back when I was in Year Four. So much for her wanting to be my friend.

When they started walking towards me – were they going to rub it in? – I spun round, grabbed Baby Pete's arm, and dragged him away.

'What's wrong?' Baby Pete was out of breath when we reached the drinking fountain. 'What's the hurry?'

'Just avoiding someone. Sorry if I hurt you.'

'I'm okay.' He rubbed his arm and looked behind him. 'Bloody hell, you've got a lot of enemies!'

'Feels like it.'

'Go to Queensland then. I'd go if I was you.'

'Yeah,' I said, with a mouthful of sweet lime frog. I would, I decided. To hell with Shelley and Toby and everyone else. 'Mum running away to the Believers is worse, isn't it? There's nothing wrong with just going to see my own brother.'

As we walked around the playground, I told Baby Pete things I'd never told anyone, not even Shelley. He didn't judge me like a girl probably would've and, because I didn't like him in a boyfriend kind of way, my words didn't get stuck and come out garbled like a two-year-old's.

I told him about the time Mum tossed Dad's address book in the oven and left it there until all the pages were black and the whole kitchen stank as bad as the steelworks, and how Dad just laughed when he got home and told her all the phone numbers that mattered were in his head anyway. I told him that Mum'd smashed so much of Grandma Bett's crockery that the whole family now used plastic plates and bowls like Grub and Lucky's. Grandma Bett said it was a waste of money buying anything else.

He wasn't shocked. The week after his mum'd died, his dad head-butted a taxi driver for being fifteen minutes late, and was sent to jail for a year. He knew what it was like to have a weird family. He said he thought I was pretty brave for a girl, especially when I was locked in the cupboard. He reckoned that if it'd happened to Sarah K, she would've died or at least pissed her pants.

'Do you ever wish your family was more like everyone else's?' I asked.

'Yeah, all the time. Not Josh's though. His dad belts him on his bare arse whenever he swears. Or Simon's. His mum had it off with old Mr Buckley.'

'No way!'

'Yeah – twice! In the Woolies car park! It was a long time ago, but.'

WE WERE DOWN PAST the basketball court when the bell rang. For the first time in ages, I was disappointed instead of relieved. I think Baby Pete felt the same. He started dawdling and kicking at the dirt with his scruffy old sneakers. By the time we reached B block, the only other person still wandering around was a snivelling kindy girl with lopsided pigtails.

What I did next was completely out of the blue. I'd never've planned anything so stupid. Even though talking with Baby Pete'd cheered me up, I still couldn't get the memory of Shelley and Toby out of my head. So, when I noticed Toby's canvas satchel in the pile of bags dumped outside the gym – the big black T made it impossible to miss – and spotted the notebook sticking out of its side pocket, I stopped still.

It looked like the notebook Toby'd had at Elijah's farewell. What was inside it? Toby's secrets? Love poems dedicated to... Shelley? The thought stung my eyes.

'Gotta go to the loo!' I said to Baby Pete. 'See you back there.'

'Oh, okay then. See ya!' Something, maybe the thought of me going to the loo, embarrassed Baby Pete. He skipped off towards our classroom, his ears bright pink.

I started heading for the toilets, but as soon as Baby Pete disappeared up the steps to C Block, I crept back to the gym. I looked around, made sure no one was coming.

Just in case someone was secretly watching me, I pretended to trip over a big blue bag with 'INXS' scrawled on it, as I reached for Toby's satchel. My heart was hammering loud as anything as I hurried away, Toby's notebook safely tucked under my school jumper. It was the first thing I'd stolen, apart from Saint Bede's letters. I felt a tingly mixture of guilt and excitement.

The afternoon dragged even more than usual. I was half expecting a kid to knock on our classroom door and announce that I was wanted in Mr Kingsly's office. I couldn't stop thinking of Toby's *stolen* notebook. Then, after school, Mum made me go to the supermarket with her before torturing me with me jobs around the house. Not until after five was I finally alone in the secret room with Toby's notebook. I examined the matt black cover. It gave nothing away. Then I wiped my sweaty hands on my jeans before opening to the first page.

The first page was blank, as was the next page, and the next. I sighed, disappointed, but I kept flicking through, and then, at last, found something. A drawing – of a girl's face. On the next page was a different face, or possibly the same face, only from a different angle. It was hard to tell. This one'd been crossed out with red pen. There were several more sketches, all in light pencil, most of them half-formed – the silhouette of a neck, the back of a head. The girl – if all the drawings were of the same person – had shoulder-length straight hair, big eyes and a small thin nose.

Who was she, this girl? She looked nothing like Shelley, I realised with relief. Me? I felt a surge of hope. Could it possibly be? If I closed my eyes and squinted, it could, but when I looked at it properly, I couldn't see any resemblance. He wouldn't draw me anyway. Why would he if he thought I was a freak? Even so, the drawings were good, beautiful even. I sniffed the paper, traced my finger over the lines Toby'd drawn. Then I snuck the notebook into my room and stuffed it under my mattress so I could gaze at it when Mum wasn't around. I still felt guilty for stealing it, but if I hadn't, I never would've seen this side of Toby. I'd heard that he was good at art, but I'd just assumed that he drew comic book-style pictures like other 'arty' boys – dragons and swords and stuff. And, anyway, he'd never find out I was the one who'd taken his book, so I had nothing to worry about. Or so I thought.

CHAPTER TWENTY-TWO

TO SAINT BEDE

*YOU MUST STOP SENDING ME LETTERS. I AM
BACK WITH MY FAMILY NOW AND THIS IS
WHERE I BELONG. I AM NOT WEAK AND I
DON'T NEED GOD'S HELP. YOU CAN'T
BRAINWASH ME ANY LONGER.*

*I DO NOT LOVE YOU, I LOVE MY KIDS AND
THEIR DAD.*

*PLEASE DO NOT SEND ME ANY MORE
LETTERS. OR I WILL TELL THE POLICE YOU
ARE AFTER ME AND THEY WILL KEEP YOU IN
JAIL UNTIL YOU DIE.*

FROM

NELL BARRETT

I THOUGHT THE LETTER looked more threatening written in capitals, but the real reason was that I was copying Mum's writing from one of her crosswords. Luckily hers is messy like mine, I didn't have to try too hard. I used thick pink flowery writing paper I'd discovered in Grandma Bett's bottom drawer. I also found a pink envelope and a stamp (and little wooden rosary beads that'd been blessed by the

Pope, but I didn't dare touch those). The letter looked pretty good and would surely be enough to scare off Saint Bede. The last thing I wanted was for Mum to get a letter from him while I was away.

Sneaking the letter into the postbox outside Woolworths was even easier than I'd hoped. We were in a queue when Mum spotted the Purple People Eater's pink sausage arms reaching from behind the 10 Items or Less counter. The Purple People Eater was in the group that'd turned against Saint Bede. People said she'd even chucked a cream bun at the door of his caravan. Mum held a *Woman's Day* in front of her face so the Purple People Eater wouldn't see her. Mum said she wouldn't be able to talk to her without using words that Believers aren't meant to say.

'Let's get out of here before she confiscates this bloody magazine for bonfire night.' Mum stuffed change back into her purse. 'One. Two. Three. *Run!* '

Lucky for me but not so lucky for Mum, just as we made it through the glass doors, one of her plastic bags split open and our next two days' worth of dinners spilled onto the concrete and started rolling away. She was kicking a can of baked beans with her desert boot when I slid the envelope into the Australia Post box. She didn't notice a thing.

I DIDN'T KNOW WHERE Queensland was except that it was right up the top of Australia and Coongahoola was a bit past halfway down New South Wales. It didn't look that far on the map on the back of my maths exercise book, but Sydney looked like it was just down the road and I knew that was forever away. Perhaps if I'd paid attention in geography I'd have had more of a clue.

The thing was, Mum still refused to believe that Saint Bede was the killer, and was adamant that Elijah stay away until they 'got the bastard'. Dad said it could take months for the case to go to court and for Saint Bede to be charged. Months to prove Mum wrong! I couldn't wait that long. I had to take control. It was up to me to bring him home and make our family normal again.

I thought about Heavenly's dream to escape from Coongahoola

– to hide in the delivery van that leaves her camp on weekend mornings. If I got a lift to Tamworth where no one knew me, I could hitchhike from there. If Josh in my class'd done it, it must be dead easy. I'd only stick my thumb out if the driver looked friendly. There was no way I'd get in a car with a man with a huge beard or anything. All I had to do was make my way to the Believers' camp and sneak into the back of the van. Heavenly seemed to think there was plenty of room. How hard could it be? I pictured myself sitting alongside crates of buns with blue Virgin Mary-shaped icing. At least I wouldn't go hungry. I wrote a list of things I'd need to take:

Stuff to pack
- Stripy sloppy joe
- Good jeans
- Dad's fishing hat (disguise)
- Toby's notebook
- Maths exercise book
- Elijah's address
- Toothbrush & stuff
- $13.90 (from Darth Vader money box)
- Grandma Bett's emergency whistle
- 1 pkt space food sticks (choc)
- 50 cents worth of mixed lollies (no mint leaves)
- Lucky bookmark
- Diary & key

On the Friday night I chickened out of going. I heard a noise outside, probably just Bubbles (Mrs Buchen's cat), but after that I couldn't drag myself out of my soft, warm bed. On Saturday night I knew I'd have to go. Heavenly'd mentioned the van leaving for Tamworth early on weekend mornings, and I didn't want to wait another week. I was terrified of going out in the dark, of climbing into a strange van, of hitchhiking, but I had to get Elijah back.

'Elijah Elijah Elijah,' I said to myself, my heart thumping so loudly I almost expected Mum to wake up. I tried to think of Elijah, of him coming home, and nothing else.

I waited until my owl clock said 1.00 before slowly sliding out of my sheets, careful not to make the bedsprings squeak. I'd gone to bed in my clothes so all I had to do was put on my Lightfoot sneakers, and grab the plastic bag of stuff I'd hidden under the spare blanket in my wardrobe.

Mum lay flat on her back with her mouth open like one of those clowns at Coongahoola Fair (only her head didn't move) snoring louder than the Irwins' lawnmower. She'd been drinking from the bottles on top of the bookshelf – her 'medicine'. She'd filled her glass four times, and I'd filled it once when she went to see if there were any salt and vinegar chips left in the cupboard. Mum normally slept well after her medicine. But this time I'd had to make sure.

The window squeaked when I opened it, but Mum's clown mouth didn't say anything and I hardly made a sound sliding off the windowsill. Elijah and I'd used to escape through the window when Mum started throwing things and we didn't have time to make it to the secret room. The trick was to land on the grass and not on Grandma Bett's agapanthus.

It was cold, even in my thick red parka, and my breath came out foggy. All I could hear was the stuff jumping about in my plastic bag and the scrunch of stones under my sneakers. I felt like the only person in the world. A tiny light was still on upstairs at the Irwins', and I thought I could see the shape of Mrs Irwin watching TV until I realised it was just a big pot plant sitting on a table. Every other window in our street was dark.

I zipped my parka all the way up and pulled Dad's fishing beanie down over my ears. It made my head itch but it was warm and smelt like cigarettes and canned tuna, reminding me of Dad. I couldn't go anywhere near Main Road in case someone saw me. I'd be safer once I reached the Believers' camp. Barely anyone there knew my name. Also Mum'd said that most of the Believers were leaving town. If I ran into Bethany I'd be doomed, but if Heavenly saw me I was pretty sure I could count on her to keep a secret. She might even show me where the van left from.

It only took a few minutes to get to River Road in the car, even when Grandma Bett was driving. And the time Elijah, Michael and I'd snuck round the back way to search for Anthea, it'd taken less than half an hour. But this night it took me ages to reach the turn-off, and I felt like crying when I looked down the long, dark dirt road. I'd never noticed that it had no streetlights.

'Elijah Elijah Elijah,' I said to myself, fighting off thoughts of turning around and running home as fast as I could. Luckily the moon was big and full and the sky was purple with enough light for me to see. Around the first corner I saw the round glowing eyes of the Believers' Virgin Mary statue staring down at me from above the gum trees. They watched me as I walked along but they didn't seem to get any closer.

After a while, my legs were as heavy as bricks and I could feel every stone on the road through my worn-out sneakers. When I made it to the Believers' camp I'd sneak into the church and sleep for a while. Then, when the sun came up, I'd search for the van, hopefully helped by the smell of freshly baked bread.

I heard noises all around me: trees creaking and animals – birds, lizards, possums, kangaroos – singing, scuttling, breathing, thumping. I was so scared that tears rolled down my cheeks. I tried to think about Elijah and how happy he'd be to see me. I summoned up his face to block out the image of a brown snake sliding out of the long grass, onto the road and around my legs. The thought of the murderer snuck in but I pushed it out again. Saint Bede was in jail so there was nothing to worry about. I looked up and into the Virgin Mary's eyes, trying to feel safe with her watching over me. I tried singing, 'Ah Mickey, what a pity you don't understand...' but hearing my small voice in the middle of nowhere made me even more scared. I thought about going home, about the rusty spare back-door key hidden under the garden gnome with the cracked face and no nose.

But I didn't think about opening the back door and tiptoeing along the hallway. I didn't get a chance to imagine my bed, the lemony smell of my flannelette sheets, or anything else. Because it was just after I thought about the back-door key waiting for me that I spotted a torch moving in the bush.

CHAPTER TWENTY-THREE

I CROUCHED DOWN SMALL LIKE A HEDGEHOG AND SQUEEZED MY EYES shut, too shocked and scared even to move to the edge of the road. Sharp stones dug into my forehead and the smell of dry dirt caught in my nostrils. My heart was beating so loudly I couldn't hear anything else. I wondered, listening to the thump, thump, thump, whether I'd hear a car if one sped around the corner. A car'd squash me flat like the possums squished along the highway. I opened my eyes and crawled to the side of the road, on my hands and knees like Grub and Lucky not so long ago, and lay on my stomach in a dusty ditch. Then I scrabbled up the bank and behind a thick bush with tiny spiky leaves, trying not to think about the red-bellied black snake that'd left two tiny holes in David Waterhouse's sister's leg. I pushed my plastic bag as far as I could reach under the bush so no one'd hear it shaking in my hands, and watched through the leaves as the torch moved up and down, getting closer.

It wasn't Saint Bede – he was in jail. And Saint Bede was the murderer, so I had nothing to worry about. And anyway, I wasn't a River Child, so I was safe. Wasn't I? I was breathing fast, like I'd just run the whole way there. I couldn't be murdered. I couldn't die, not now. I'd thought a bit about dying for a while, but really, deep down, I preferred being alive. Father Scott was right: I had lots to be thankful for. Especially now that everyone was talking to me again at school. Besides, there was so much I hadn't done yet. I'd never been to a Blue Light Disco. I didn't know what it was like to kiss a boy I actually liked (not just one I was forced to kiss while playing dares). I was still confused about sex. Even though Nathan Taylor claimed to have done it several times and explained it to us in minute detail, I couldn't see why anyone'd want to. And since running away was probably a massive sin, if I died right now I'd probably go straight to hell.

I was touching the whistle Grandma Bett'd given me, envisioning what'd happen if I blew it as hard as I could, when the torch disappeared. For a moment I thought I'd imagined the whole thing, but then there it was again, like one eye of an animal, watching through the trees. I don't know how long I'd stared at it before I realised it wasn't coming closer. I guessed that whoever was carrying it was resting and'd stuck it in a tree or somewhere. I stretched my arms and shook the pins and needles out of my hands.

The ground was cold and I was shaking so hard my teeth were chattering, like cartoon teeth. I didn't want to think about this, what someone was doing with a torch out here. Were men still taking turns to go on patrol, even after Saint Bede was caught? That was possible. I prayed it was the case.

Just then I heard a scraping sound, the kind Grandma Bett would say made her spine tingle. The torch still wasn't moving, but the sound came from the same direction. I searched the sky for the Virgin Mary's shining eyes but there were too many branches. Although I was only Catholic when Grandma Bett was around, I'd felt safer knowing that the Virgin Mary was watching over me.

I was wiping my nose on a dry crinkly leaf when the scraping stopped and the torch started moving again. I lay with my cheek on a cold sharp stone and pine needles tickling my skin, sniffing back tears and trying to breathe as quietly as possible. The crackling snap of feet through the bush got louder and louder and I soon heard another sound as well. A low hum. Humming, then singing. Deep and croaky, like Nana Butcher with a bad cold.

The torchlight grew bigger and brighter as the big, long shadow stepped down onto the road, still singing. The torchlight shone next to me, behind me. I sucked in my breath to make myself as flat as the ground I was lying on.

He – I could tell it was a man – crossed the road towards me singing, 'Three blind mice, three blind mice...'

He sang like a kindergartener, or like Dad in the shower, loudly and out of tune, like he didn't care if anyone was listening. My legs were shaking out of control, and my arms. Could it be the murderer? I almost wanted to jump up and yell, 'Here I am!' I almost wanted him to kill me right away because I couldn't bear waiting for him to find me. Instead I closed my eyes, clenched my fists and stopped breathing altogether.

When I opened my eyes again, he was only a few metres away. He had something in his hand – a stick, it looked like – and wore a duffle coat and a hat. A cowboy hat! I covered my mouth with my hand. I felt like laughing out loud. Mr Lothum! It was only Mr Lothum!

CHAPTER TWENTY-FOUR

I watched Mr Lothum pick up something, a pine cone maybe, throw it in the air and try to whack it with the stick (he missed), then toss the stick away.

'Mr Lothum!' My voice sounded small and out of place in the dark night. I was so relieved to see him, I nearly started bawling.

Mr Lothum spun around, the bush crunching under his boots.

'It's only me.' I stood up and waved. 'Gracie. Gracie Barrett. Can you help me? I'm on my own and I got a bit scared.'

I grabbed my plastic bag, but it caught on a branch and my things spilled onto the ground. I quickly stuffed them back in and rushed over to Mr Lothum.

Mr Lothum stood there, saying nothing. I wondered if he was embarrassed that I'd seen him playing with the stick.

'Can you walk with me? Back home?' I couldn't bear for him to say no, so I took his hand. It was so cold it made me shiver.

Mr Lothum cleared his throat and looked over his shoulder. 'Yes, of course. But it's so late. What–'

'I was stupid,' I butted in. 'I was going to get a lift to Tamworth and make my way to Queensland to get Elijah. But I can't. It's too dark and–'

'Your parents? They know your... plans?' It was always surprising to hear how deep Mr Lothum's voice was.

'No. They'd kill me! Please don't tell *anyone*.' If he told Mrs Lothum, Mum and Dad'd know about it before breakfast time. 'I'll never do it again.'

Mr Lothum bowed his head. His hand was trembling.

'Please?' I begged.

'I won't say a word.' He was still looking at the ground. 'But, Gracie. That was a very dangerous thing to do.'

'I know that now. I promise I won't do it again.'

I meant it. Just minutes before, I'd thought I was going to die – I'd never been so scared in my life. My body was still shaking, and I'd always thought 'shaking with fear' only happened to people in movies. The sky seemed darker, more black than purple, and the tree branches looked like long spindly fingers reaching out for me. There was no way I could've kept walking to the Believers' camp, no way I could've hid in any van.

'Good.' Mr Lothum said. 'I'm relieved to hear it.'

I'd thought the men'd stopped patrolling once Saint Bede was locked up, but maybe Mr Lothum didn't believe it was Saint Bede. He was definitely weird, but it was kind of nice to see someone out here trying to protect us, in case it turned out that Saint Bede was innocent. Where were Constable Stewy and the sergeant? Probably safely tucked up in their beds.

'Can you walk me to the turn-off, please?' I said. 'I'll be okay from there.'

Mr Lothum's hand grew warmer as we walked back down River Road. I babbled on a bit, about the bush and how dark and eerie it was, how brave he was to be out there alone with a murderer on the loose, and how I'd never try this again. He didn't answer, didn't add anything, but after a while he began to hum. He hummed 'Three blind mice' over and over as we walked, hand in hand, down the long, dark dirt road. I liked his humming, his voice. I found it soothing. It made me feel safe.

I said goodbye to Mr Lothum as soon as we reached the first streetlight, and sprinted all the way home, not even stopping when I had a stitch. I didn't feel the stones through the thin soles of my shoes or the tiredness in my legs. Busting to go to the loo made me run even quicker. I reckon I ran almost as fast as Elijah could, maybe even faster. Just before the turn-off to Devon Street, near the spot where Shelley'd broken her arm falling off her BMX, I tripped on a pot-hole and landed on the cold tar on my knees, felt the blood wet under my jeans, but I kept going. I didn't notice if any houses still had their lights on, or anything else; the only thing I noticed was how fast I was running.

It was still dark when I lifted the gnome who'd lost his nose to Elijah's cricket bat, and picked up the key ring with the little grey plastic steelworks building. The back door opened with a long, slow creak and every floorboard I trod on groaned. It was warm inside and the safe hum of the fridge nearly made me cry. I could still smell the spicy mince Grandma Bett'd poured over our mashed potatoes and carrots the night before. I crept into the toilet, careful not to slip on the Tonka truck Grub'd parked next to the bath. I'd never been so relieved to see the 'Lord bless thy loo' sign hanging above the basin. I walked along the hallway, past Dad's snoring, and into my room. My owl clock said 5.08 a.m. Mum'd rolled onto her side and her head'd slipped off the pillow, but she looked dead asleep. I sniffed the lemony smell of my soft warm flannelette sheets and tears came pouring out. I was home again, but I hadn't rescued Elijah and I knew I'd never be brave enough to try again. It was freaky out there in the dark, even if the torch man turned out to be only Mr Lothum. I was never going to do anything like that again.

I wasn't sure what time I finally fell asleep, but when Mum yelled out to Dad to put the kettle on it felt like I'd only just closed my eyes.

'Here you go. Thick-as-mud coffee, toast, and the crossword you were too sloshed to finish last night,' Dad said, carefully placing Grandma Bett's special silver tray on Mum's lap. I'd opened my eyes just wide enough to watch without them seeing that I was awake.

'What are you after?' Mum poked the toast with her finger. 'Why the special treatment?'

'Oh, come on, Nell. It's Sunday mornin'. Does there need to be more reason than that?'

'Not usually, no, but I know you too well. Too well for my own – Oh God, my head!'

'You nearly polished off all the good stuff, what d'you expect?' Dad yawned and stretched his arms. His hairy white tummy poked out from under his Balmain footy jumper. 'I better go and have some Weetbix before Grub gutses them all.'

'Well, ta, Robbie. And thank Bett for me too.' Mum stirred her coffee. 'It's obvious she made it. The toast's buttered properly and there are no crumbs floating in the coffee.'

Dad didn't say anything as he backed out of the room, but he didn't close the door as quietly as he could've.

Mum laughed before slurping her coffee. 'Hey Gracie, you still in there?'

I moaned and buried myself under the covers.

'I was just going to give you this toast. It's the jam you like, too sweet for me, feel sick just looking at it – but never mind,' Mum said.

My stomach growled at the thought of jam on toast and I was sweating under two blankets, but I was still wearing my jeans and T-shirt so I had to stay hiding. If it wasn't for that and if my knee didn't sting when I bent it I would've thought I'd dreamt what happened the night before. But lying there listening to Mum click her pen and read out the crossword clues, things didn't seem so bad. I'd talk to Mum and Dad about Elijah, I made up my mind. Even if Mum refused to believe that Saint Bede was the murderer, it was a while since anyone'd been murdered, so maybe she'd agree that it wasn't so dangerous any more. I missed Elijah, and I knew they did too.

When I woke again, Mum's bed was empty and her nightie lay in a pink pool on the floor. I threw off my blankets and quickly changed into clean clothes. But when I unpacked my plastic bag, dug out my maths exercise book, toothbrush, diary, bookmark, food and money stash, I discovered that Toby's notebook was gone. I shook my clothes. A few pine needles, the whistle and a Space Food stick fell onto the bed, but that was it. I sat on the bed, my mouth dry and my head spinning. The notebook must've dropped out when my bag snagged on the branch. That was it then. There was no way I could get it back. I flopped onto my back, mourning the loss of Toby's pictures. The only thing that made me feel better was that at least now the notebook could never be found in my room. The drawings were etched on my mind anyway. This way, Toby'd never know I'd stolen them.

Apart from the fact that I ate my way through two bowls of rice bubbles instead of one, everything felt normal at breakfast. Grub and Lucky were under the table, giggling as they tried to stick cold blobs of play dough on my bare feet. It didn't bother me. I swung my legs, playing along. Grandma Bett was swirling tea leaves around in her teacup while reading *The Sunday Telegraph*. The door to Mum and Dad's room was closed and I could hear Mum laughing from behind it. All we needed was Elijah back and everything'd be perfect.

'What've you been up to, possum?' Grandma Bett asked suddenly, frowning and folding up her newspaper.

'Nothing. Why?' I hoped my voice wasn't too shaky.

She reached over and raked her fingers through my hair. 'Pine needles!'

'Oh, yeah. Yesterday I was lying on the ground. I was reading. A book.'

'You're a funny one. Didn't you have a shower last night?'

'Yeah, I did. But I didn't get my hair wet. I'll wash it tonight.'

'Good girl. Looks like it could do with a brush now, too.'

I combed seven pine needles out of my hair. I hid them in the bin and washed my face and hands in case they still carried signs of the night before. Then I went into the living room and lay down on the couch with *The Chocolate War*. Mum and Dad were still in the bedroom and Grandma Bett was vacuuming the hallway outside their door. Lucky and Grub sat in front of the TV trying to guess what Mr Squiggle was drawing.

I was so glad to be home I decided I wasn't going anywhere all day. I'd just read my book and relax. But Mrs Irwin ruined all that. At first I thought a bird was squawking from the wattle tree, but it got louder and louder. Soon I realised it was Mrs Irwin's voice and that she was following it up the driveway and up the steps to our front door. This time she didn't even bother to knock.

'Where's yer mother?' she screeched over the sound of the vacuum cleaner. She'd burst into the living room and was leaning against the wall, clutching a blue and white packet of Peter Jackson cigarettes and breathing fast. Her short hair was almost as grey as it was blonde and the lines around her eyes and mouth looked like they'd been drawn on.

'In her and Dad's room.'

'What?'

'She's in her and Dad's room.' Just then the roar of the vacuum cleaner wound down and Grandma Bett walked in, red-faced.

'Jane! What is it?'

'Oh God, Bett – s'cuse my language – but holy hell! I've got to talk to Nell.'

'Well dear, she was a little bit busy a moment ago.' Grandma Bett tugged at the little gold cross hanging around her neck. 'I'll just go and check.'

As Grandma Bett tapped on the bedroom door, I stared down at the brown carpet so my eyes wouldn't catch Mrs Irwin's. Dad's voice sounded far away, but his 'Shove off!' was loud enough for us to hear. So was Mum's giggle. She sounded like a girl my age.

Mrs Irwin walked across the room, an unlit cigarette poking out from her glossy pink lips. She squinted up at Ken Done's painting of the Sydney Opera House, before crossing the room again. Grub and Lucky acted like she wasn't there, except when she walked in front of the TV they stretched their necks to see around her big tracksuit-panted bum. Lucky didn't even notice that snot was sliding from her nose and hanging dangerously close to her mouth. Life was much easier for three-year-olds.

'I'm sorry, Jane.' Grandma Bett's face was still red and her forehead was shiny with sweat. 'Could you come back in, say, erm, deary me, an hour or so?'

'Do you mind if I wait? I really don't want to be alone. You've got no idea what my imagination's like.' Then she yelled, 'SORRY NELL!' so suddenly and loudly that the twins' eyes came unstuck from the TV. They turned their heads and stared at her. 'There. I've said it.'

None of us said anything. Mr Squiggle carried on squiggling, but the rest of us were quiet. Then we heard the bedroom door click open and Mum's slippers scuffing along the hall.

'Just ignore her!' Dad was saying in a loud whisper. 'Nell, come back!'

But Mum walked into the living room, dressed in Dad's Mr Tickle boxer shorts and Jim Beam T-shirt, and sank into the brown beanbag. Dad followed in his black shorts and Balmain jumper, with a grumpy look on his face. He nodded at Mrs Irwin and let out an exaggerated sigh as he sat on the floor.

'What's going on?' Mum asked.

'I'm saying sorry to you. I was wrong. About him.'

'About him?' Mum pointed her foot at Dad. 'Or Saint Bede?' The thick black hairs on her legs made me think of the cactus we were growing in our classroom.

'The Bede fellow. I don't think it's right, what you've been doing with him, not by a long shot. But I was wrong. I hate the fact that I was wrong, but there's nothing I can do about it.'

'Move your legs, Gracie, so Jane can have a seat,' Grandma Bett said. I pulled my knees up to my chin, my left knee stinging.

'I don't want to sit. I can't. My nerves! I hate to be the one to tell you this but–'

'Another kid's been taken,' Mum said, as if she'd known all along.

No, not a murder, I thought. Saint Bede was the murderer. I was sure of it.

'Last night,' Mrs Irwin whispered. 'My first thought was that your Bede fellow'd escaped. But no, Gazza checked with Stewy. He's still locked up.' Mrs Irwin slid down onto the couch next to me anyway.

It couldn't have been last night. My mind was spinning. Not near the river. I'd have seen something. Mr Lothum would've done something. Saint Bede was the murderer!

'Surely not!' Grandma Bett cried. 'Who?'

Mrs Irwin made a terrible noise. I thought it was a laugh at first, but she sniffed, a horrible snotty sniff. I wanted to cry too, to scream.

'Another River Child. One of the Muller twins: Abigail.'

Abigail Muller. The girl with Dad's Jersey cow eyes. I looked over at Dad. He was as still as the statue of the Virgin Mary, staring at the wall.

'Freckly girl, not much to look at, poor dear, but that's beside the point,' Mrs Irwin said. 'She doesn't deserve to have her life taken away from her. Oh, her poor, poor mother.'

I could only just make out what she was saying over the thumping of my heart.

'I tell you what,' she said. 'My boys aren't even River Children and I'm going grey with the worry of it.' She pulled at her short, sticking-up hair, making me think she might go bald with the worry of it too.

'When was this?' Grandma Bett talked softly into her praying hands.

'Yesterday sometime, afternoon, night, not sure. I heard it from Derek who heard it from Gaz so it's a bit hazy. Yesterday arvo Abigail went to her dad's place over on Ross Street after her tennis lesson, while Sammy – he's the twin – was playing soccer. There was a bit of a mix-up about whose house Abigail was staying at. Lyn thought she was staying at her dad's. So, you can imagine Lyn's shock when Abigail's dad rang this morning to see if the twins were keen to go fishing. Called the cops right away, but...' She dug a lighter out of her pocket and looked at Grandma Bett for permission to use it.

Grandma Bett nodded, her hands still praying. Dad wiped the corner of his eye with his hand. Tears?

Mrs Irwin kept talking but I'd disappeared into the thick cloud of smelly smoke she was blowing towards me. Had Mr Lothum seen anything? Was that why he was so quiet and weird? Would he be able to help the police?

'Gracie! Gracie!' Grandma Bett clicked her fingers and I realised that Mrs Irwin'd stopped talking and they were all watching me. 'Are you feeling all right?'

I nodded, but I didn't say anything. This wasn't right. I'd wanted the killer to be Saint Bede. I'd wanted him to stay in jail so Mum'd never go back to him.

'My boys are the same,' Mrs Irwin said. 'Jonathan didn't say one word at lunch, not one. And Toby's been keeping to himself for a while now, shutting himself off from me. It's the shock. Can you blame them? In our day we could play anywhere, do anything, without fear of some loon carrying us off into the bush.'

God, it could've been me, I realised. Fat lot of good Mr Lothum was. This could've been Mrs Irwin telling my family that I was dead.

'Gracie, you're biting your lip! Your mouth's bleeding.' Mrs Irwin grabbed my arm with her brightly-painted claws. 'I really should say sorry to you, too.'

I looked at her. I'd forgotten how to speak.

'For the way the boys've treated you. Toby and Jonathan. I told them to stay away.'

Mrs Irwin turned to Mum. 'I just didn't know what the hell was going on! With you all and those Believer people! Derek just shrugged it off. But he's been best mates with Robbie since school, and he's a – bloke. He doesn't lie awake all night worrying about things like I do. But I was just protecting my sons from... I don't know what. I've been awful! I'm sorry.'

We stayed sitting long after Grandma Bett'd walked Mrs Irwin to the door and told her to be strong. We all stared at the TV, though

I couldn't tell you what came on after *Mr Squiggle*. I was waiting for Mum to say 'I told you so' to Dad about Saint Bede, but she didn't.

Instead, she said, 'What're we going to do?'

'What *can* we do?' Dad kicked at the pile of *New Idea* magazines on the carpet.

'There must be something!' Mum replied. 'We can't live like this.'

'Yeah, well, we tried patrollin'. Waste of bloody time.'

'So, what? You've given up?'

'Well, what's the point, love? We can't be out there every minute of the day. It's just not bloody practical. There's only a few of us – Dez, Gary, Tommy, Pongo, Joey–'

'Mr Lothum,' I said, without thinking.

'James?' Dad glanced at me, yawning.

'I saw him – on his way there,' I said, quickly adding, 'the other day.'

'Yeah? Didn't know he was on the roster, but good on 'im for havin' a go. Doesn't even have kids to worry about. Course he'd shit himself if he ever busted anyone.'

'What do you mean?' I asked.

'Oh, you know, old James's always been a big softie.'

I nodded. 'He cried when his kitten died.' I wanted to add, 'But he helped me when I was scared to death,' and, of course, I couldn't.

'Yeah, not many blokes cry, not like you sheilas anyway,' Dad said. 'But James isn't like most blokes. He's a bit simple, always has been. Even back at school. He 'ad this pet bat.' Dad flapped his arms the way a bat might. 'James didn't have many mates, so he was really into his animals. Brought a wombat to school once; or was it a roo? Dunno. But anyway – the bat. He brought it to school, now and then, in a pickle jar. That's where he kept it – with holes in the lid so the thing could breathe. It didn't bother anyone – just slept all day. But. Shit, yeah.'

'What? Did it die?'

'Not exactly. Jethro and Kev, they were tough bastards, seniors, wrestled the jar out of his arms, set the bat free in the hall.'

'That's right! I remember hearing about that,' Mum said. 'Didn't it go crazy then escape out the window?'

Dad nodded. 'Odd thing was, James didn't say nothin', didn't go off his nut at 'em. He just curled up in a ball on the hall floor and bawled his eyes out. Like a little girl. S'pose to him it was like losing his best mate.'

'Poor Mr Lothum,' I whispered.

'Yeah,' Dad said. 'He was older than me, but he seemed like a little kid. Still does in a way. I've always felt sorry for the poor bloke.'

'And he's the only one still looking out for the town?' Mum said. 'God help us!'

Mum was holding Dad's hand, something that'd normally make me happy. But I wasn't happy. I bit hard into my thumb. I wanted to cry. Everything was wrong. The town wasn't safe at all. I could've died! And, if Saint Bede wasn't the murderer, who the hell was?

CHAPTER TWENTY-FIVE

I<small>T SEEMED LIKE THE WHOLE WORLD WAS IN LIMBO FOR THE NEXT FEW</small> days. My family didn't know what else to do, so we just did what we normally did. For me, that was going to school. Only twelve kids turned up in our class all week. Mr Friend didn't even bother shaving. He said there was no point in going on with algebra until the others were back, so we mostly did silent reading while he sat in his chair staring at the swirly carpet and making frog noises with his tongue. Shelley's desk was empty and I heard Sarah K say that Shelley's dad was thinking of taking her and Billy back to Dubbo. I realised it didn't worry me what Shelley was up to any more.

On Monday morning Baby Pete sat next to me at the spare desk with the broken lid. He smiled, showing off all of his crooked teeth, and I tried my best to smile back. I didn't know what to say, though, so I pretended to concentrate on my book.

'Can you believe it?' he asked me while Mr Friend was outside telling some giggling Year Fours to keep it down.

'What?' I looked up from my book.

'The murder, dead-head!' His freckles were glowing.

'Oh. That. Yeah. It's terrible.' I looked back down at *The Chocolate War*.

'It's like we're living in a real-life horror movie. Have you seen *Friday the 13th*?'

'I don't think so.'

'You should! It's real scary.' When I didn't reply, he started whispering, 'You wanna know something freaky? Josh's dad was part of the search party that found the first dead girl. Remember Anthea? He saw the body and everything! He said–'

'I don't want to know!' I said it louder than I'd meant to.

'It's not that bad. It's just that the murderer must be the Incredible Hulk or something. He–'

'Shut up, will you!' I put my hands over my ears. A few other kids turned around and looked at me like I was mental. I laid my head on the desk.

'Sorr-eee!' Baby Pete made it sound as if I was the one who should be sorry, not him.

I lay with my cheek flat on the cold, hard desk reading words scratched into the wood: *Andrew Fuller sux, JJ woz 'ere 1981, Midnight Oil rules!, JD + CL 4 eva.* Anything to stop me thinking about what Baby Pete'd been saying. Then I heard Mr Friend come back inside and I wiped my eyes on my jumper sleeve before holding the book up to my face. Baby Pete didn't say anything else, but he moved back up the front next to Josh after lunch and stayed there the rest of the week.

After school that afternoon, I found Mum at the kitchen table with *The Coongahoola Times* sprawled in front of her.

'The really tragic thing is that we must know this – this monster.' She scribbled over the headline, MURDERER STRIKES AGAIN, with a blue pen.

'Who on earth could it be? That horrid Baptist, Ken Knowles? Now, he's a nasty piece of work, but he's a bit of a mummy's boy and totally spineless. Gerald Buckley? He's angry enough, but too fragile. A few years back, maybe.' She went on to consider half the men in Coongahoola – including Dad.

'What?' I slammed my cup down on the bench. 'Dad?'

'Well, yes, he's your father, but you've got to keep an open mind.'

'Dad is *not* a murderer.'

'I agree with you. I was just *considering* him. You're right, your dad's not evil. He's got a good heart deep, deep, deep down somewhere. But, even so, he's also not the most innocent bloke around. You might think he's perfect, but he's not.'

'And *you* are?' I dropped my cup into the sink and walked out. How could she talk about Dad like that? She and him were supposed to be back together! I stormed into my bedroom and slammed the door so hard that my Year Four netball medal fell off the wall.

Coongahoola was on the TV news again. This time I didn't feel proud of seeing our town on television. For some reason they showed the steelworks and they'd filmed it through the barbed-wire fence so it looked more like a jail than somewhere your dad'd go to work. I'd always thought it had three chimneys, not six, and I'd never noticed how thick and black the smoke was that poured out of them. They also filmed three senior boys from Coongahoola Central walking down Main Road laughing and drinking beer, and old Mr Buckley spitting on the footpath just outside the bakery. What made it even worse was the scary music they played at the same time. It reminded me of what Baby Pete'd said, about living in a real-life horror movie. Hearing Constable Stewy didn't make me feel much better. He took too long to answer the questions and when he finally got around to saying something it was usually, 'Ahm'.

The latest murder was talked about non-stop on Radio Coolio. One lady who didn't even live in Coongahoola called to say why didn't the Believers just ask the Virgin Mary who the murderer was? That made Dad smile but he hid it behind his hand and Grandma Bett shook her head angrily.

No one was shocked when on Tuesday night the man on the radio announced in a soft, sad voice that Abigail Muller's body'd been found. It was news we'd been waiting three days to hear. Grandma Bett didn't bother turning off the radio. She just looked across the table at Mum and Dad, tears spilling out of her eyes and her hands praying on her lap. When the radio man said that Abigail was found wearing her white tennis dress, Dad said, 'Oh, for fuck's sake!' and slammed the tomato sauce bottle down on the table. No one saw me spit my peas into my lemon cordial.

The radio man also said that the police had found, 'in the near vicinity', what they believed was Abigail's tennis racket, as well as something they described as an 'item of interest'. At last – some hope! The tennis racket could have the killer's fingerprints on it, couldn't it? And what could the 'item of interest' be? A wallet? A bit of clothing? Maybe now the police had a good chance of tracking down the killer.

I thought about Mr Lothum. What had he seen that night? Maybe he'd seen it happen, but was too scared to do anything about it. Maybe he'd just curled up on the ground and started crying. Or started singing that silly nursery rhyme. Maybe he'd been singing to take his mind off what he'd seen.

Every day I checked the box for letters from Saint Bede and was relieved not to find any. Mum never mentioned him or talked much about the Believers. I heard her telling Dad that only thirty caravans out of more than a hundred and fifty were still at the camp, and that all those who stayed were on Saint Bede's side. Apparently, Bethany was waiting for Saint Bede to be released before she decided what to do, and I guessed that Heavenly was waiting there with her.

Mum was friendly on the phone to Bethany, but she laughed when Dad jokingly talked in Bethany's silly American accent. I can still remember her laughing because it sounded weird. Laughing seemed like a thing of the past.

Then, after school on Wednesday, it happened: one of the things I'd been dreading most. I was the one who opened the door – unless you count Grub and Lucky who were each clutching one of my legs with sticky jam fingers – and my first thought was that I was done for. There, on the WE ME mat, in brown sandals, black trousers, long white gown and a giant gold cross, stood Saint Bede.

'Is your mother at home?' he asked in his loud American voice, without smiling. It was as if he'd never met me before, as if he'd never put his arms around me, or stood so close that I'd nearly choked on his BO.

A million things ran through my mind. None of them told me what to do next. A smarter person would've said that Mum was away or that Mum never wanted to see him again. But I didn't say anything. Saint Bede put his hand in his pocket and dug something out. I was still frozen in the doorway a few moments later when I heard Mum's slippers scuffing along the hall. In Saint Bede's hand was a pink envelope, Grandma Bett's pink envelope. With my handwriting on the front.

CHAPTER TWENTY-SIX

'GRACIE, WHO IS IT? YOU'RE NOT MEANT TO OPEN THE – OH,' MUM said, seeing who our visitor was and slowly turning the handle on the squeaky screen door.

'Bede? Hello. How – how are you?' she asked in the soft, kind voice she used for the twins when they'd been good.

'I'm just dandy, no thanks to you.' Saint Bede pointed a finger at Mum. It was an unusually small finger, like a kid's, but it still wasn't the nicest thing to have waving in your face.

'What?' Mum took a step back, squashing my toes. 'What do you mean?'

'Don't play dumb with me, woman, you know what I mean.' Saint Bede's face shone an angry red and little bits of spit fired out of his mouth. 'Turning your back on your husband-to-be. Or should I say your *brainwasher*?'

He screwed up the pink envelope and threw it over his shoulder. It bounced down the stairs and landed on a pile of leaves on the path.

'What are you talking about? You've been locked up. And you're NOT my husband-to-be.'

'You're right about that. I wouldn't lower myself to your standard – even if you were only going to be wife number four.'

His top lip curled as he spoke. I wondered if his spit'd burn if it landed on my skin.

'What are you on about?'

'I was wrong about you. You're no angel. You may look all right on the outside – though you're no picture compared to my other wives – but inside you're rotten. You've got the devil inside of you.'

He talked in a horrible American voice that belonged in a movie, not on our front verandah.

I couldn't think what to do, what to say. Lucky started blubbering.

'You've gone mad. You're bloody mental!' Mum said.

'I can see it in your eyes right now. There's something very dark inside you. A shadow where your soul should be.'

'Get lost! Get away from my house you – prick! Or else I'll call the police.'

'Who? Your buddy Stewart? Go on, call him. I'm out on bail. A free man!'

'Sounds like you should be locked up again.'

'Is that so? You'll know what it's like to be imprisoned – when you go to hell!'

Grub suddenly pushed past Mum and, standing on the tips of his dirty little toes, yelled, 'Get away from our mum this minute or you'll be in big trouble!' It was probably the longest sentence he'd ever spoken.

'Come on, kids, inside.' Mum grabbed Grub's fraying overall straps and yanked him back. She shoved the three of us into the hallway and pulled the screen door shut.

'You and your spawn.' Saint Bede pressed his face against the mesh, squashing his nose and forehead and breathing warm prison-food breath all over us. 'You're all going to hell!'

'Fuck off!' Mum slammed the front door and locked it. She put her arms around me and Grub and Lucky, and her whole body was shaking. Saint Bede kept screaming at us, scary stuff about Mum being a dirty Lucifer-loving whore and the fires of hell. Then there was a big bash on the door and another and another. I squeezed my eyes tight, certain he was going to break through the door and kill us all. Finally, we heard our gate creak open, and then slam shut.

I started breathing again. Mum's tears flowed down onto my head, wetting my hair. I buried my face in her soft pink bathrobe. She smelt like coffee and mothballs. Lucky cried louder and soon Grub and I were crying too. The noise of the four of us together was worse than anything I'd heard before, except maybe the sound Sebastian made when he died.

'What a fool I've been, Gracie. Such a bloody fool!' Mum stood up, blew her nose so loudly that Lucky covered her ears, and dabbed at her eyes with one of Dad's big brown hankies.

'It's okay now, Mum. He's gone,' I said. But what about the letter? It was right there on the path where anyone could see it.

'Thank Christ your grandma was out. Don't say anything to her, or your dad, will you? Any of you! And, keep away from the door. I don't want any of you going outside for the rest of the day. I don't trust that – creep.'

'Creep man, creep man!' Lucky blurted out an hour or so later, as soon as Grandma Bett started taking off her trench coat. Mum let out a tiny laugh even though her face was still puffy and pink.

Grandma Bett promised she wouldn't say anything to Dad, but she told Mum that she should tell him herself.

'Honesty is the key to a good marriage,' she said, digging around in her coat pocket. Turning away from Mum, she pulled out something crumpled and pink. The envelope! She quickly slid it into the pocket of her green cardigan. Then she asked Mum if she wanted a nice hot cup of tea.

I WAS RELIEVED THAT Mum'd never want to go near Saint Bede again. But I still couldn't relax. I barely had any fingernails left to chew, but that didn't stop me from nibbling away on my fingers. When I wasn't worrying about Grandma Bett working out that I wrote the letter, I was thinking about the murderer. Everywhere I looked there were reminders of him and what he'd done. In the newspapers that Grandma Bett no longer bothered to hide, on the TV she no longer bothered to turn off, in the number of police cars we saw on Main Road, on the faces of the kids at school. Everyone was waiting for him to kill again. It seemed like it'd never be safe for Elijah to come home.

Then, as if I didn't have enough to worry about, Josh told our class that his dad'd heard that 'the item of interest' the police were investigating was some kind of sketchbook. I thought nothing of it at the time. Only that night did it dawn on me. I was just lying there, watching a repeat of *Dr Who*, when Josh's words came back to me, and I realised that the 'sketchbook' could be the notebook I'd lost in the bush. I sat up in a panic. Hadn't the 'item of interest' been found somewhere near the tennis racket? I shivered at the thought that Abigail could've been murdered near where I was hiding. But the notebook didn't have Toby's name on it so they'd never be able to trace it to him. Or, could they?

I chewed on my nail, gnawed the side of my finger. What'd I done? I wanted to scream, to punch something. What if the police connected the notebook to Toby? Would they think he'd something to do with the murder? Would he be a suspect? And all because of me! I couldn't let that happen. I'd have to pray. What else could I do? I'd pray that the police never traced the notebook to Toby. I wasn't sure if I believed in God, and if I did, whether it was the Catholic God or the Believers' one, but I spent the rest of *Dr Who* and all of the *ABC News* on my knees on the living room floor, begging him to listen.

Abigail's funeral was held at St Luke's, the Catholic church. Mrs Muller was in hospital suffering from shock (I imagined her lying in bed, her blonde hair standing up in spikes as if she'd stuck her finger in a power point), so Grandma Bett told Mr Muller not to worry, that she and Father Scott'd take care of everything.

I'd had enough of funerals. I didn't want to go. I told Mum that my stomach hurt, but she said that a stomach ache was nothing compared with what the Mullers were going through. Apparently Sammy hadn't spoken a word since the night his twin died. People said he'd actually felt the pain of Abigail dying, of the murderer's fingers squeezing her neck. When his mum gave him the terrible news the next day, there were already tears on his cheeks and he just nodded like he knew already.

Mr Muller shuffled up the aisle in stonewash jeans and a pale blue shirt. I thought about the kids at school reckoning that our dad was also Abigail and Sammy's dad, making them our half-sister and brother. But I couldn't believe that, not seeing Mr Muller make his way up the aisle like an old man, his face thin and grey, and his body shrunken. Sammy trudged along behind in his wrinkly school uniform, hands folded together and head bowed down. I wanted him to look up. I wanted to see if his eyes looked different now that the other half of him was dead. I knew it was wrong, but I wasn't the only one. All the other kids were watching, hoping to catch a glimpse of his face, too.

I didn't need to turn my head far before I spotted Mrs Lothum. Even dressed in black she was impossible to miss. Her orange hair was shining between Mrs Clark and her mum, Old Mrs Clark, halfway down on the left. Mr Lothum was there too, next to her. He caught my eye and quickly looked away. Weird. He'd walked me to safety that night – he'd pretty much *saved* me – so why didn't he want to look at me? I turned to face the front. I must have made a noise because Grandma Bett took my hand and gently squeezed it, and Mum mouthed, 'Are you all right?'

I still don't understand what happened to me next. I was paying attention to Abigail's Aunty, Madeline I think her name was, speaking about Abigail's life. I was listening to the part about how close Abigail and Sammy'd always been and how, when they started school, Abigail'd kicked up a big fuss because she had to wear a dress instead of a shirt and shorts like Sammy. Abigail couldn't understand why she had to be different from her twin. I pictured a five-year-old Abigail, red-faced with rage. Then I remembered Abigail as a ten-year-old, as she had been until... that night.

I squirmed, accidentally knocking a hymn book off the seat. It landed on the wooden floor with a loud thump. I couldn't get

Abigail's face out of my mind – the curly blonde hair, the freckles, the shy smile. I imagined her in the bush, in the dark, under the gaze of the Virgin Mary. What'd happened? What did the murderer do to her? It must've hurt like hell. How could dying not hurt? She must've screamed, so why didn't I hear anything? Could I've done something? Could I've saved her?

I suddenly noticed how warm it was in the church. My dress was clammy with sweat – even though it was a cool, cloudy day outside – and there wasn't enough air, not for all the people crammed inside, not for me. I was going to faint. Faint, or throw up on Mrs Jackson in the row in front. I slipped out of my seat and fled down the aisle.

'Abbi had a gentle nature. She was generous and caring,' Abigail's Aunty Madeline was saying as I splashed my forehead with holy water. 'She didn't deserve this, she didn't deserve to–'

I stuck my fingers in my ears as I ran the last few steps to the church door. Outside, I leant against the cold brick church wall and breathed deeply – breathed in the fresh cool air, air that hadn't already been breathed by everybody else.

'Gracie, what is it?' Grandma Bett was behind me, her handbag in one hand, a balled-up hanky in the other.

I couldn't talk. I shook my head, stared at the ground, chewed on what was left of my nails.

'Let's just sit down here, shall we?' She led me by my elbow. 'Next to this nice bottlebrush.'

We sat there, on the cold soggy ground, silent apart from Grandma Bett's sighs, until Abigail's coffin was carried out. Sammy, Mr Miller and four men I didn't know placed the coffin in the back of the long, shiny black car that was parked in the churchyard. People streamed out of the church after that, and the yard filled with forlorn faces and hushed voices.

Grandma Bett stood, brushing the grass off her best dress, but told me to stay resting. Shelley and Hannah walked past, arms around each other, their eyes red. Baby Pete nodded to me as he headed towards the car park, looking even tinier than usual as he tried to keep in step with his muscly dad. The Irwins wandered by too, but if any of them noticed me they fortunately pretended not to. Mum and Dad rushed over, full of questions, and Grandma Bett assured them I was fine, that I'd just had 'a funny turn'. Then, Grub and Lucky climbed on me for a 'fam'ly cuddle' and I began to feel better.

I was thinking that maybe I could handle going to the wake when I spotted Mr Lothum, standing next to the shiny black car, the *hearse* Grandma Bett said its correct name was. He touched Abigail's dad's shoulder before shaking his hand. Then he saw me watching and, just as he'd done in the church, turned away.

What'd I done? Why couldn't he look at me?

'Can we go now?' I asked. My throat was dry, my voice raspy. 'I want to go home.'

CHAPTER TWENTY-SEVEN

THE NEXT DAY WAS JUNE THE FIFTEENTH, MUM'S BIRTHDAY. SHE DIDN'T want a fuss, said she felt 'guilty as hell' every time she smiled, let alone actually enjoyed herself. But it was her thirtieth birthday and Dad insisted they do something out of the ordinary. He took the day off work and persuaded Mum to arrange for Mrs Lothum to babysit Grub and Lucky.

'Poor Abigail Muller hasn't even been in the ground for twenty-four hours. How d'you expect me to kick up my heels?' Mum said, but she took ages deciding what to wear and I could tell she was happy that Dad wanted to spoil her.

Grandma Bett was cleaning the church that morning and offered to drop me at school on the way. She was humming along to 'Yellow Submarine' as she pulled up in front of the school gate.

'Just a minute, Gracie,' she said as I reached for my bag.

'Mmm?'

Grandma Bett gave me a quick look, sucked in her breath. 'Gracie, I know you wrote a letter to that Bede fellow.'

I let go of my bag and looked down at my hands, at my ugly chewed-up fingernails, waiting for a long lecture about how it was wrong, that it was against the law and blah blah blah.

'It worked.' Grandma Bett smiled at me. 'You're a very clever girl, Gracie. But–' She took her hand off the steering wheel and tapped my knee. 'It still is the wrong thing to do and it's even against the law.'

'But he wrote to Mum first! He said things only Dad should say. *That's* the wrong thing to do. I had to stop him.'

'So, you stole your mother's mail, too?' A new set of wrinkles dug into Grandma Bett's forehead.

'Mmm, yeah. Sorry.'

'Don't apologise to me. I'm not angry and I'm not going to tell your mother. But I do want you to promise me something.'

'Not apologise to Saint Bede!'

'Good heavens, no! Good riddance to him. Just promise me you'll look after yourself.'

I relaxed. 'Okay.' I was getting off lightly. For a moment I'd thought she was going to force me to face Saint Bede again. Or at the very least drag me back to confession.

'Yesterday, at the funeral, I was worried about you, *really* worried, Gracie. All the stress you've been under lately. It's just not healthy for someone your age. Try to take a step back from it all. Reflect on the good things in life and remember that we *will* get through this. Be gentle on yourself.'

'Okay, I will. Promise.' I smiled, trying to look like I didn't have a worry in the world. I wondered whether Father Scott'd talked to her. Did he spill the beans about me wanting to die? Surely him sharing my confession was against God's law, and would make Father Scott a sinner too. It didn't really matter though. I wasn't in trouble – and my plan'd worked. I'd got rid of Saint Bede!

THE SCHOOL DAY STARTED well enough. Baby Pete asked if I'd hang out with him at lunch. I lost count of how many laps of the playground we walked. The more I heard about his life – he had a sister he'd never met! – the better I felt about mine. I couldn't bring myself to share the news about my mum and dad spending the day together, though. It seemed unfair, like I'd be letting him down.

It was only when the after-lunch bell rang that everything went horribly wrong.

A group of kids was hovering outside our classroom, whispering. Shelley, Sarah K, Hannah, Josh – they were all there, as well as others I can't remember. At first I thought it was me they were talking about, and my stomach tightened. Baby Pete must've thought the same thing. He gave me a nervous glance. What'd I done now?

But no one paid any attention to me. No one rolled their eyes or curled their lip in a sneer. I relaxed, and even offered Shelley a smile (not that she noticed). Even so, I stood outside the circle, next to Baby Pete. I still wasn't confident enough to be part of the group.

'Yeah, Jonathan's big brother,' Josh was saying.

'He's in my sister's class – she sits next to him!' Samantha said, playing with her red curls.

'He seems too sweet though. He couldn't have.' Sarah K said.

'Yeah, he could've. He did! With 'is bare hands! You gotta watch the quiet ones. That's what my mum says,' Josh said.

'That's 'cause your mum's got the biggest mouth in Coongahoola,' Baby Pete laughed.

'It *must've* been Irwin, but. They found his sketchbook filled with sicko drawings – of kids!'

Irwin? Sketchbook? Josh was talking about Toby's notebook! His drawings weren't *sicko!* And they couldn't have traced it to Toby. It wasn't possible. Was it? I'd prayed that this wouldn't happen. Thanks, God. Thanks for nothing! The sandwich I'd eaten for lunch was rising, stinging my throat.

Baby Pete whispered, 'You okay?'

I shrugged, clenched my teeth. No, I wasn't okay. Today was meant to be a good day. It was Mum's birthday. She and Dad were celebrating – together. I was going to 'reflect on the good things in life'. Everything was supposed to get better.

'Yeah, and the drawings were of the kids he'd slaughtered.' Josh wouldn't shut up. 'That's what my dad said.'

'Do *you* know anything about it, Gracie?' Shelley asked. She probably didn't mean anything by it. She sounded friendly enough, but at that moment I hated her, wanted to shove her hard onto the asphalt. Yes, I knew something about it. And I wished like hell I didn't.

'No, I don't think so. About – what?' The words came out in one shallow breath.

'About Toby Irwin being a psyco killing maniac,' Sarah K answered, and I felt like my head was about to explode. 'The cops came at lunch and took him away. He your boyfriend? Why doesn't that surprise me?'

'It wasn't him!' I yelled. They all looked at me, their mouths hanging open, but I didn't care. They nudged and smirked at each other, but it didn't bother me. I didn't give a stuff what they thought any more. 'It was *not* Toby Irwin.'

'It was, but. They've got *evidence.*' Josh's fat cheeks were pink with excitement. 'Anyway, if it wasn't your Bede man, who else could it be?'

Who else could it be? I stared at Josh, my mouth dry. *Who else?* That's when I realised. I leant back against the brick wall to stop myself from falling. There was only one person it could be. How could I have been so stupid?

I pushed past them all, past Shelley, Josh, Sarah K, Samantha, Hannah and even Baby Pete, and I ran. Without saying anything else, without grabbing my bag. I ran across the playground and out the school gate, past the Coongahoola Central sign with its stupid motto 'Striving for Excellence' – what was the point of striving for anything in a hole like Coongahoola? – and down Henderson Street.

I was beyond crying, beyond anything. I thought back to that night. Hiding in the bush, scared out of my brain. I remembered the singing, *Mr Lothum* singing like he was the only person in the world. *Three blind mice, three blind mice.* I could see the boots – black boots – on the ends of his long legs, crunching through the dry bush. I could see the stick thing – the tennis racquet? – in his hand.

How could I've been so stupid? I was a moron, a complete moron. And now, because of me, Toby was in trouble. Big trouble. He was a suspect for murder!

I ran and ran, only slowing to cross the road. If I got knocked down dead by a car, no one'd ever know the truth about Mr Lothum. I didn't bother keeping my head down. I didn't care who was driving past. Let them stop me! I'd broken all the rules: leaving the school grounds without permission and being on the streets without an adult. But I'd got involved in a murder and rules no longer applied.

I didn't realise I was heading for home until I'd turned down our street. What do you do when you know something this bad? Who do you tell? Mum. I'd tell Mum. Mum or Dad. I'd even confess to Grandma Bett if I had to. She'd be disappointed, they'd all be pissed off, but that was beside the point. I had to save Toby. They'd know what to do. Someone had to help me.

I kept my eyes on the grass as I cut across the Irwins' front lawn. I wondered if Mrs Irwin knew where Toby was, what he was being accused of. If she came outside, if she tried to talk to me, I wouldn't be able to handle it. How could I admit to her what I'd done? I'd probably just drop dead with shame.

Our driveway was empty. I wasn't expecting Grandma Bett to be home yet, but I'd hoped Mum and Dad were still there.

I bashed on the door. No answer.

'Muuuuum!' I called, praying Mrs Irwin wouldn't hear me. 'Daaaaaaaad!'

No answer. I was on my own. Normally I couldn't get away from my family and had to hide in a stupid little room just to get some peace. But now that I actually needed help, where was everyone?

I had to do something, and fast. How would Toby be feeling? What was going through his head? I picked up a stone from the driveway and scratched a message onto our verandah's rotting boards.

Gone 2 police.
G x

Then I ran like hell to the bus stop.

CHAPTER TWENTY-EIGHT

I'D BEEN TO THE POLICE STATION ONCE BEFORE TO PICK UP DAD. I CAN'T think why he was there – it was years ago – but I remember Gary was there too, the veins in his forehead pulsing with anger, and Dad was covering Gary's mouth to muffle his swear words. That night (it must've been night because Elijah and I were in our pyjamas) Constable Stewy was the only policeman there, and I thought he looked lonely, sitting at an old wooden desk just like my teacher's.

But now the station was buzzing with police I'd never seen before, slamming down phones and ordering each other around, the air hot and thick with unanswered questions. I felt like fleeing back out the door.

'Gracie?' The voice made me jump. I scanned the room until I saw Constable Stewy waving me over. My heart was thumping. It was too late to run.

I zigzagged through the sea of sweaty blue uniforms and sank down in the worn-out brown chair that faced Constable Stewy's desk.

'Excuse the chaos,' Constable Stewy said. 'Can't hear yourself think in here any more. They've sent fifteen more officers down from the city – a special force devoted to the case. Been working non-stop the past week.'

I thought about the row of shiny police cars in the school car park, the police men and women none of us kids had seen before marching across the playground as if the whole school was about to be arrested.

'Cuppa tea? Milo?' Constable Stewy picked up a chipped white mug with *I love my Daddy* written on it.

I shook my head. 'I've got something very important to say. I need to talk now.'

'Okay.' Constable Stewy nodded, frowning.

'It wasn't Toby,' I said. 'You've got to let him go.'

'Um, Gracie. Hang on–'

'I heard you'd got Toby Irwin. You can't lock him up. It wasn't him!'

'We haven't locked up anyone, Gracie. Yes, it's correct that Tobias Irwin is here – he's in with the sergeant, having a chat, answering a few questions. But no charges have been laid.'

Constable Stewy's chair farted as he leant forward. 'Are you feeling all right? Can I get you something? A glass of water?'

'I know who the murderer is! I saw him. It was me who dropped Toby's notebook. I shouldn't have been there, but I was.' I stopped, bit my lip, tried to breathe.

'Gracie. Please. Relax, and start at the beginning – slowly,' Constable Stewy said, and I noticed how old and tired he was looking. His blue eyes'd sunk deep into his face and his red hair was speckled with grey like a bad case of dandruff.

I wondered if he'd heard that I'd lied about Saint Bede. *Dirty liar! Dirty liar!* Would he believe me? He had to. I had to save Toby.

Constable Stewy scribbled in his exercise book as I talked. He wrote down everything, even the bit about the Virgin Mary's eyes watching over me, and I had to say a few things twice, practically yelling to be heard over the ringing phones and constant chatter. He was a slow writer, but he didn't stop, not even when his phone rang. When I'd finished, he read over his notes, scratching the mole on his nose.

I shook my hands, stretched out my fingers. I hadn't even realised I was sitting on them until they'd started tingling with pins and needles.

'Thank you, Gracie,' Constable Stewy said. 'If you can spare me a few more minutes, I'll just go and get Sergeant Colby.'

Constable Stewy left through a glass door, under huge framed photos of Mayor Banks and Mayor Kirk, inviting in a cold draught. I wrapped my arms around myself. I was staring at a photo of Constable Stewy's four smiling, freckly kids when I felt the next burst of cool air.

Constable Stewy and the sergeant marched in, side by side. Toby shuffled in behind them, his face as white as Constable Stewy's coffee mug. I looked away, tears welling up.

'Miss Barrett?' Sergeant Colby marched over to Constable Stewy's desk. While Constable Stewy's boots squeaked on the shiny white floor, the sergeant's stomped.

'You've kept this to yourself for – what was it? *Six* days?'

'I'm sorry! I didn't know then. I didn't know what I'd seen.'

'Tell me, Gracie, what do your parents think of you roaming the streets at night?' A shiny black gun poked out of the sergeant's holster. I shivered.

'They don't know. They'd be angry.'

'E-e-easy, Sergeant. She's d-d-done the right thing.' Constable Stewy looked small beside the sergeant. He stood with his back straight and hands by his sides like a kid on detention.

'She wanders around alone at night and has been withholding crucial information. This is hardly a miss goody-two shoes, is it?'

The station was quiet except for the soft, persistent ring of a phone on the other side of the room. The other police had stopped what they were doing to examine me.

'She's a good k-k-kid.' Constable Stewy's face had turned the same red as his hair. 'She's Elijah's sister – remember the one–'

'Yes, yes, I know,' the sergeant snapped. 'The three of us should discuss this further in my office. If she's not making this up–'

Just then the foyer door swung open and Mum and Dad stumbled into the station, holding hands and pushing their way through the crowd. Grandma Bett rushed in after them, her hair fluffed up and her grey cardigan inside out.

'What's going on?' Mum's voice was loud, drunk. 'Bett said you left a strange message on the doorstep. What're you doing here?'

Everyone was staring at me, including Toby. I couldn't bear to look in his direction, but I could feel him glaring, waiting for an explanation.

'This is turning into a spectacle!' the sergeant said. 'Gracie, we need to talk in private.'

But I couldn't wait any longer. I wanted everyone to know, especially Toby. 'I was there the night Abigail died.'

I wiped my eyes with the backs of my hands, but I couldn't stop the tears from pouring out. 'I accidentally dropped Toby's notebook and – they reckon it was him. It wasn't! I saw who it was.'

'*You* saw the murderer? Why the... Why'd you ... What–' Mum shook her head. 'God, I've had a drink too many.'

'Who was it?' Dad asked, letting go of Mum's hand. 'Gracie, who'd you see?'

'This is police information!' The sergeant's face was red, his eyes bulging.

'Mr Lothum.'

I'd meant to yell the name, to spit it out, get rid of it once and for all, but 'Lothum' came out as a whisper.

'Mr Lothum?' Toby sounded scared.

'*James* Lothum?' Dad frowned. 'Are you serious?'

I nodded.

'You're *absolutely* sure?' Dad asked.

'I am now,' I whispered.

The sergeant cleared his throat. 'Okay. Enough! We'll pay the man a visit, bring him in for a chat. Stewart! Put a call out. We could need reinforcements.'

'*James* Lothum?' Mum said. 'You're fucking – *sorry* – kidding me. I need to sit down.' She stumbled over and sank into Constable Stewy's chair.

'Keep it down, please!' the sergeant said. 'I understand your distress, but it's against the–'

'For Christ's sake.' Dad closed his eyes and rubbed his forehead. 'James! I've worked with the bloke for twelve, thirteen years. Knew he wasn't the full quid, but I just thought he was a big softie. Geez, I've bought 'im beers and everythin'. The bastard! He went after my own fuckin' son!'

'His mother had a few serious mental health issues.' Grandma Bett stared at the wall. 'But he was a good boy. Polite. Left school, worked at the steelworks like most decent young men. What on earth?'

'They're on their way to Watson Close, Sergeant,' Constable Stewy said, holding what looked like a high-tech walkie-talkie. 'Told them to wait for further instruction.'

'I've always thought he was like a harmless pup.' Mum jumped up so suddenly I thought something'd bitten her. 'Oh my God!'

'Mum? What's wrong?'

'The twins!' she screamed. 'The twins are there! Shirley Lothum's got Grub and Lucky!'

CHAPTER TWENTY-NINE

'PUT YER FOOT DOWN, MUM. KEEP ON THEIR TAIL,' DAD SHOUTED. WE were following the sergeant, Constable Stewy, two other policemen, and Toby, and they'd sped off, lights flashing and siren wailing, before I'd even done up my seatbelt. If the twins weren't in danger, if we weren't on our way to the Lothums', and if all the bad things that'd happened that day weren't my fault, it would've been the most exciting thing ever.

'But they're speeding!' Grandma Bett's voice was shaky.

'They're cops, Mum!' Dad said. 'And they're hardly going to arrest us – it's our kids!'

'How can this be happening?' Mum was in tears. She sat slumped next to me on the back seat. I'd nodded at her seatbelt but she'd ignored me and left it undone.

'They'll be alright, Nell,' Grandma Bett made the car jerk as she suddenly accelerated. 'Shirley won't let anything bad happen.'

'Yeah? I hope you're right,' Mum said. Then she poked my arm, her sharp fingernail digging into my skin. 'Why, Gracie? Why'd you do such a thing? Why'd you go out at night? After what happened with your own brother!'

'It was him I was going to see! Elijah! To bring him home, but Mr, Mr... *He* was there and I got scared. I didn't know what he'd done then, but–' I realised how ridiculous my story sounded.

'Remember dropping Elijah at the airport? He's in another state! We're protecting him from doing something stupid like you just did.'

'I was going to get a lift, in a van that delivers the Believers' buns and stuff to Tamworth. From there I was going to – hitchhike.'

Mum laughed but tears were rolling down her cheeks. 'I can't believe this. I just–'

'It's not as silly as it sounds.' Dad turned to look at me. 'She could've got away with it. I hitched a lot of rides in my teens.'

'Robbie! You're not helping!' Mum lifted her arm as if she was going to whack the back of his head, but then she dropped it and sighed.

'Well, I can't see what's wrong in wantin' to see her brother,' Dad said. 'Wantin' it so much she was brave enough to sneak away at night. Personally, I reckon she deserves a bloody medal. Good on ya, Gracie.'

I didn't say anything, didn't want to make Mum any angrier. But it felt good to hear Dad sticking up for me. Maybe what I'd done wasn't all bad.

'I'll leave the disciplining to you in future then, shall I?' Mum was saying.

'You're hardly a saint of a mum. You been half pissed ever since that head-case you were screwin–'

'Please! Can we turn our attention to something else?' Grandma Bett butted in. 'Like a prayer for Gabriel and Lucy.'

'You said they'd be fine!' Mum cried, but she started mumbling softly which I guessed was her praying.

I stared out the window, at the giant gum trees flashing by, gum trees like the ones in the bush by the Bagooli River. Please God, make the twins be safe. They had to be. They must be! Or, or else I'd–

Grandma Bett took a sharp turn into Watson Close and pulled in behind Sergeant Colby and Constable Stewy, skidding our tyres on the gravel. I undid my seatbelt, ready.

Dad's door'd swung open before the car even stopped. 'Stay here,' he said.

'Wait! I'm coming!' Mum leapt out of the car, and I followed. Three more police cars were parked across the road, and Toby was walking off down the street. Heading straight for his place, no doubt.

'Be careful!' Grandma Bett cried after us. She called for me to come back and wait in the car, too, but I pretended not to hear.

The sergeant and another policeman had already gone inside the Lothums' house and Constable Stewy was halfway up their front steps. When he saw us approaching, he jumped back down and sprinted across the lawn.

'I'm going to have to ask you to stay here. Sergeant's orders.' Constable Stewy held up his palm like a stop sign.

'Don't give us that shit!' Dad yelled. 'I'm getting my kids.'

'C-c-come on, mate,' Constable Stewy said, rubbing his nose. 'Don't make things worse.'

'Our twins are bein' babysat at this address,' Dad said. Then he nodded at Mum and me. 'We're here to collect them.'

'Robbie, Nell. I urge you, do *not* enter the house,' Constable Stewy pleaded as Dad, Mum and I climbed the Lothums' crumbling steps.

Someone was coming up behind me, and at first I thought it was Constable Stewy, but then I heard Grandma Bett catching her breath. She grabbed my hand and began whispering, 'Hail Mary full of grace,' as we stepped onto the doormat and through the Lothums' front door.

It was dark inside – all the curtains were closed – and there was a strong smell, like the stink of cleaning products in our secret room, but the house seemed as it'd always been. I don't know what I was expecting to see – blood stains on the lino, a knife on the table? – but I was surprised to see the kitchen, at least, looking so normal.

'My babies!' Mum sobbed, and my stomach heaved. Grub?

Lucky? We raced through to the living room. But then I saw their sweet little dirty faces. They were cross-legged on the carpet, watching the Lothums' black and white TV, clapping their hands along with Benita from *Play School* as she sang, 'Big Ted, Big Ted, tucked up in his bed.' I took a deep breath, then breathed out slowly. The twins were safe!

'Oh, thank you, Lord. Thank the Lord you're all right.' Mum covered the twins in kisses, and they tumbled back onto the carpet, squealing.

I spied Mr Lothum's cowboy hat sitting on the couch, just a couple of metres from the twins, and felt a wave of sickness.

Then we heard a cry from somewhere along the hall. 'This is where it ends! It's the end!' It was Mrs Lothum's voice, but it sounded crazy, like a madwoman's. 'Got that, James? This is the end!'

'Robbie, this is an o-o-order.' Constable Stewy stood in the doorway, hands on his hips. 'Take the children and leave. Now!'

'All right, all right. Keep your hair on. Coming.' Dad picked up the twins, tucking one under each tattooed arm. 'Let's get you home.'

I blinked as I stepped out into the blinding sunlight, and walked straight into a policeman about seven feet tall. 'S'cuse us, love,' he said, pushing past.

'What's going on?' Mrs Anderson called from the front lawn where a small crowd had gathered. 'Why are the police here?'

'All will be revealed,' Dad said. 'Soon enough.'

'Must be questioning Shirl, right?' Mrs Anderson said. 'Since she knows more about everyone in this town than we know about ourselves.'

'But you wouldn't need *four* police cars for that,' Heidi Anderson said. 'Someone must be going to jail!'

'Shirley? No! Never in a million.' That was Andy Hall's wife. I forget her name.

'Oh my God. D' you think? How could– I'd never've guessed!' Heidi said.

'Me neither, but she has been acting strange lately, hasn't she?' Mrs Anderson said.

That was when Constable Stewy stepped out of the Lothums' front door, followed by Mr Lothum and the sergeant. Mr Lothum's hands were behind his back and his head was bowed.

'That's not–' Mrs Anderson started. '*James!* Handcuffed!'

'James Lothum! Bloody hell! I never–' someone cried.

'Shhhh – look.'

Closing the front door, then walking down the steps with two other policemen, was Mrs Lothum. She wore what looked like a pink dressing gown and her hair hung down over her face.

'Jesus, she looked normal enough a couple of hours ago,' Mum whispered.

'Child killer!' Mrs Lothum screamed, running towards the car Sergeant Colby was forcing Mr Lothum into. 'He killed them all!'

'Stand back please, Shirley,' Constable Stewy said.

'I saw the boy's blood, Michael Sanders' blood – couldn't get *that* out of his clothes with Cold Power!' Mrs Lothum yelled as two of the other policemen took her arms and led her to another police car.

'Well, fuck me dead!' It was Graham Anderson. By that time, he and the three Wilson boys had joined the crowd.

As Dad placed the twins on the back seat, Grandma Bett wrapped her arms around Mum and me, and the three of us began to sob.

'C'mon, let's go,' Dad said to us. 'Let's get the hell away from here.'

CHAPTER THIRTY

I KNOCKED ON THE IRWINS' FRONT DOOR, AND TRIED TO SWALLOW. My mouth was dry. It'd been hours since I'd had anything to eat or drink. The thought of food made me dry-retch, but I was craving a drink of water.

We'd only just got home from the Lothums'. My mind was still reeling from all that'd happened, but I had to talk to Toby. I didn't want to. I would much rather've stayed holed up at home, but I knew I'd never be able to sleep if I didn't go.

'Gracie?' It was Jonathan. I could tell by his smirk that I'd been a recent topic of conversation.

'Is Toby here?'

'Yeah, but I dunno if he wants to see you. Hang on a sec.' He turned his back. 'Tobyyyyyyyyyy! It's Gracie.'

Jonathan faced me again. 'Yeah, sorry but he's not–'

The door was flung wide open and Toby elbowed his younger brother out of the way. He'd changed out of school uniform into faded blue jeans and a black T-shirt with *The Clash* written on it. His face hadn't changed, though. It was still pale and tired-looking.

'What're you doing here?' His hair was wet and dripped onto his T-shirt.

'I'm really sorry.' I didn't want to say anything with Jonathan standing just inside the door, but I didn't know when I'd get another chance. 'I didn't mean to get you involved. Honestly. I was on my way–'

'Yeah, yeah, to get Elijah – I got that. But why'd you have my book? I thought I'd lost it.'

I took a deep breath. 'I… took it. Sorry!'

'You *stole* it? How? Why would you?'

'At school. Out of your bag, but only 'cause I was upset – after seeing you and Shelley.'

Toby blushed. 'Shelley? The one with the funny hair?'

'Um, yeah. At the tuck shop.'

Toby frowned down at his bare feet, as if trying to remember. How could he have forgotten? He and Shelley were definitely standing together when I saw them, and they'd started walking towards me.

'Gracie Barrett!'

I jumped at the sound of her voice.

Mrs Irwin squeezed into the doorway next to Toby. 'Haven't you done enough damage for one day? Have you come to traumatise my son even further?'

'I came to say sorry. And that they've taken Mr Lothum away. They've got him. We're safe now.'

'Amen to that! But, Gracie, Toby said you *knew* about this. Days ago!'

'I didn't know it was him.'

'How could you not know? You saw him! Down by the Bagooli River – in the middle of the night. Are you thick?'

'Mum!' Toby said. 'Don't.'

'No, I'm not. It's a long story,' I was determined not to lose it, not to cry. God, I hated Mrs Irwin. 'I was going to get a ride to–'

'I've heard all that nonsense. So, what went through your head when you saw him? Or do you make a habit of meeting strange men in the bush?'

'No. I just thought he was on patrol.'

'All right. So what'd it *feel* like to be out there with him in the middle of the night? You must've felt something.'

'I was scared.' A large tear slid down my nose. 'But not scared of him. He was, um...' I couldn't stop the tears.

'Leave her, Mum!' Toby said. 'Gracie, it's okay.'

'No, it's not bloody well okay!' Mrs Irwin screeched and pointed at me. She wore dark red nail polish and a gold ring with a 'J' on it. 'You were hanging around with a killer in the middle of the night. That makes you an accomplice in my book!'

'No,' I said. 'No, you're wrong.'

'Even worse,' Mrs Irwin's face was so close that I could smell wine on her breath. 'You tried to frame my son! I was right not to trust you, Gracie Barrett. With your mum running round with that criminal Bede, and God knows what else going on behind your walls. I warned Toby to stay away from you, but you *still* managed to drag him into it.'

'But I. It was–'

'No, Mum,' Toby said. 'You've got it all wrong. You haven't heard everything.'

'I've heard enough! The last few months I've been terrified out of my mind.' Mrs Irwin continued. 'I've lost my hair, my looks, my nerve, my–'

'Shut up!' Toby yelled. 'Just shut up, Mum.'

Mrs Irwin stared at Toby, stunned.

'She's said sorry, Mum. It was an accident.' Toby had sweat glistening on his forehead. 'Look at her – she's just a girl, a scared girl. She's no crim! I told you why she was out there. It was all just one terrible fuck-up.'

It was hearing Toby's words, Toby standing up for me, that made me lose it. I started sobbing, my whole body shaking. Neither Toby nor Mrs Irwin knew what to say. Toby looked at his feet, wiggled his toes.

'Look, Gracie,' Mrs Irwin said, in a gentle tone I'd never heard her use before. 'Okay, I believe you didn't mean to get mixed up in all this, and I'm sorry for blaming you. God, I should be over the moon, dancing for joy now that the murderer's locked up.

'But, listen: today – this morning – there was a knock on the door. It was Constable Stewy, standing there, right where you're standing now. On *my* doorstep. He came to our house before going to the school, you see. I thought one of the boys was missing, that was the first thing that came to mind. *It's one of my boys.* Then Stewy, looking all nervous and pathetic, says, "I need to talk to Tobias Irwin in relation to Abigail Muller's murder". His words!

'Gracie, I tell you – that was almost as bad as him saying my son was dead. Toby – a murder suspect! So look, I shouldn't have gone shooting my mouth off at you. But I've had a bitch of a day, all right? I just need to make sense of everything, all the shit that's been going on.'

I nodded, tried to say 'Okay', but I started bawling again, my whole body heaving.

'Come in, love.' Mrs Irwin took my hand. 'You can't go home like that. Come inside and have a sit down. I'll get you a tissue.'

I hadn't stepped inside the Irwins' house for ages, not since before I'd started liking Toby. It stank of cigarettes, but being there didn't feel as weird as I would've expected. Mrs Irwin ordered Jonathan to go and watch TV, then she swept Toby's maths homework up off the kitchen table and pointed at a chair. Toby plonked down in the chair next to mine and his mum sat facing us.

I took a deep breath and blinked back tears. I hoped my face didn't look as ugly as Mum's did when she cried.

'James Lothum.' Mrs Irwin reached for a red cigarette packet on the windowsill. 'James *bloody* Lothum. Who'd have thought it? And, living on our street the whole time! And, Shirley – that poor bloody woman. No wonder she's got a screw loose. She's married to a murderer! A child murderer! And all because of one stupid, stupid night.'

'Stupid night?' I wiped my eyes.

'The River Picnic! Surely you know about that.' Mrs Irwin lit a cigarette. 'Toby, pass her the tissues.'

'Yeah.' I quickly blew my nose as politely as possible. 'I've heard some things. But I don't really know much.'

'No? Well, that's probably not a bad thing, Gracie. God, *James Lothum!* I've suspected most blokes in this town, but he wasn't even on the radar.'

'Can you tell me? About the… picnic?' Normally I wouldn't be brave enough to ask, not an adult anyway, but there was nothing normal about this day. 'I want to know.'

I'd just discovered who the Coongahoola murderer was. Why stop there? It was time I heard the truth about the town's other dark secret. I wanted to know why I still had nightmares about that night, even though I'd only been two at the time and couldn't remember a thing. And why, even though the nightmares didn't make sense – they were mostly shadows and sounds – they left me with a feeling of dread. What'd happened at the River Picnic that haunted not only me, but the entire town?

Mrs Irwin frowned, blowing a mouthful of smoke towards the ceiling. 'How much do you know?'

'Just bits I heard at school.'

'Mr Bailey's wife drowned.' Toby said. 'And they never found out why.'

'And Stu Bailey thanked the Lord for a week – did you hear that part?' Mrs Irwin said. 'Thought all his Christmases'd come at once.'

'I heard he gave all her stuff away the next day – to St Vinnies. Do you reckon *he* killed her?' Toby asked.

'Who knows. There was never any proof. But a lot of people were sus for a while. God, it could've been anyone. *Anything* could've happened that night, and that woman sure did rub people up the wrong way.'

'What about Mr Lothum?' I asked. 'Could he have–'

'Could he've killed her? Well, there's a thought; but, dunno, I doubt it. She was a big woman, built like a truck. And I think he was probably a bit busy with–'

'With?' I asked. The sun was boring through the window, forcing me to squint.

'With Shirley, of course.' She stubbed out her cigarette, slid back her chair. 'Now I'd offer you a proper drink, Gracie. God knows you probably need it. But your grandma would burn me on a stake. So, here's a juice – orange.'

'Thank you.' I took a big gulp.

'Juice, Toby?' Mrs Irwin asked.

'Beer?'

'All right, but just one,' she said firmly.

Mrs Irwin handed Toby a can of VB and poured herself a large glass of white wine before sitting back down. 'I'm not really sure I want to get into it all, the goddamned River Picnic.'

'Come on, Mum,' Toby said. 'We've got a right to know.'

'Please,' I said.

Mrs Irwin looked at me, thought for a moment, and sighed. 'Oh, all right, I probably owe it to you after going off like that. But where to start?' She stared into her wine.

'We'd never had anything like it before, and we sure as hell haven't had since.' She lifted her glass and sipped her wine, then sighed again. 'Okay, so it was organised by the bigwig who runs the steelworks, Frank Watson. Fat guy, real smart-arse. He was mayor at the time and the picnic was just before the election. A big party to get the community together – that's what Frank said. Well, did it ever! So we'd all vote for him again, anyone could see that, but we didn't care. Parents, kids, babies and animals, all camping out together. You must've been there?'

I nodded. 'But I was only two.'

'Too young to remember and probably just as well! Mind you, it was innocent enough in the daytime. There were three-legged races, Pete Lander's band playing, a barbecue, kids running everywhere. The usual family stuff. Toby, I remember you riding around on a blue tricycle with some other little kids. You were having a ball!'

Toby nodded. 'Sometimes I think I remember bits. But I dunno. Were people flying kites? I think I remember kites.'

'Probably. There was all kinds of family stuff in the afternoon. But then, come evening, it was like the whole of Coongahoola'd gone mad,' Mrs Irwin said. 'Even though it's always been a bit of a blur, just the mention of that night still gives me goosebumps. It's hard to explain, but it was a very – unnatural experience. I actually feel slightly *ill* when I think about it, to be honest. And I'm not the squeamish type. I lived in Sydney as a teenager, wandered through Kings Cross once or twice, and saw all sorts of shit going on there. But, everyone, every*thing* went wild at the picnic – even the animals! Graham Anderson's pit bull was put down the next day. Graham made such a fuss about that, but God, the mess it made of little Andy's nose. Then there were the cats. They were celebrating in their own way – screaming like blooming banshees.'

'What about Toby? What was he doing then when this was going on?' I glanced at Toby.

'He was fine. We made a little bed for him in the back of the station wagon – remember that Tobes? – and he was out to it by dark. Thank the Lord! As for the others... The papers talked about kids as young as six wandering away from the river and roaming the streets in packs. Like dogs!'

Mrs Irwin lit another cigarette and sucked in a mouthful of smoke. 'As I said, it's a bit of a blur. Must've had quite a few of these that afternoon.' She tapped her glass with a fingernail. 'It started with burnt snags being thrown, but soon it was beer bottles. Those kids chucked them at bus shelters, cars, houses. Smashed Toby's nan's kitchen window, kicked her letterbox over – scared the poor bat half to death.'

The sound of smashing glass – that was in my nightmares! Could it've been the sound of all those bottles being chucked? What about the shrieking, the horrible shrieking and moaning? I drank the rest of my orange juice in a couple of mouthfuls. The sun in my eyes and Mrs Irwin's smoke were making my head hurt.

'But why?' Toby asked. 'Why'd everyone go – nuts?'

'Oh, there's a reason. There's a very good reason why everyone went mad that night. It would've just been an ordinary old community picnic, with a handful of yobbos and plenty of pissed people, if–'

'If?' I said.

'If it wasn't for Deirdre Buchen's mushroom soup.'

'Soup?' Toby scoffed. 'You're bullshitting.'

'I'm not – and Toby, I've talked to you about your swearing. It *was* all because of soup. Unbelievable, isn't it?' Mrs Irwin laughed, and I counted five fillings in her yellowish teeth, but I could tell she didn't really think it was funny.

'Deirdre's granddaughter – she was a wild one, that kid – and those little bitches she hung around with offered to go mushroom picking, help Deirdre make her famous soup. Well, Deirdre usually got her mushrooms from Woolies. How was she to know that the only mushrooms growing in Coongahoola were those ones that send you loopy?'

I frowned. I'd heard about Deirdre's granddaughter. Doreen. She was sent away to boarding school after robbing the Post Office with a toy water pistol. But I didn't know anything about mushrooms that send you loopy.

'Magic mushrooms!' Mrs Irwrin said.

'You haven't heard of magic mushrooms?' Toby looked at me.

'Jesus, your grandma keeps a tighter rein on you than I thought,' Mrs Irwin said. 'Most of us didn't have a clue that there was anything wrong with the soup, but I'm sure half the kids knew the score. They went back for seconds. Stuffed themselves silly. Ha – literally! Deirdre later said that some of the mushrooms looked a bit odd, but her granddaughter swore they were premium quality. And that Deirdre was a real tight-arse – she was never one to look a gift horse in the mouth.'

'You ate some?' Toby asked

'Oh, yeah! And so did your dad, and Gracie's mum and dad and, well, half the bloody town. It should've been a bloody hoot, really. But it wasn't. It was wrong. Especially with what happened – all those kids. That part was real creepy.'

'The River Children?' I asked.

'Yeah, that.' She sucked her cigarette. 'Now, Gracie, surely your mum's told you about sex?'

My cheeks burned. I hoped Toby wasn't looking. 'Not really, but I know about it anyway,' I said. 'From books.'

'Books?' Mrs Irwin shook her head and made the tiny plastic koala earrings bob about. 'Well, what happened at the picnic you won't find in books – not in books that your olds'd let you read anyway. If there's another word for orgy, I don't know it, so I'll just come out and say it. An orgy went on – that is, heaps of people had sex. Some of them were married anyway, just getting into the spirit of things, enjoying the novelty of doing it out in the fresh air. Others weren't. Some got carried away and did the business with someone they weren't married to, or in some cases, two or more people they weren't married to.'

Toby snickered into his beer.

'Oh.' This part wasn't much different from what the kids at school had said, but I'd never in a million years believed it could be true. The idea of people I knew, *old* people I knew, having sex made me want to throw up.

'Yeah, and a hell of a lot of sperm got past the goalie, as they say, because nine months later, women were dropping babies left right and centre. Not me, of course. You know full well Jonathan's not a river kid. Just between you two and me, Dez'd had too much soup – not a good combo with Jack Daniel's, that's for sure.'

'Yuck, Mum!' Toby's cheeks were red, too.

Mrs Irwin ignored him. 'I was pissed off about it that night, but it was a bloody blessing to me later. When all those kids were born. It's a bit weird, isn't it? I know your Elijah's one of them and he's turned out okay, though I've had my doubts about him in the past. But Janet Cole dropped a sprog, Sylvia Benson too, and various others – including Shirley Lothum.'

'Mrs Lothum?' I'd forgotten she'd had a baby, a baby she'd named her kitten after. 'Her baby was a River Child?' Mrs Lothum'd *had sex?* I couldn't bear to think about it.

'Yep, Sebastian. Probably would've been better if she'd been too sloshed to remember – half the women didn't have a clue who the dads were. God, what a nightmare to discover you were up the duff with James Lothum's kid.'

'What was wrong with him? Back then?' I asked.

'Well, we sure as hell didn't know he was a serial killer! But he was ugly as sin and never said boo. Didn't even have enough balls to make a speech at his own wedding. And for a social butterfly like Shirley Lothum, getting hitched to him must've been like a life sentence.'

I nodded, picturing Mr Lothum getting married in his stupid brown hat.

'So, that's it, kids. Screwed up, isn't it?' Mrs Irwin lifted her glass. 'To the River Picnic!' She poured the rest of the wine into her mouth.

'I'd better go now.' I stood up. 'Thanks for the juice, and for telling me everything.'

'Oh, that's not everything.' Mrs Irwin let out a little burp without covering her mouth. 'I don't think anyone can give you the full story. But that's probably the best you're going to get.'

'Just as I thought,' Toby said, swirling his beer in its can. 'This whole town is nuts.'

I felt lightheaded as I walked across our lawn in the bright sun. A kookaburra watched me from the wattle tree, but didn't make a sound. What a mental day, I was thinking. Even the kookaburra's speechless. Since waking up that morning I'd confessed to the police, the killer'd been caught, I'd been inside Toby Irwin's house, and I'd heard the truth about the River Picnic. I didn't want to see or talk to anyone else. I'd had more than enough for one day. I headed straight for my room and collapsed on the bed, a million thoughts spinning around my head.

CHAPTER THIRTY-ONE

It didn't take long for Mum to stop being angry with me for running away. She said that she thanked the Catholics' God as well as the Believers' God and even the Anglicans' God that I'd come back to them in one piece.

'At last we can celebrate a return to normal life!' Grandma Bett clapped her hands. She shouted us fish and chips for tea, accidentally buying a piece of fish for Elijah, which was lucky because after barely eating for a week I was ravenous. Grub and I were still crunching on the last of the salty chip crumbs when we heard a *tap tap tap* on the front door.

'Blimey!' Dad came in carrying a huge cane basket of pink and red flowers.

'Gum blossoms,' Grandma Bett said, as we all crowded around to sniff them.

Dad ripped a little, silver star-shaped card off the basket and read out loud:

To dear Gracie

These flowers are just a small token of our appreciation of you for being such a brave girl, and saving the lives of our children. We are indebted to you forever.

With all our hearts
The Hartleys, Landers, Parsons & Haberfields

I would rather've been famous for something else, like being the lead singer in a band (if I could sing). But I was pretty happy with being famous for catching a murderer.

At school, Mr Friend asked me to stand on the platform and tell everyone what'd happened. It was about the twentieth time I'd told the story so I said it without too many 'ums' and when I got to the part about Mr Lothum chasing me down River Road and me escaping into the bush (which I'd added to the story around the tenth time I told it), the whole class clapped, whistled and woohooed as loud as anything.

Then at the end of the Tuesday morning school assembly, Mr Kingsly called me onto the stage and gave me a special award. I didn't have to do anything except smile and hope my face wasn't the same colour as the red brick wall I was standing in front of. The award looked exactly like the netball trophy I'd won in Year Three, except the little gold plastic ball'd been taken out of the little gold plastic girl's hands, leaving a small hole. You could hardly see that a ball'd been there. It looked like a girl reaching for the sky. On it was the school motto 'Striving for Excellence' and the words: 'Awarded to Gracie Barrett for bravery. May 1984.'

Shelley sat next to me in class as if we were still best friends. She gave me a cassette tape with New Order on one side and The Cure on the other, and said I was welcome to come over to her house any time I wanted. I loved the tape – it was so different from Mum and Dad's records. I spent ages lying on my bed listening to the lyrics, but I didn't really feel like going to Shelley's house.

In the playground, boys smiled and said hello to me, not just the ugly ones like Baby Pete and fat Andy, but the good-looking ones with spiky hair and coral necklaces, like Nathan Taylor. So many people asked me to hang around them at lunchtime – even Sarah K and Hannah – that I couldn't choose. I ate my lunch in the library instead, between the A–H and I–O shelves because most of my favourite authors' names began with C and J.

People kept sending stuff to our house, all of it addressed to me. I made a list:

Good stuff:

- 1 x $20 note
- 3 x boxes of Darrell Lea chocolates
- 1 x tape from Shelley

OK stuff:

- 4 x bunches of flowers (2 in baskets)
- 12 x thank you cards
- 9 x letters (5 typed, 4 handwritten)
- 1 x Michael Jackson tape
- 1 x clay dove that changes colour when it's hot or cold

Stuff I didn't want:

- 4 x sets of rosary beads
- 3 x Believers prayer books
- 1 x Phil Collins record
- 1 x photo of Saint Bede in a frame (Mum let me rip up the photo)
- 1 x lock of Abigail Muller's baby hair

Around that time I also received the first letter in ages from Elijah:

Dear Gracie

I couldnt believe it when Mum called, not even when I talked to you. Ive told everyone at school and one kid even wants your autograph (hes a dickhead but so dont bother sending one).

I wouldnt of guessed it was Mr Lothum, but it makes sense. The voice I heard that night was a creepy deep voice a lot like Mr Lothums. Remember that time he got me to mow the lawns and take all that wood out of the shed and only paid me 50 cents! I spose at least he didn't chop me up!!!!

Its all right here now (its hot even in winter!),

but I still want to come home. Hope its soon.

Give Lucky and Grub Chinese burns from me (just make them soft ones cause I actually miss them.)

From Elijah

PS: If you get to go on TV can you say your brother is called Elijah because not all the kids at school believe your my sister.

I DIDN'T GET TO go on TV, but the news reporter mentioned "a young girl who had been instrumental in helping police with their enquiries". Although he didn't say my name, anyone with half a brain knew that the young girl was me.

We also had more visitors that week than we had at Elijah's going-away party. Even Mayor Kirk dropped in for afternoon tea. Grandma Bett sprayed the house with her Lily of the Valley perfume, covered the kitchen table in the special white lacy tablecloth she kept at the top of the linen cupboard, and served up a big plate of lamingtons. Mayor Kirk talked about having a special school-free day named after me, but he was either joking or changed his mind when he saw Grub weeing in the hallway, because he never mentioned it again.

'I hear you've saved the town.' Nana's mouth stretched into a smile and her warm wrinkly hand squeezed my elbow. She'd never had anything nice to say about me before. She was always too busy saying great things about Elijah. She and the Butcherer were at our place congratulating me when Mum got the call about Mrs Lothum.

'They've put Shirley in hospital. That was Jane,' Mum said, hanging up the phone.

'Did *he* get her?' I asked, imagining Mr Lothum trying to kill her through the bars in jail.

'Who? Oh, no. Nothing like that. Nervous breakdown,' Mum said.

'How very convenient.' Nana shook her head.

'What does that mean?' I'd heard of nervous breakdowns, but what exactly broke down? Her brain? Arms? Legs?

'She's messed up. Can't cope.' Mum sighed. 'S'pose we'd better go and see her. Find out what the hell happened.'

'Why would you talk to her? Are you forgetting what *he* could've done to Elijah?' The Butcherer sat up in his armchair, suddenly awake. 'That woman was in on it.'

'Shhhh! She's Gracie's godmother. She just found out something was going on, that's all. And it's obviously taken its toll.'

'She gossips about everything else. How'd she manage to keep her mouth shut about this?' Nana grumbled.

'She's told the police everything now though,' Mum said. 'Enough to have James put away for good, I hope.'

'Well *I* ain't going anywhere near her.' Dad yawned. 'Specially if she's in a bed. Could all be an elaborate plan to get me in the sack.'

'You hardly need encouraging, son. I'd keep quiet if I were you!' the Butcherer said, pushing himself up out of the chair.

'Settle down, Poppy. It was a joke!' Mum said. 'You really think she'd go to that much trouble for a couple of minutes with him?' Mum reached to pull out the elastic on Dad's tracksuit pants and let it snap against his belly. 'Then again, you running into Nurse Audrey'd be a bit of a worry.'

'That was ages ago!' Dad said. It was, but none of us would ever forget the row when Mum found out what'd been going on. It sparked off two weeks of yelling, plate-smashing, door-slamming and furniture-kicking, of slapped-together school lunches, sloppier-than-usual dinners and tight-lipped goodnight kisses.

'Seems like yesterday to me. Anyway, me and Gracie'll go. Gracie deserves an explanation. What do you reckon, pet?'

'I dobbed him in. She'll hate me!' The thought of seeing Mrs Lothum made me want to run and hide under my bed, like Grub did when he was told to eat his carrots. I was happy being a hero, but I was trying not to think about what'd actually happened. I'd told the story so many times I didn't even think about the words as I said them. They meant nothing by now. I was sick of the Lothums. Scared of them, too. I didn't want to hear any more about either of them, let alone see them. Why did I have to go and talk to her?

'Oh, codswallop!' Mum flicked through the *New Idea* Nan'd given her. 'She knows you did the right thing. Besides we're probably the only people talking to her. She'll be desperate for the company.'

CHAPTER THIRTY-TWO

IT WAS WEIRD TO THINK THAT ONCE UPON A TIME IT WAS MRS LOTHUM taking me to the hospital to visit Mum. That was back when the twins were born: the first day I saw their squashed little faces, and the first day Elijah and I played at the hospital. As Mum and I pushed open the heavy glass door, I remembered that smell, of cleaning stuff mixed in with the smell of sick people, so strong it almost burnt my nose. The squeak of my sneakers on the glossy orange floor reminded me of the day Elijah ran smack bang into old Mrs Clark, knocking her and her walking stick to the ground and sending her glasses flying. We were shooed out to the car park after that. We still played chasing, but it wasn't the same without the nurses yelling, 'That's enough you two!' and the kids in the children's ward cheering us on.

This time we didn't walk through the swinging grey doors to Maternity.

I jumped up to peek through the window, though. I was curious to see who was in Mum's old bed and whether she'd been lumped with two babies like Mum had, or just one. I also wanted to delay seeing Mrs Lothum for as long as I could.

'Gracie! Don't be so nosey,' Mum said.

'There's no one there! Whole place is empty.'

'What do you expect? Who'd put themselves through the hell of giving birth if there was a chance of losing the kid to some nutcase? Just you wait, there'll be babies everywhere nine months from the day *he* was locked up.'

I was thinking about that and imagining her and Dad having another baby – another girl maybe, only less of a sook than Lucky – when a lady in a white uniform and navy blue shoes stepped into the corridor. I knew who it was without looking at her face.

'Congratulations, Gracie!' Nurse Audrey squeezed me tight, as if we were good friends, as if my dad never used to 'pay her visits of a *non-medical kind*' (the words Mum'd screamed at Dad – at the time I didn't have a clue what she meant).

'You're a brave girl. Bet you're pretty popular now, eh?' She stepped back and searched me with her dark brown eyes.

'A bit.' I wasn't sure where to look. My eyes were now at the same height as the giant shelf her 'Audrey' badge sat on. Elijah was right: 'bazoobas' was a perfect name for them.

'A bit? I bet all the boys are lining up to go out with you! How are those adorable twins? They must be big now. How old are they – two?' She was talking like Mum wasn't there.

'Three. And a half.'

'You're joking! And what about–'

'We've come to see Shirley,' Mum said with her hands on her hips and her chin stuck out, as if Nurse Audrey was going to tell us to get lost.

'Shirley Lothum?' Nurse Audrey finally looked at Mum. 'You're a braver woman than I am. I'd rather have nothing to do with her. Second door on the left.'

'How much perfume does that woman pour on?' Mum muttered when Nurse Audrey'd got halfway down the corridor. 'The smell of her was bringing back all sorts of memories. None of them good, believe me.'

The first thing I noticed about Mrs Lothum's room was how quiet it was. It took a moment before I spotted her in the bed next to the window. She had the whole four-bedded room to herself, but most of the space was wasted. She'd shrunk so much she almost wasn't there. Her grey face blended into the pile of pillows it was propped up on, and her body was like a little speed-hump in the white bedspread. I relaxed a little. This wasn't a woman to be scared of. She wore the same blue hospital gown as Mum'd worn when she had the twins, and no make-up. Only the hair was left of her old self. It sprayed off her head like the Coongahoola park fountain, as shiny and red as ever. It looked wrong and more like a clown's than a godmother's, but without the hair I would've wondered if it was really her.

She was facing the doorway, staring right at me, like she'd known we were about to walk through the door. She lifted a hand to wave us over but had to cough lots and swallow twice before her voice worked properly.

'Thank you. Thank you so...' She licked her lips. They were dry and peeling, and the same greyish colour as the rest of her face.

'Sorry, Shirl. I forgot to get you anything.' Mum looked at the table next to Mrs Lothum's bed. She only had a box of tissues and a glass of water with bits floating in it. 'Flowers or even a card. Just wasn't thinking right. Thought Gracie and I'd come for a – chat.'

Mrs Lothum shook her head slowly, which seemed to take a great deal of effort. 'Sit with me, please sit with me.'

Mum plonked down in the visitor's chair, sliding her handbag to the floor. I perched on the arm. I didn't want to be there, didn't want to commit to sitting down. I looked at the floor and bit my thumbnail.

'I will never, ever take you for granted again. I love you both. I can't tell you how much.'

Mum and I glanced at each other. It was Mrs Lothum's voice, but the words seemed to belong to someone else.

Mrs Lothum reached out her hand for me to touch or maybe even hold. It was the colour of cardboard. I shivered and pretended I hadn't seen it, instead gazed around the room at the grey patches on the wall where the paint'd peeled off and the framed photo of the Queen, which must've been ancient because she looked younger than Mum.

Then I said, 'I didn't realise it was him. I didn't realise for six days.'

Mrs Lothum's eyes were wide, scared. A deep noise rose from her throat, clearing the way for a torrent of words: 'I thought every phone call, every knock was the sergeant. I was washing, always washing and scrubbing – *his* clothes, the sheets, the carpet, walls, anything he touched. Anything that could've–'

I blinked back tears. Was I meant to listen to this?

'But why, Shirley?' Mum leant forward. 'Why didn't you say anything? How could you stay with him? Why didn't you just tell the cops?'

Mrs Lothum looked even uglier when she cried. I wondered what Dad'd call her if he could see her grey face scrunched up and wet with tears. Maybe Davros from *Dr Who*. But he probably wouldn't call her anything. He'd probably just feel sorry for her like he did the Andersons' dog, Buffy, when two of its legs were broken and bent up in slings.

'All right, just tell me what happened. Please.' Mum put her hand on Mrs Lothum's shoulder, then seemed unsure and took it away again. 'He wasn't always bad, was he? He wasn't what you'd call a talker, but I had some okay conversations with him. Had a chat about fishing once. We used to all meet up at the pub, remember? What happened? Why'd he do it?'

'Why?' Mrs Lothum reached for a tissue and blew her nose loudly. 'Why?'

I jumped up and crossed the room, trying to think how to get out of there. I didn't want to hear about Mr Lothum. I hated him. I didn't care *why* he did it. He was obviously a nutcase. All that mattered was that he did it and that now he was locked up.

'I'm thirsty. Can I buy a coke?' I asked.

'There's a water cooler in the corridor just outside the door,' Mum said.

'The picnic.' Mrs Lothum twisted her mouth into a half smile. 'Everything comes back to the picnic.'

Chapter Thirty-Three

WHEN I SHUFFLED BACK INTO THE ROOM HOLDING A FOAM CUP, MRS Lothum was staring straight up at the ceiling, saying nothing. Her mouth was drooped in an upside-down smile. I wondered if she'd fallen asleep with her eyes open. I only knew she wasn't dead because her breathing was so loud.

Mum patted my knee as I sat down, and I noticed she was wearing her wedding ring again. The fake diamond glistened under the bright hospital light. I could taste dust in my water, but I drank it anyway.

'Robbie Barrett. I can still see him, clear as day, in his grey school shorts.' Mrs Lothum didn't turn her head to look at us, to check that Mum was nodding or to catch her rolling her eyes.

'Erm, Shirley, what's Robbie got to do with James?' Mum asked, chewing her little finger.

But it was as if we weren't there.

'He chose Nell, not me. Nell. Accident or not, Nell was the one who got to have his baby.' She glanced at me, her eyes red and sore-looking, then back at the cobwebs on the ceiling.

'We get the idea, Shirley. Can we move on to James now?' Mum said.

'Gracie was born, I got over him. I got over *Robbie*. Life went on until,' Mrs Lothum paused.

'The River Picnic,' I said. 'Everyone ate magic mushroom soup. Mrs Irwin told me.'

'Oh, she did, did she?' Mum frowned. 'I thought you couldn't stand her. When did you two talk?'

'The other day. After Mr Lothum was arrested. I just asked her.'

Outside somewhere a siren screamed – police car, fire engine or ambulance, I never could tell the difference. It made me feel like I was back there at the picnic in the middle of all the madness.

'A disturbing number of babies,' Mrs Lothum continued. 'So very disturbing.'

'The River Children,' I said, hoping Mrs Lothum wouldn't go into any more detail, especially not with Mum around.

'One of them was mine.'

'Yes,' I said. 'Sebastian. Same name as – your kitten.'

'One and a half bowls of soup.' Mrs Lothum was speaking again as if we weren't there. 'And I ended up with *him*.'

I winced at the thought of Mrs Lothum *ending up with* Mr Lothum.

'Hey, another siren,' Mum said. 'What's going on out there?'

Mrs Lothum didn't seem to hear anything. 'All that acne at twenty-four, and shy as a mouse. But my parents: "Shirley," they said, "you do the right thing – you marry that man".'

Mrs Lothum mumbled something about not loving Mr Lothum but being prepared to make it work, willing to do anything for 'our baby, our little Sebastian'.

I tried to picture Mrs Lothum as a mum, boring her poor baby to sleep with her non-stop talk.

Mrs Lothum took a deep breath. 'He'd just got his third little tooth when he died. Cot death, they said. But they were wrong! It was the steelworks. The steelworks killed him!'

'What are you talking about, Shirley?' Mum asked.

'Remember our old place next door to the steelworks? On windy days the washing'd turn black. Pollution. It was the steelworks that killed him.'

Mum sighed. 'What medication have they got you on, Shirl?'

'Black as charcoal: all those little nappies and teeny tiny singlets,' Mrs Lothum said.

'And you told the cops this?' Mum asked. I couldn't tell if she believed what Mrs Lothum was saying.

Mrs Lothum laughed, but her face stayed sad. 'Coongahoola would die without its blessed steelworks.'

'Couldn't you have had another baby?' I hoped it wasn't a bad thing to ask.

Mrs Lothum reached for her glass of water, took a sip and swallowed loudly. It was a bad thing to ask, I knew, when I noticed shiny wet patches under her eyes. Somewhere in the hospital, people were yelling, shoes were squeaking, doors were swinging open and closed.

'I've never forgotten my son,' Mrs Lothum said in a soft, sad voice.

Just then the door to her room swung open and a nurse with long, blonde curly hair rushed through with an armful of sheets.

''Scuse us, Mrs Lothum.' She threw the sheets onto one of the empty beds. 'I think you're going to have company.'

'Something to do with all the sirens? What's going on out there?' Mum asked.

'Well, I'm not s'posed to say anything that'll cause her any stress.' The nurse nodded at Mrs Lothum. 'But I've got a strong feeling we'll be using this room, so what can we do, cover her head with a pillow? There's a fire, ladies. A big one. Those Christian people – Believers, Bleeders, whatever you care to call them – their camp is on fire.'

Chapter Thirty-Four

'NO ONE KNOWS HOW MANY PEOPLE ARE OUT THERE. COULD BE FIVE, could be fifty,' the blonde nurse said, tucking in a bed sheet with *Coongahoola Community Hospital* written along the edge. She said that both ambulances were on their way to the camp.

Heavenly! I thought. God, poor Heavenly.

'But, but what happened?' Mum asked.

'Who knows? Can't say it surprises me. Wouldn't surprise me if a bomb went off on Main Road. If aliens landed in the middle of Woolies, I wouldn't even blink. As soon as I've got the money, I'm gone. We came here two years back when my man got a job at the steelworks...'

She kept talking but I stopped listening. A big fire in Coongahoola! I shivered, remembering Heavenly telling me about bonfire night, how 'Father' always looked for 'sinful material' to burn. Could that have anything to do with this?

We'd had fires before. A few houses'd burnt down, and old Mr Buckley lost most of his shed while barbequing chicken sausages, but nothing big like this. Coongahoola'd be on TV again. What would the world think of our town now?

I watched as the nurse lifted the mattress and tucked in the sheet, folding the corner in perfect straight lines. Mum never bothered to lift my mattress when she helped me make my bed. She didn't even move the bed away from the wall like Grandma Bett did. It probably explained why the sheet always came untucked as soon as I lay on it, and why the first thing I saw every morning was the dirty blue and white stripes of my lumpy old mattress.

'I'll be out of your hair now,' the blonde nurse was saying. 'You all right, love?'

'Love? You all right?'

Mrs Lothum jerked like you do when you fall downstairs in your dream, then she said a tired ,'All right'. A rope of red hair hung over her nose. She didn't seem any more stressed than before, but maybe she'd reached the maximum level.

'I'll be back in a bit,' the nurse said as she left.

'You're worried about – the saint?' Mrs Lothum asked Mum, brushing something invisible off her bedspread.

'Bede? No. Not at all. To be honest, he's a part of my life I'm trying to forget.'

'I wanted *him* to get the blame.' Mrs Lothum's voice was cold.

Mum touched her wedding ring, then twisted it round and round. 'Turned out he wasn't such a nice person. *Saint* Bede – ha! He certainly wasn't a saint. I wouldn't trust him – but I wouldn't put him down as a murderer.'

'But that makes me bad, bad, bad, bad.' Mrs Lothum rubbed her eyes. 'Especially when he and you were–'

'We were doing very little actually, Shirley. But this isn't about me. Can we get back to James? I still don't understand. People lose kids every day. It must be bloody awful, but they deal with it – eventually. *You* dealt with it.'

When Mrs Lothum coughed, her whole body coughed and I thought she was about to drop dead. She gulped the rest of her water and held up her glass for me, I guessed, to refill.

Standing next to her bed, handing back her glass of water, I got a whiff of something so horrible it reminded me of opening Dad's fridge when he lived with Gary. When I realised it was Mrs Lothum's breath, I stepped back. No wonder she looked so bad. She smelt off, like a forgotten carton of milk.

'So sad, so lost.' Mrs Lothum's shaky hand dropped her glass down on the bedside table, spilling a bit of water. 'Always talking, talking and singing to a baby who'd been buried years ago. Slept in the baby's room, even when we moved house, just set up the room as if Sebastian was still with us. He doesn't have much of a voice – don't suppose that matters when you're singing to an empty cot.' Mrs Lothum's throat made another horrible noise, and then she sang, 'Three blind mice, three blind mice, see how they run, see–'

'Don't,' I said. 'Please stop.' My stomach tightened. I felt like throwing up.

'I suppose I don't have much of a voice either,' Mrs Lothum said. 'Ha! So James and I do have something in common.'

Mum squeezed my hand. 'I'm sorry you have to listen to this, pet. But we need to know. We need to know why. Please keep going, Shirley. But perhaps without the singing.'

'I know where it comes from. The madness. His mum. When James was around fifteen, she fed him nothing but peas for a month. Peas! Breakfast, lunch and dinner.'

Mum stood, her face red and her jaw clenched. 'Okay, so he was messed up. Come on, Shirley, who isn't? What about Gerald Buckley? Ken Sanders? Saint Bede! And most of the Believers? Jesus, I'm hardly an advertisement for sanity! Thing is, the picnic was years ago, Sebastian died years ago.

'What made James decide to start taking the lives of innocent children last year? You can't blame that on peas! You lived with him. You protected him. You must've asked him something.'

Mrs Lothum stared at Mum as if she couldn't understand English.

'What made him do it, Shirley?' Mum demanded, her clenched fists digging into her narrow hips.

'He said he opened the door on that Halloween night.' Mrs

Lothum took a deep breath. 'He saw the boy, chocolate smeared on his face, a River Child just like our Sebastian, standing where our boy should've stood–'

'So, so he just – on the doorstep?' Mum'd kicked off her shoes and was walking around the room in black-stockinged feet.

'Something in him just broke.' Mrs Lothum was staring at the ceiling. 'Peas. Nothing but peas. See what happens when you eat your greens.'

'Okay, and I heard you found out after Michael Sanders? How'd you find out?' Mum looked ready to punch someone – probably Mrs Lothum if she didn't already look nearly dead.

'Tomato sauce,' Mrs Lothum whispered.

'Tomato bloody sauce?'

'Slopped tomato sauce all over his – soiled shirt, then chucked it in the washing basket.' Mrs Lothum's whole body seemed to be shaking.

'Okay. And you'd washed tomato sauce-soaked shirts before without asking questions?'

Mrs Lothum shook her head and tucked her pale pink arms back under the bedspread. 'The Sanders boy. He was the one who – put up a fight.'

'God Almighty,' Mum said, squeezing her eyes shut.

The only way I could listen was by pretending it wasn't real, that this wasn't a real person Mrs Lothum was talking about. That this was a made-up kid, not *Michael*. Poor, poor Michael.

'Sauce washed off in cold water but then there was blood, soaked deep into the flannelette, and I asked him where he'd gone in his Blundstones the night before – I'd heard them clomping along the hallway, see, I'm not completely stupid – and he just stared at me.

'I said, did you kill that little boy, and he nodded and I fell on my knees and he said, "please move out of the way of the television, I want to see the weather forecast for tomorrow".'

Mrs Lothum took a breath, tears streaming down her face. 'I

screamed at him. I screamed, promise me, you've got to promise me you won't do it again, but he just took off his hat – that damned Akubra...'

Mrs Lothum didn't finish what she was saying – she was crying too hard. I wished she'd blow her nose but if I passed her a tissue I'd risk getting her nervous breakdown germs. I looked away, down at my sneakers, at the bit of rubber coming off the toe. The room was quiet except for the sounds of Mum and Mrs Lothum crying. Tears slid down my cheeks.

Mrs Lothum started talking again, but I let the words drift away. I'd heard enough. Then there was another siren. Two sirens, wailing louder and louder. The blonde nurse poked her head into the room, saw Mum and Mrs Lothum's faces, then looked at me.

'Um, hate to interrupt, but the patients will be here soon and I don't think you'll want to be around when we get them inside,' she said.

Mum tore a tissue out of the box and blew her nose with a honk. 'Time to leave, anyway. Pass me my bag, Gracie.'

'I haven't had tomato sauce since,' Mrs Lothum said in a wobbly voice. 'I'll never be able to eat tomato sauce without–'

Mum dug around inside her bag.

'Nell?' Mrs Lothum sounded like she was going to start bawling again.

Mum pulled out her keys and snapped her bag shut. 'I'll come again. In a couple of days. You take care of yourself.'

We ran down the corridor, Mum's keys jiggling and our shoes squeaking like Elijah's and mine used to when the hospital was our playground. We smelt the smoke as soon as we reached the car park, and we covered our mouths with our hands to keep from swallowing it. Seeing smoke wasn't new. It normally sat in a cloud above the steelworks on the other side of town. But this smoke was black, and it covered the sky like a blanket.

'Forgive us our trespasses and lead us not into temptation, forgive us our trespasses and lead us not...' a voice was screaming over and over. It was a man's, I think, and it came from the stretcher being wheeled out of the ambulance.

'Don't look!' Mum whispered. I kept my eyes fixed on the ground. A Red Skin wrapper blew across the tarmac and I wondered if the man on the stretcher'd dropped it, if he'd been enjoying eating a Red Skin before the fire came along and ruined everything.

As we drove out of the car park, Dr Bryce sped past in his silver car. Mum turned on the windscreen wipers to sweep away the pieces of ash that floated onto the glass. We drove home without saying a word.

CHAPTER THIRTY-FIVE

As the front door creaked open and we stepped into the warmth, it felt just like a normal day. One of Lucky's yellow duck gumboots stood on the scratchy brown mat, the other lay halfway along the hall with a pile of half-chewed jigsaw puzzle pieces. We followed the sound of the twins blabbing away, and the smell of rissoles cooking, to the kitchen.

'Oh! It's you two.' Grandma Bett glanced at us as she reached into the cupboard and pulled out a bottle of tomato sauce.

Tomato sauce. I looked away.

'I want Daddy!' Lucky cried. She and Grub sat at the table, Grub swinging his fat legs and Lucky swinging her skinny ones.

'Good to see you lot too.' Mum dropped her handbag on the table and scooped up a handful of squashed-looking beans from Lucky's plate. 'I guess you know about the fire? It's madness out there.' She shoved the beans into her mouth.

'Of course, love. It's awful, and I'm relieved you're home. It can't have been an easy drive. I was just – hoping it was Robbie.' The sauce bottle went 'blop' and a big dollop of red blobbed onto Grub's plate, drowning his mashed potato.

James slopped tomato sauce all over them. I shook my head, tried to shake the thought away.

'I don't suppose you know that he went to help?' Grandma Bett asked.

'Help?'

'With the fire.'

Mum stopped chewing. 'You're kidding! When'd he go?'

'Oh, a couple of hours ago, maybe more. Called to say he was going straight from work. I'm sure he'll be here soon.' Grandma Bett reached into the fridge.

'Must be plenty of help there already. Been hearing sirens all afternoon.'

'Certainly. Robbie's probably just offering moral support. What does he know about fires?' She pulled out an opened tin of pears.

'Enough to keep his fags alight twenty-four hours a day,' Mum said.

'And firecrackers too, when he was a lad. Those dreadful ones that go *screeeeeech bang!* – Thumbelinas or something.' Grandma Bett sniffed the pears and pulled a face.

'Tom Thumbs? No, they're just little ones. I think it's rockets you're thinking of. That's right, he planted some in the school incinerator. Nearly took Mr Jamison's head off,' Mum said, kicking her shoes off under the table.

'Oh Nell! The strife he used to get into … Gracie, what's wrong? You look a little bit pale. Sit down. I'll get your tea off the stove.'

'Don't want any, thanks.'

'Rubbish, child! You need your tea. Oh, almost forgot – how was Shirley?'

Mum rolled her eyes. 'A mess. Admitted turning a blind eye to him. Didn't want to be known as the "monster's wife", afraid of losing everyone. Only reason I can forgive her is she's a complete wreck. Let's talk about it later – did my head in today.'

I ate some watery beans and carrots, but couldn't face the rissole. I felt queasy at the thought of dousing it in tomato sauce. Besides, it was still pink and squishy inside. Grandma Bett must've decided there was enough fire in Coongahoola already without risking burning our tea. I didn't say anything though. I knew she was worried about Dad. When she and Mum were putting the twins to bed, she sang their bedtime *Amazing Grace* so softly that I could hardly hear her 'saved a soul like meeeee' over the tick of the Virgin Mary clock. Normally I could hear it in the secret room, even with cotton wool stuffed in both ears.

Outside the living room window, the sky was dark and foggy. A few pieces of ash floated down like dirty snow. How unlucky is Heavenly, I was thinking. Her dad's only just out of jail and now their camp's on fire. If I was her, I would've gone nuts years ago – the moment Saint Bede started burning books. She was obviously a stronger person than me. I was too weak even to talk to her at school, in case someone saw me. People'd been saying I was a hero – about catching Mr Lothum and everything – but really, when I thought about it, I was pretty gutless.

I was still staring out the window when Grandma Bett came in with the shiny silver biscuit tin under her arm. The biscuits were only for special occasions. Grandma Bett kept them hidden in her room so Grub couldn't find them. She slid the tin across the coffee table to me. Did the Believers' camp burning down count as a special occasion? I took an oval biscuit with pink cream in the middle, but its sickening sweet smell made me think of the Red Skin wrapper in the hospital car park and I suddenly felt like puking.

I was sneaking the biscuit back into the tin when Mum ran in, Dad's little radio in her hand and her wet hair dripping onto her bathrobe. 'News!' She placed the radio on the table and turned up the volume.

It was the same old voice that'd been delivering bad news for as long as I could remember.

'...still struggling to contain the blaze on the bank of the Bagooli River which started at around two o'clock this afternoon. The number of people hospitalised has reached four, with three others confirmed dead. The cause of the fire is yet to be determined, and police are urging motorists to stay away from River Road.'

251

Dead? People were dying! Not Heavenly, *please*.

'Oh my God! It's bad. Really bad!' Mum's hair drip, drip, dripped onto the kitchen table. 'How typical – James is finally locked up, then a bloody fire rips through the town and wipes out everyone else. Bett – what are you doing under the table?'

Grandma Bett opened her eyes. 'Talking to our Lord. It may be too late for some, but I'm praying for their families, and for the casualties, and anyone else in danger.'

Mum tapped her fingers on the coffee table, waiting for Grandma Bett's lips to stop moving. 'So who'd he go with?'

'Just a moment.' Grandma Bett crossed herself and sat back up in her chair, smoothing down her long grey skirt. 'Derek and Gary and a few others, I think. Frank told them they could take the afternoon off if they were prepared to help out.'

'Did they have proper equipment?'

'Not sure, love.'

'Because firemen wear special fireproof clothes, you know.'

'Yes. Actually Robbie's Uncle Terry was–'

'And those overalls of Robbie's – he might as well be wearing nothing. Oh God!'

'What? What is it?'

'Was he wearing his flanny this morning? I can't remember. God, you know what they say about flannelette!'

'Highly flammable, but surely he'd–'

'Bett, it goes up in a flash!' The way Mum threw her hands in the air you'd think wearing a flannelette shirt was like wearing a bomb. 'Jeez, I've no idea what he was wearing this morning.'

'Nell, please sit down. I'll put the kettle on.'

'He had the blue chequered shirt on.' I remembered him at the table crushing up his Weetbix with a fork before drowning them in milk and sugar. He'd made funny faces at the twins, making them laugh until Lucky wet her new heart undies (then Grub laughed harder, but Lucky started blubbing).

'Bloody hell!' Mum said.

'Nell, he'd know, others'd know, not to wear a flannelette shirt near a fire. Besides, he's probably just filling buckets, wetting towels, that kind of thing. Rolling his dreadful cigarettes. You know our Robbie, he's more of a spectator.'

'Yeah, I s'pose, but God, I don't know.' She stood up, frowning. 'I need a drink!'

I heard wine dribbling into a glass, wine from the box that lived on the top shelf of our fridge. Mum came back holding her *Coongahoola Central School, Form 4, 1969* wine glass with both hands as if it was the most precious thing in the world. She drank it quickly, returned to the kitchen and trickled more wine into it.

'What good will that do?' I asked. Mum's glass was filled to the top and she walked slowly so she didn't waste any on the carpet.

'It's helping me relax!' she snapped, before gulping down half the glass in one mouthful. 'What business is it of yours anyway?'

'It's not my business,' I said carefully. 'It's just that you always say you need a drink when something's wrong.'

'And?' Mum took another sip. 'So?'

'So – it never makes things better.'

'It doesn't? How do you know? How do you know how a drink makes me feel?'

'Because mostly it just makes you even more angry. Or cry.'

'What are you on about?' Mum said, but she sounded more surprised than annoyed. She was looking at the glass like there was something wrong with it.

'And what if Dad needs you?' I asked. 'To pick him up or something.'

Mum was quiet for a while. 'You're probably right, it won't help, not really.' She walked over to the dining room table and, with a big splash, emptied the wine into the vase of dying flowers.

'Well, I suppose the gum blossoms do look a bit thirsty,' Grandma Bett said. 'Good decision, Nell. There are other ways of dealing with your worries.'

'Hmm, maybe I should call Stewy. See what's going on.'

'I think he'll be rather busy, don't you? I'm worried too, but we're not helping anyone. What about Gracie? Poor girl's been through quite a lot today.'

'I'm all right.'

'Sorry, pet,' Mum said. 'You're a good kid. And all that stuff Mrs Lothum came out with this morning – enough to give you nightmares for years! Ignore me. Your dad'll be fine.'

'He had a T-shirt on too. The purpley one, Manly Sea Eagles,' I said. 'Would that burn?'

Mum and Grandma Bett looked at each other. 'Perhaps you should watch the television,' Grandma Bett suggested. 'Think about something else for a while.'

I tried watching TV but there was only a boring show about platypuses or rugby league, so I sat at the window instead. I pressed my face against the cold, wet glass and stared into the darkness. Mum was walking around the house talking to herself about flannelette, and Grandma Bett'd sunk back onto her knees, this time holding her rosary beads, the special ones that'd been blessed by the Pope. I wasn't worried about Dad dying. He was my dad and somehow I knew he'd be all right. But I felt sad for Heavenly.

'I can't do this,' Mum said, stepping into her shoes. 'I can't wait around doing nothing.'

'He can't be far away,' Grandma Bett said.

'Well, there's no harm in me going to see, is there? Can I take your car?'

'Nell, you can't go!'

'Why not?' Mum picked up Grandma Bett's keys.

'You're all worked up. And you've been drinking! You can't go in this state.'

'But I can't just sit here and you're not my–'

'I'll go!' Grandma Bett said. 'I'll go and see what's going on, then I'll come back and tell you. You having an accident is the last thing this family needs.'

Mum thought for a moment. 'Straight back? Without popping into the church on your way past?'

'Yes, Nell,' Grandma Bett said. 'As soon as I've seen Robbie. My keys, please.'

CHAPTER THIRTY-SIX

GRANDMA BETT'D BEEN GONE FOR NEARLY TWO HOURS – AND MUM'D called her all sorts of names – when the front door clicked opened. I jumped, and Mum must've too because her *New Idea* dropped onto the carpet.

'Robbie!' Mum cried.

'Dad!' I said.

Dad's face, arms, T-shirt and overalls were smeared with black. His flannelette shirt was stuffed under his arm, still clean and blue. He smelt like a barbecue.

'Youse all okay?' he asked. He wasn't smiling.

'Of course,' Mum said. 'Now that *you're* here.'

'Yeah? Well, it's not all roses.' Dad flung his shirt onto the back of a chair.

'What do you mean?'

'I mean, fat lot of good I was. Got him out, but it was probably about twenty minutes too late.'

'Who?'

'Whats-is-name – Bede.'

'Saint Bede.'

Dad looked at Mum, at the tears sliding down her face. 'I'm sorry, Nell. It's fuckin' mental. I've never seen anything like it. It's like... It's like hell. It's still blazin' like – blazin' like fuck. I just I did my best and then I got the hell out.'

'I'm not crying for him, you silly man.'

'Nah? Well you should be. He's – deceased. I know it for a fact. Hate to be the one to break it to you.'

'Robbie, I'm crying for you!'

For a few moments, it was like in the movies when the mum cries and the dad hugs her and you know that everything's going to be all right. I could've watched them forever, standing there hugging and crying and getting black stuff from the fire all over each other. But then Mum pulled away from Dad and said, 'Where's your mother?'

'Mum?' Dad looked around the room as if she might be sitting in a chair in her dressing gown and slippers reading the Bible.

'She follow you back?' Mum asked.

'What d'you mean?'

'Well, she went to the – she went to find you. Because I–'

Mum fell to her knees. 'Oh no!'

CHAPTER THIRTY-SEVEN

EVEN THOUGH DAD TOLD MUM SHE WAS OVERREACTING, I THINK WE ALL knew then that something'd happened to Grandma Bett. I thought of her on her knees under the table before she'd left, praying for everyone in Coongahoola. Everyone except herself.

'I'll go back,' Dad said. 'Can't see for shit out there. Maybe she pulled over.'

'No, Robbie. You're not going back.'

'She was looking for *me*. How can I hang around here and wait?'

'Call Constable Stewy. He might've seen her.'

'God, I hope so,' Dad said.

'Stewy's not there,' he said a minute later after slamming the phone down. 'Some young cop from Sydney's answering the phones. The kid's clueless. Sounded twelve years old. I've gotta go!'

'I know,' Mum said, her eyes and nose running.

'I won't get close, promise.'

'You'd better not.'

'I'm just going to bring your grandma back, okay?' He turned to me and raised his fingers in a Scout's Honour salute.

I nodded but the tears flowed anyway. I couldn't believe what was happening. When would life become normal again?

'For Christ's sake, don't give her that Scout's Honour bullshit!' Mum said. 'Just go! And make sure you bloody well come back.'

'It's all my fault,' she said when he'd gone. 'My own bloody fault.' She disappeared into the kitchen and I heard the fridge opening and the wine cask pouring. But this time it was dribbling into the sink. I heard water splashing out of the tap and washing the wine away.

When Dad came home, Mum and I were staring at the test pattern on the TV. I was still sitting in the same spot on the couch as I was when he left. I don't know what time it was, or how long he'd been gone. His face was streaked white where the tears had run down his sooty cheeks. He opened his mouth to speak, but no words came out.

CHAPTER THIRTY-EIGHT

ANDY HALL'D SPOTTED GRANDMA BETT DOUBLED OVER A FEW METRES from where her little blue Hillman was parked on River Road. She'd died from breathing in too much smoke. It was probably better than being killed by the fire, but it seemed so unfair since she'd never smoked a cigarette in her life. They reckon she'd only just got out of her car, which means Mum and I must've been the last people to see her alive.

There was more bad news. The other seven people who died were Believers who'd still lived at the camp, including Saint Bede and Bethany. And Heavenly.

Everyone said the fire was lit on purpose, but no one'd been caught and Constable Stewy looked down, probably at the reflection of his own worried face in his shiny black boots, when a TV reporter asked him if the police had any leads.

'The Catholics are saying that the Virgin Mary did it. Y'know, that spooky statue of theirs,' Dad told us. 'She'd had a gutsful of the lot of them and set their caravans on fire with her blazin' eyes.'

But he didn't believe that – none of us did. We couldn't believe that the Virgin Mary was responsible for what happened to Grandma Bett. Other people said the fire was started by the Believers who'd turned against Saint Bede. Mum said there was even a theory that Heavenly did it – that her dad'd finally pushed her over the edge. But Dad reckoned Saint Bede'd lit it himself: 'He lost the plot and took them all down with him.'

I didn't know what to think. I had trouble comprehending the fact that I'd never again see Grandma Bett sitting at the kitchen table or rushing off to church. And that Saint Bede and Bethany and Heavenly also no longer existed. Nothing made sense. I didn't like the thought of Heavenly being driven to do something so awful, but was that better than having had someone else do it to her? Her own dad? I couldn't decide. I tried to tell myself that it was just an accident – a bonfire gone tragically wrong. What did it matter now, anyway? They were all dead.

Dad ended up on the *ABC News* as well as in *The Coongahoola Times* and *People* magazine. The firemen'd been busy searching empty caravans when Dad arrived at the fire. They didn't know which ones belonged to who. Dad knew which caravan was Saint Bede's, though. He confessed to us that he'd visited the camp before, that he'd found out exactly where he lived. He'd been angry with Saint Bede for trying to steal Mum, and wanted to do – or at least say – something to Saint Bede, but never got up the courage. Even though Dad was too late to save him, everyone said he was going to get a bravery award for risking his life trying.

'First you get a trophy and now your old man's up for an award,' Mr Irwin teased, trying to make me smile. 'Who's doing what to the mayor is what I want to know.'

In those first few days after the fire, it felt like the world had ended. It looked like it too. The fire'd swallowed all the gum trees, leaving only black stumps sticking out of the ground like old Mr Buckley's rotten teeth – right along the river almost to Amanda Ferguson's. It made the whole town stink. I held one of Grandma Bett's hankies over my mouth when I was outside, trying not to breathe the air because I was scared of what I might inhale. The fire'd stopped burning and the remains of the Believers'd long been taken away, but I couldn't help wondering what was in the air that made it so thick and suffocating.

I was surprised that life went on, that the sun shone through the smoke and people drove out of their driveways and went about their usual business. I was surprised, not because of what the fire'd done to the town, but because Grandma Bett'd died. It didn't seem right that people were acting like it was just another week.

Grandma Bett was the first person in our family who'd died. Grandad was dead, but he'd died before I was born, so I didn't really know what to feel about him. Mum'd never even met him, and all Dad ever said was that he was 'a top bloke', and Grandma Bett could never speak his name (Samuel) without her chin going wobbly and her eyes filling up. In fact, the only person who ever told me about my grandad was Mrs Lothum. I asked her about him once when I was at the Post Office.

'Oh, he was a charming man,' she said, as she slapped a stamp onto a big brown envelope. 'Your dad worshipped him, was never quite the same happy-go-lucky fellow after he died. And it was obvious your gran loved him dearly. Except for–'

'Except for what?' There were eight photos of him on Grandma Bett's dressing table and only six pictures of Jesus and two of Pope John Paul II. I couldn't imagine her not liking anything about him.

'His language. It wasn't his fault. He was in the war so you can't blame him for saying a few obscenities. But it was the blasphemy she objected to the most, or so your mother told me. You know, the *Oh my Gods* and the *Christ Almightys*. Your gran thinks that's what killed him.'

'But – she told me he slipped off the roof.'

'Yes, he did. But he slipped *after* saying "Jesus Christ!" *After* catching his trousers on a tile. I'm sure there's nothing to it. Most people think it's rubbish but still, you won't hear many people in Coongahoola saying "Jesus Christ" for that very reason.'

It was true. I'd never heard anyone say *Jesus Christ* (although I'd heard plenty of *God Almighty's* and *For Christ's Sake's* which were surely just as bad) and I'd never been brave enough to say it either. But for me it was always the thought of Grandma Bett dragging me to confession that stopped me, rather than the thought of dropping down dead.

I DON'T KNOW WHAT Father Scott said to Mum as he sat at our kitchen table with watery red eyes drinking milky tea out of Grandma Bett's St Francis of Assisi mug, but she stopped crying, changed out of her nightie and dressing gown, and started writing lists of what needed to be done.

Dad even helped, calling Grandma Bett's cousins in Canberra and Yass, and poking his head into the secret room to give me a list.

My jobs were to write a eulogy for the funeral, answer the phone, and take the flowers or cakes or casseroles or prayers or rosary beads from the people who came to the door.

Even though I can remember all the other funerals we went to that year and the year before, Grandma Bett's is a blur. I suppose it's because I watched hers through tears. I can only think of snippets.

Watching Mum and Dad and Gary and Mr Irwin carrying Grandma Bett's coffin down the aisle as we stumbled over the words to 'Sons of God', Grandma Bett's favourite hymn. The coffin was huge, making Grandma Bett seem much bigger than she really was. It was made of pine, and painted faux-mahogany with brass edging. Stan, the funeral director, had helped us choose it from a thick catalogue of coffins. The four of them gently set it down on a metal stand. It was so close to where I sat I could've reached out and touched it.

Kids sneaking looks at me on their way back from communion, and me thinking, It's my turn now, I'm the person who's lost someone in my family. This is what it feels like, and it feels awful. It felt awful because, even though it was Grandma Bett's funeral, I expected her to be sitting next to me, saying 'Hush', and 'Turn around', and singing the hymns louder than anyone else – especially since they were her favourites.

Father Scott talking into his microphone in a quavery voice, and when he returned to the altar after communion, me noticing that his black trousers had the shape of an iron burnt into them.

During his eulogy, he'd asked us to try to think of an occasion when Bett had put herself before anyone else. I couldn't.

I can't remember reading my eulogy, but the other day I found what I'd written tucked inside the children's picture Bible Grandma Bett gave me when I was six:

I've known Grandma Bett since the day I was born. Mum said that in the first few days of my life, Grandma Bett was the only one who could change my nappy without accidentally stabbing me with the pin, and that one time she sat up with me all night when I was vomiting and by morning she was vomiting too, but she still sat in the chair by my bed, wiping my forehead with a cold washcloth.

Even though she was strict and didn't let us watch anything rated AO, she was the kindest person I've known, and the second holiest after Father Scott. She went to mass three times every week, cleaned the church and read Father Scott's sermons to make sure they made sense. She prayed all the time – even during her favourite TV shows if she had to. She never said a rude word and hardly ever yelled. She shouldn't have died. But she has, so I just want to say goodbye from me and Elijah who, after Uncle Boyd convinced Mum, is now staying in Queensland till he finishes his end-of-term tests, and Grub and Lucky who won't go to sleep at night anymore because she's not here to sing Amazing Grace to them.

She was the best grandma ever. Without her my family wouldn't still be together – Dad'd be sitting with Gary and Mr Irwin or worse, a lady, and Mum'd probably be sitting on her own, possibly even drunk.

So thanks Grandma Bett and goodbye from your loving granddaughter. I hope that heaven is nice and God makes you a saint.

We walked to the cemetery after the funeral. I didn't notice who came with us but we were surrounded by people, some of them crying loudly, and Father Scott said a few more prayers. As Grandma Bett was lowered into a dark hole, I felt that part of me was being put there with her. Mum and Dad and I threw some pink roses onto the coffin and I wondered if I'd ever run out of tears.

The last rose I threw in was for Heavenly. I said a prayer for her in my head, asking God to take care of her and to tell her, if possible, that I was sorry for being such a bad friend. I couldn't go to her funeral – she and her parents were being buried at another Believers' camp in Newcastle – so this was a chance to say goodbye via Grandma Bett. I didn't think Grandma Bett'd mind. Heavenly was a Believer, but it's not like she'd been given a choice, and if anyone could forgive her, it'd be Grandma Bett.

At the wake, I just stood there and let peoples' lips brush my cheek and their hands squeeze me. I heard them whisper that they were very sorry and felt them pat me on the back. I was like a rag doll.

'Never mind that strange little man with the glasses, your grandmother was Coongahoola's true saint,' Mrs Buchen said, between bites of her ginger kiss.

Shelley asked if I wanted to hang out at her place one afternoon soon, but I shook my head. I didn't even have the energy to think up an excuse. Baby Pete asked me to come to his place too, and I thought that might be okay because his mum'd died. I wanted to ask him about that, and how long it took him to feel normal again.

Even after the wake, the day wouldn't end. The Irwins, Andersons, Wilsons, Mrs Jones and I forget who else followed us to our house, still talking about the time Grandma Bett gave them a cutting from her garden or went to the chemist to pick up their prescription. Mum and Dad'd stopped talking long before then – they were just nodding and smiling sad, tired smiles.

I don't know how long I'd been sitting in the brown beanbag, staring at the bookshelf, when I realised that Toby was kneeling on the carpet next to me.

'It's shit what happened,' he said, when our eyes met. 'Your granny was a top lady.'

'Yeah. Thanks.' I was sick of saying thanks. I was sick of people saying sorry. But I knew there wasn't much else to say.

After a minute or so of neither of us speaking, Toby said, 'You should come over again sometime.'

'To your place?'

'Yeah. If you want. I'd make sure Mum was out of the way.' Toby pulled at the fraying thread in the knee of his acid-wash jeans.

'What about Shelley?'

'Shelley? You want me to ask her as well?'

'No. I just thought that you two were, um, I saw you two near the tuck shop. Together. That's why I took your notebook, remember?'

'*Stole* my *artwork*, you mean,' Toby said, but he was smiling. 'I remember, but I was only asking her something. That's all. I don't like her.'

'Oh.' I thought back to that day, seeing them standing there, together. 'You were looking at me, though. Both of you.'

'We were? Well, that's 'cause we're dumb. And, also 'cause I was asking her something about – you.'

My heart lurched. 'What?'

'Um.' Toby sighed, and fiddled with his shoelaces. He had a navy blue shirt on and looked really nice, a bit like an angel with his curly hair. 'I was sorry for being a dickhead at Elijah's party. I was just asking her what to do about it.'

'Oh, what'd she say?'

'Not much. She said she doesn't know you very well anymore.'

It was true, probably truer than Shelley realised. 'Okay. I probably will, then – come over sometime.'

'Great. Um, can I just show you something?'

For a moment I thought he was expecting me to go somewhere right then, and I was about to say no. This was Grandma Bett's wake. I was staying home, no matter what. But Toby shuffled over and held up something he'd been concealing under his knees.

266

An art pad. He thumbed through the pages then handed it to me, licking his lips nervously.

It was a drawing, of course. In black ink this time, not pencil. I recognised the face – it was the girl from his notebook. Toby was obviously very talented. This drawing was amazing, so much better than the pencil versions, but – then I saw it. She had *my* eyes. *My* hair. *My* lips. My lips are a bit too thin if you ask me, but Toby'd recreated them perfectly. The girl *was* me. And I actually looked – almost beautiful. I had to concentrate hard to keep my eyes from watering.

'I was pissed off that you stole my book,' Toby said as I handed the pad back to him. 'But only 'cause they were just rough sketches. It took me heaps of practice to get – to get you *right*.'

I nodded, but couldn't think of anything to say. I didn't know what to think. Toby was a brilliant artist. *And* his subject was me. But Grandma Bett was dead, and that changed everything. I couldn't let myself feel anything but grief. It wouldn't be right.

'Okay, then, um, I'll see ya round, Gracie.' Toby leapt up, and practically ran out of the room. I think he was embarrassed. I hadn't said anything, not even thank you.

'Bye, Toby,' I whispered as I heard the screen door close behind him.

I'd thank him another time. I'd tell him that the drawing was brilliant and I loved it. But not today. Today my thoughts were with Grandma Bett. I was tired and my eyes were sore from so much crying. I stood up, feeling a bit spaced out. I'd hardly slept since before the night of the fire. I wanted to escape everyone, but didn't feel like sitting in the secret room with Lucky and Grub. Instead, I went and opened the door to Grandma Bett's room and crept inside. Everything was just how she'd left it, and as I lay on her bed, smelling her smell from the blue cardigan I found folded on her chair, I pretended she was still with us.

CHAPTER THIRTY-NINE

EVEN WHEN WE WERE DRIVING OUT OF COONGAHOOLA, PAST ALL THE boring shops selling sinks and tiles, it still hadn't hit me that Elijah was coming home. We'd left our house and all the bunches of dying flowers and were on our way to Sydney. Elijah's plane was landing at 3.40pm, and all six of us were going to sleep in a motel on the way home, but it still didn't seem real.

'Look!' Grub yelled. He'd climbed out of his belt and was kneeling on the seat. 'Cows are fighting!'

I turned to look between the splashes of bird poo on the car window and saw two cows joined together. Both were black-and-white like the little plastic cows in our toy farm set, and it looked like one was giving the other a piggy-back ride. But I knew what they were doing from biology at school. I looked away, my face burning. Mum started giggling like she was about ten years old. I hadn't heard her laugh since before the fire.

'Get 'im! Get 'im!' Grub cried, his brown trousers slipping down to show off his new Felix the Cat undies.

I imagined what'd happen if Grandma Bett was in the car. She'd be kneeling on the floor, down with all the old chip packets, Paddle Pop sticks and Grub's vegemite crusts, whispering Hail Marys for the lot of us.

'See that?' Dad asked, taking a hand off the steering wheel to point at a grey wall standing all by itself on a hill.

'What is it?' Barbed wire snaked along the top of the wall and, even when I stretched my neck, I didn't come close to seeing what was on the other side.

'James Lothum's new digs. Sherlwood Prison.'

Jail! I shivered, thinking of what kind of people were behind that wall. People as bad as Mr Lothum. I was glad it was a long car drive away from our house and it didn't look like an easy place to break out of.

'What about Mrs Lothum?' I asked.

'Ha! She'd have a field day with all those blokes! But nah, they don't take sheilas there,' Dad said.

'It's unlikely that she'll go to jail,' Mum said. 'She was playing bridge the night Nigel went trick or treating; plenty of people of confirmed that. She was in the dark until – Michael. And she's probably suffered enough in her own head.'

Mum'd visited her the day after Grandma Bett's funeral. This time she took the lavender she'd snuck from the Irwins' garden (Toby and I'd busted her from his living room window), a bag of oranges and three Mills & Boons she'd finished reading, but I stayed at home.

'If she does, it won't be for long. God knows what she'll do with herself – poor woman.'

'They'd be doing me a favour locking her up. You know, a bloke can't take his shirt off to mow the lawn, case she gets wind of it and drops by for a perv.'

'Oh, you love it, Robbie! Besides, the only reason she gets wind of it is 'cause your gut's so big, she can see it from her kitchen window.'

We all laughed at that. Well, all of us except Lucky who was asleep with dribble making a slobbery pool on her red skivvy. Dad could make his stomach go round like a balloon when he breathed out, but he wasn't really fat. Not like some of the dads you see with big wobbly white bellies and flabby faces that melt into their necks.

Even though it meant that every woman in Coongahoola would've liked to marry him, I was quite happy with the way Dad looked.

I stared out the window as we drove into a town that a million-year-old sign said was called Bunderga. I recognised things I'd seen on our last trip to the airport. There was a giant old-fashioned clock stuck on the side of a red brick building, still ten minutes slower than my digital watch, and a hairdresser's called *Hair Today* with *Gone Tomorrow* spray-painted in ugly black letters underneath. The place was a bit like Coongahoola but with a whole different lot of people we didn't know. I wondered if this town had a family just like ours, a person just like me.

Then the car jerked and the engine growled as Dad sped up to overtake a slow white van. The van had a big dent in its front and could've even been as old as our car. As we passed, I saw a boy looking at me from the back seat. It was only a few seconds, but long enough to tell he was about my age and good-looking – even better looking than Toby (I'd never admit that to Toby, though) – with spiky blonde hair and a big smile. It was also long enough to see him stick his middle finger up at me.

I was shocked, my nose tingling, ready to cry. How could he be so mean? But before I'd thought, I made a fist and stuck my finger up at him. I pressed it against the window so he could see it clearly.

'Stuff you, white van boy,' I said in my head. The funny thing was, he smiled again, and not in a mean way. He smiled like he thought I was okay for sticking my finger up at him. Maybe he even thought I was pretty cool.

It made me think for a bit: my family wasn't normal, but we were still together, and Mum had said that after a while we'd stop feeling so sad about Grandma Bett. And Elijah was coming home! I looked back at the white van, lost in the grey cloud that followed our car everywhere it went, and even though I couldn't see the boy or his smile any more, I smiled back.

ACKNOWLEDGEMENTS

I COULD WRITE ANOTHER WHOLE BOOK'S WORTH OF ACKNOWLEDGEMENTS, but I want to publish this one before another decade passes, so in short, a big thanks to:

Penelope Todd, my mentor turned editor and NZ publisher, for your support, advice, dedication, expert editing and much more. I owe this book to you.

To Lindy Cameron, of Clan Destine Press, for bringing *All Our Secrets* to Australia.

To Emily Gale, for your encouragement and guidance all those years ago. Thanks for believing in the story.

To the Wellington Writers Group – Janis Freegard, Sarah Anderson, Niamh McManus, Chris Hobley, Mark Stephenson and Phil Evans – for your valuable feedback and support.

To Annabelle Court (photographer) for the great profile shot. You had a difficult subject to work with but you pulled it off.

To Mum, for fuelling my love of reading, proofing an earlier draft of *All Our Secrets*, and being nothing like the mum in this book.

To Damien Lane, for your great suggestions and creating my website (including the photography).

To Natasha Clark and Jenny Mainwaring, for your careful last-minute proofreading.

To my family, Allan, Tess and Matilda, for not begrudging me the many hours I've spent on my laptop (or for not letting on you that you did).

And to all the friends and family who kept asking me how my book was coming along. Yes, you! Thanks for not giving up and sorry it took so bloody long.

THE AUTHOR

JENNIFER LANE

Jennifer was a winner of New Zealand Book Month's *Six Pack Two* competition in 2007, and her short stories have been published on both sides of the Tasman.

She lives in Wellington, New Zealand, with her husband and two daughters, but feels equally at home in New South Wales, Australia, where *All Our Secrets* is set.

All Our Secrets was first published in New Zealand by Rosa Mira Books (2017) and won the Ngaio Marsh Award for Best First Novel in 2018.